THE DOOMSDAY KIDS

BOOK 2

NESTER'S MISTAKE

KARYN LANGHORNE FOLAN

K SQUARED BOOKS

The Doomsday Kids: Book 2—Nester's Mistake

Copyright © 2014 by Karyn Langhorne Folan

Cover Image by www.fiverr.com/alerrandre

Editing services provided by Judy Danish & Natasha C. Watts

This is a work of fiction. All of the characters, names, incidents, organizations, and dialogue in this novel are either the products of the author's imagination or are used fictitiously.

Published in the United States of America by K Squared Books.

TABLE OF CONTENTS

Chapter 1: Shoot First

Chapter 2: He's Baa-ack!

Chapter 3: For Elise

Chapter 4: The Coming Storm

Chapter 5: The Onion Cure

Chapter 6: Nester's Girls

Chapter 7: Amaranth Looks Out

Chapter 8: The Animal in the Barn

Chapter 9: Mercy Killings

Chapter 10: A Kiss in the Snow

Chapter 11: Pillowcase Talk

Chapter 12: Dude, That's My Foot

Chapter 13: In His Blood

Chapter 14: Don't Talk to Strangers

Chapter 15: The Hoard

Chapter 16: Presents for Doc Watson

Chapter 17: The Whole Truth

Chapter 18: Who Let the Dogs Out

Chapter 19: Where There's Smoke

Chapter 20: Light It Up

Chapter 21: Fire Fight

Chapter 22: Doc Watson's Ghost

Chapter 23: Puppy Love

Chapter 24: Goodbyes

Book Three: Amaranth's Return

1

SHOOT FIRST

Lilly was dead.

I didn't have to touch her or get any closer to her to know it. Her face had drained of color and even the ugly red lesions had lost their anger, washing out to dull sores.

Feelings crowded in on me like a fat man on an airplane, spilling into places where they shouldn't have been. All the crap we'd been through since the nukes dropped over Washington rushed back to me in a nasty blur. After weeks of hearing about Liam's family's "Mountain Place," this was supposed to be our haven. This was supposed to be our safety. Liam's father was supposed to be here to help us. And instead, Lilly was dead and Liam—

There was no mistaking the gunshot that split the cold air wide open—and now Liam was swaying like a rotten tree in front of me, gripping his side. My glasses were broken—cracked right down the middle of the nose bridge and hanging from my ears in two pieces—but I didn't have to have seen what happened to know that Liam had been shot.

A strange-looking boy and girl stood between us and a house that looked like Abe Lincoln's original log cabin. The girl was tall and slender and maybe twelve or thirteen and the boy was half her size and age. A shotgun lay on the ground and the girl held a pistol loosely in her hand like she'd forgotten about it.

Liam glared at them, his eyes ablaze with fury, clutching the wound like he could knit himself back together by willpower alone.

"Who are you? Why are you here? What are you doing on *our* land—" he yelled and then stopped. His features twisted and his eyeballs rolled up like cartoon window shades. I slipped my arm under his shoulder right before he kissed the ground.

"We need to get him inside!" I cried. "Now!"

"Get the door, Marty!" the girl yelled.

Amaranth, Liam's girlfriend—I guess that's the best word for her—struggled to help me shore Liam up, but Rod Wasserman muscled her out of the way.

"I'll help Nester," he told her. "You help Amy bring Lilly home."

The way he said "bring Lilly home" made something twist inside me, blocking my throat. I thought of my dead brother, Nate, buried alone on a railroad track, covered by rocks. Homeless in death. Blackness rose inside me like water and I had to fight for a few seconds to keep from drowning.

"Open the door, Marty!" the girl repeated, moving to help Amaranth and Amy with Elise and Lilly. She had wild brown hair worn in two puffy pigtails, gray eyes and skin the color of watered-down tea. She wore an old-fashioned loose brown coat over a pair of rubber black galoshes. I knew instantly that she was a "mixie"—the name my mom gave to kids who were biracial. Once, I'd have spent some time checking her out like a test tube specimen, trying to guess what combo of races would give you that look.

There's no time for that ish, man.

That's what Nate would have said.

The boy—Marty—hesitated, taking us in dubiously. For a split second, I saw us as he probably did: Amaranth

2

Jones was a quivering mess of fading bruises with a .22 rifle strapped to her shoulder. It was probably out of ammo—but Marty didn't know that. I probably didn't look much better, with my broken glasses, my mud-coated Afro and my clothes crimson with my dead brother's blood. Rod Wasserman looked like a horror movie scarecrow: stick thin, burned and his left eye covered with a patch. At only seven years old, tiny Elise Gomez was wailing over Lilly like she'd come unhinged. That left Amy Yamamoto, who wore her John F. Kennedy High School cheering skirt over the top of Nate's old fouled jeans. Her face was pinched and cut and she looked as hungry as she probably was.

In short, we looked like a band of pirates whose ship had been sunk. If I'd been in Marty's shoes, I'd have run for the door all right—and locked it from the inside.

"Quick, Marty!" This time anger snaked through the girl's words. "You didn't mean to hurt him, but we gotta help 'em fix him, if we can! Think of Mr. David—what he asked us to do! Now get the door and hold it for 'em. And then you bring them blankets from upstairs. And put on another pot of hot water. And bring some clean towels—"

The boy frowned disapproval at us, but he grabbed the shotgun off the ground and hurried toward the cabin at the girl's command.

Rod and I half-lifted, half-dragged Liam up the three steps of the wide front porch and into the cabin. My busted glasses stayed on my face by the strength of my ears alone. Everything and everyone around me was as blurry as a bad selfie, but there was no missing that we were entering a *home*—or the closest thing to one any of us had seen in weeks.

We stepped into a mudroom the size of a large coat closet with hooks for coats and benches on either wall. Marty stood sentry over the next door—the real one that actually led to the house. As we passed him, I saw that his body was pint-sized but the angles of his face, the few zits

3

peppering his chin and the eyes all said twelve or thirteen. Nate's age—

"Lilly!" Liam snapped into consciousness just as the toes of his wet sneakers scraped across the threshold. "Lilly!" he screamed, slapping at me like I was keeping him from something. "Where's—"

"She's right behind us," I told him, ducking the wild swings that threatened to finally send my glasses flying. "She's coming. Right behind us. You gotta calm down, man—"

"Lilly!" Liam kept fighting us like we were the enemy. Rod bent, sagging under his weight.

"I got him, I got him," he hissed to himself, ignoring Liam's flailing arms and frenetic screams. Wasserman kept saying the words over and over under his breath like he was *The Little Engine That Could.* "I got him. I got him. I think I can, I think I can..."

Sounded stupid...but it helped.

We maneuvered our burden down a single step into an open room warmed by a bright fire in a huge coal stove. An old-fashioned braided rug lay over a plank floor and a shabby corduroy couch faced the front door with a couple of mismatched rocking chairs on either side of it. A pair of cheap bookshelves and a cluttered desk filled the wall. There was a window above the desk with the shutters on the inside of the house, not the outside. A long wooden table with six straight-backed chairs dominated the other side of the room, segueing into a short corridor lined with shelves that looked as deep as they were wide. There was another room back there, but it was too far away and I couldn't see anything about it without my glasses. But even without $20/20$ vision, I could tell the whole place was neat and clean, warm and bright.

"Thar's beds up the stairs." The girl pointed to the loft above us. "You can take him—"

"The couch," Rod panted, lurching toward it with the

4

last of his strength.

The girl pushed aside a battered coffee table.

"Hey!" I cried, suddenly stupid. "That was ours! My mom left it on the curb as trash a couple of years ago, but it disappeared before the garbage men arrived the next morning! Man, your dad took it? That's...crazy...."

If I'd had any breath left, I'd have laughed: a stupid coffee table Mom had thrown away had survived the end of the world but she and Nate and just about everyone else we'd ever known—

Hopelessness corkscrewed from my throat to the pit of my stomach, making my eyes sting. I blinked a couple of times trying to clear it, but it wouldn't go. I had to stop because I couldn't breathe, couldn't see, couldn't make my body move the few more steps forward. Rod propelled himself on and Liam slid off my shoulder. He nearly fell before I made my body move.

Katie—that was what the "mixie" boy called her, Katie—dropped a sheet over the couch's worn fabric and helped us ease Liam onto it. Then she ran to the back of the room, her oversized boots slapping the steps of an unseen staircase.

The front door slammed behind me and I turned, the two pieces of my glasses swinging away from my face as Amaranth and Amy struggled into the room carrying Lilly. Elise trailed them, sobbing disconsolately and trying to catch Lilly's arms as they flopped loose and useless from her shoulders.

"Put her on the table." Marty cleared a tumbler and a stack of books with a single determined sweep of his arm, but took care when he lifted a rectangular black box out of the way. The crackling sound of static told me it was a radio. The boy set it on the desk, lowering the volume slightly.

Liam's eyes fluttered open, zeroing in on the boy.

"Who *are* you?" he demanded. "Who *are* you? What

5

are you doing here?"

Even as messed up as he was his voice was a bull whip that cracked across the room and flayed the kid like a beating out of *Spartacus*. Marty's coppery cheeks flamed red, but he didn't say a single word. I didn't blame him: Liam couldn't have hurt anyone if his life depended on it, but his eyes were full of TV psycho crazy.

"Who are you?" Liam shouted. "Why are you living here?"

"Stop screaming, man—"

"Don't tell me what to do, Nester." Liam wanted to sound all badass, but he didn't have the strength to even keep himself upright. He sank back against the couch, groaning, his hand hovering over his blood-soaked side like it hurt too much to touch. "I want to know... what...they're doing here," he hissed.

"And they'll tell you. Later, man." I reached out to lift his jacket. "First, I gotta see what I can do about that bullet hole—"

Liam slapped my hands away.

"No. Now. Right... now." He was trembling, shaking so hard I was scared for him.

"Okay, but you're losing blood. Stop flailing around. Lay still and let me--"

"Please, Liam. Please, let Nester stop the bleeding." Tears wet Amaranth's cheeks—the ugly kind that made ropes of mucus stream from her red nose. She wiped the snot with the arm of her dirty coat and cut her eyes at Marty like she wanted to rip him apart with her torn, mud-coated fingernails. "Tell him what he wants to know. It's the least you could do considering—" The tears came faster and her chest heaved. "This is all your fault. He—we—"

"She's right: tell him," I interrupted, because it was clear she was losing it and none of us needed that. I nodded at Marty, adding the word *quick* with my eyes. "Tell him before he hurts himself."

6

Marty just shrugged.

"Marty didn't mean to shoot nobody," Katie said, reappearing with a tower of towels and blankets in her arms. She plopped them onto Mom's coffee table, then stepped into Liam's line of vision. The patchwork of old and oversized clothes she wore reminded me of a movie I watched once about the Depression. "All kinds of scary people been showing up here—"

"From the prison. Over in Herriman," Marty interjected. "Bad folks, looking for food and stuff—"

Katie nodded. "Mr. David—your Papa—told us that would happen. He said after a couple of weeks, when all the stuff folks got on hand is gone, they'd start coming--"

"And he was right," Marty continued. His words made him sound old—much older than the youthful high-pitched tone of his voice. "None of 'em have made it this close to the house yet. There's a few booby traps out along the drive—"

"He knows that, Marty," Katie rolled her eyes. "He probably helped Mr. David plant 'em—"

"Do I look like a convict to you?" Liam interjected. The effort of the conversation was taking its toll on him, but he was too stubborn to lie back. "I was carrying—carrying—" his voice quavered and his eyes shifted toward where Lilly lay. "What kind of convict carries a little girl...?"

"Liam," I said, leaning close to him. "Let me..."

He didn't resist—I don't know if he even heard me—so I lifted his wet jacket and the slick T-shirt.

There was a lot of blood—the bullet had sliced him open below the rib cage, making a trough in his skin about an inch wide and three inches long. The wound was ugly—ugly enough that my stomach rolled as I sopped the oozing blood with the towel. Was there a bullet or a fragment in there? Had it hit anything vital inside? I couldn't tell. I couldn't see anything but—

Blood.

And then suddenly, I was back in that tunnel and Nate was screaming and there was blood everywhere.

I'm not going to make it, my little brother said in my memory. *I'm not going to make it...*

I shook my head, clearing the past and pressed my frames together with one hand, reaching for another towel with the other. Amy dropped it into my outstretched hand with fear in her eyes.

"You was a stranger and—" The two kids spoke in a weird tag team exposition and it was Katie's turn.

"And Mr. David, he told us to shoot first and ask questions later," Marty finished.

"When I saw you come running up from Mock Lake, I thought you might be Liam Harper and the little girl might be Lilly. Your Dad described you real good--"

"But he didn't say nothing about the rest of 'em. We started thinking about those folks—the bad ones—who came up here before. Started thinking they might have got some kids in their gang. Started thinking the whole thing might be some kind of trap—"

"Or that you was running from them, bringing 'em right up here to us. So I came down with the gun, and I told Marty to hang back." Katie's eyes circled the room, appealing to each of us before landing back with Liam. "We ain't got no one but each other. Been just me and Marty since—"

"Since our mama passed a while back."

Katie paused a moment before adding in a soft, pleading voice. "You got to understand. Marty was just trying to protect me."

I glanced at Liam and saw two things: first, nothing she said had moved him and second, that he wasn't going to be conscious much longer. He was breathing too fast and his lips looked almost blue in the low light. He blinked like he was having trouble focusing. The second towel I'd pressed into his abdomen was already soaked.

8

"Why are you living here? Why did my Dad let you stay?" A flicker of something like jealousy twisted his lips. "We—we aren't—related or anything, are we?"

Katie blinked in surprise.

"Gosh no! You think Mr. David—" she blushed, roses lighting the dusk in her cheeks. "No. We got our own papa."

"Somewhere," Marty added sardonically.

"We're used to being on our own. But Mr. David was always nice to us—"

"We'd been stayin' over on old man Watson's farm next door. Mr. David caught us swimming in the lake one day."

"We didn't know anyone was here. We'd been swimming there most of the summer. Never seen nobody. I was scared at first—"

"Ain't never seen a man with metal legs before," Marty drawled.

"Hush up, now. Ain't polite to talk about stuff like that, Marty—"

"Well, it's true. I ain't holding it against him."

Katie ignored him. "We didn't see him again for a while after that—not until just around the time the other kids were going to school. That's when he hired us. To check on the animals when he was down in Washington. He paid us a little money and he always said we could come here any time." She quirked an eyebrow at him. "He never told you 'bout us?"

Liam stared at her but didn't—couldn't — answer.

"Then Mr. David came up and stayed," Marty said. "Longer than he had ever before. He said he came to work the pumpkins, but he seemed kinda..."

"Sad," his sister finished.

Liam's eyes filled with tears.

"Seemed like he wanted some company," Marty added, studying Liam closely. "Like there was something

9

troublin' him."

Liam suppressed a sob.

"And, right about then we didn't have much food left and no money." Katie studied the black rubber toe of her boots. "And neither one of us had been to school in a while for one reason and another—"

"I don't want to go no more anyway," Marty muttered.

Katie sighed. "It's been hard for us both. Harder for Marty on account of him being so small for his age—"

"How old are you?" It wasn't relevant to the story, but my curiosity overcame me.

"Twelve," they answered simultaneously. "We're twins," Katie clarified.

It was all I could do to keep from staring at him after that. To keep my eyes from crawling all over him, I studied Liam's wound.

*Think, Nester...*I told myself, letting the ballad of Katie and Marty fade from the top of my mind. If the bullet had pierced any internal organ, Liam probably wouldn't be talking so much: he'd be dead or nearly so by now. I held the left lens of my glasses over my eye and peered closer. The bullet had caught the skin just above his hip bone and ripped it away, but as far as I could tell, that was it. It was bleeding like Old Faithful. The remaining skin around it was blackened and burnt.

"We was kinda in a bad way until Mr. David stepped up," Katie continued. "Made sure we had enough to eat—"

"Said we could come over here and he'd give me— both of us—lessons. He's a powerful good teacher. Better than most of 'em—" Marty pointed toward the shelves near the door. Most of the books had titles like *The Sustainable Farm* and *Survival Medicine* but I saw titles like *Call of the Wild, Great Expectations* and *Hatchet*—all stuff we had to read in school, too. There was even a row of brightly-illustrated children's books, the kind of stuff you'd read to

10

Elise or Lilly.

"Never cared much for reading before, but I liked them stories he got about life in the wilderness—" Marty continued before Katie interrupted to take her turn.

"So that's why we come that day, to keep up with our school work," Katie said. "We was sitting right there at yonder table—" She nodded to where Lilly lay, then looked down at her boots again. "Sitting right there when it suddenly got dark in the middle of the afternoon. Mr. David, he said, 'Looks like a storm rolling in' and we went back to work. We didn't think nothing of it. Just kept working 'til suppertime—"

"Weather gets funny up here in the late fall. Can be sunny one minute and snowy the next."

"He was cooking when your Mama came through on the ham radio. That's when Mr. David checked his phone and realized it weren't working—"

"He talked to her?" Liam's voice was a ragged whisper. "*After* it got dark...after the bombs...that was when he talked to her?"

Katie nodded.

"What—what—"

"She said she'd talked to you. Reached you at your school and told you to get Lilly and get up here. 'But there wasn't enough time.' That's what she said: 'There wasn't enough time.' She said that a few times. Sounded like she was crying. And Mr. David, he said, 'Don't worry, Sandy. Liam, he's a smart kid. He got Lilly and he'll take care of her. They're probably sitting in The Hole complaining about how bad the MREs are right now.'"

Rod chuckled a little at the memory of the bad old days—the eight days in the bunker under Liam's house nicknamed "the Hole." At the time I'd thought nothing worse than the Hole would ever happen to me: eight, long, sunless days in a stinking underground bunker. Eight hot, boring and miserable nights. The whole time, Nate had

11

whined. He was hungry. The military meals-ready-to-eat were nasty. His stomach was grumbling. His only other subject was his boredom: his phone wouldn't work. He missed his iPad. He missed playing *Call of Duty* and *Grand Theft Auto.* It seemed to me that every word that came out of his mouth was stupider than the one before. If you'd told me then how much worse it would get—that our days in the Hole really were the "good times" —I wouldn't have believed you. I would have told you this kind of hell could never happen in America. I'd have told you that shit like this didn't—couldn't— happen to nice suburban kids like us.

But it had. The bombs had fallen and everything had changed. Now, Nate would never be hungry or bored again because he was dead. And Liam was on the way to dead, bleeding like crazy right in front of me.

"Go on," I barked, grabbing yet another towel. Katie's head snapped toward me, her eyes flashing, but I didn't apologize. "You need to finish this. Quick," I explained nodding toward Liam's pale face. "What else did they say? Where was she? Anything about other survivors or--"

"They got a little mushy. 'I love you' and all like that. Then your Mama said she'd try to contact him again as soon as she could. So before he left, he told us to mind the radio. Keep it in batteries and turned on—"

"But we ain't heard nothing since he left." Marty nodded toward the device on the desk. "Just static—"

"Then he grabbed the gas cans and loaded them and the rest of his gear into the old truck—"

"The engine turned right over 'cause it didn't have no computers in it—"

"And he took off. Said he was going to get you and Lilly but you might make it without him. That he'd be back and to wait—"

"Lilly! They're alive! They're—" Liam sounded dazed

12

and hysterical, as though he was talking to his own dreams. He lurched upward, fighting toward a new destination, and then collapsed. As if someone had pulled an invisible plug inside him, the last bit of color drained out of his face. Sweat pearled on his forehead.

I slapped his cheeks with my fingertips. "Liam! Stay with us, man! Liam—"

"What is it?" Rod pulled himself to his knees, crawling closer to the couch, alarm etched into his face.

"I don't know, but it isn't good." I told him. "We gotta do something... and fast."

2

HE'S BAA-ACK!

I dropped to my knees beside the couch and yanked off Liam's jacket. Then I grabbed his filthy sweatshirt at the neck and ripped it straight down the middle.

"What are you doing?" Amaranth rushed forward like I had taken a knife to him.

"Getting him out of these dirty clothes," I snapped, tearing Liam's T-shirt away from his body the same way and pressing the towel harder against the wound. "You want to be useful, help me. Otherwise, go away."

She backed off, trembling from head to toe, either from cold or fear or a combination of the two. Didn't matter. She got out of my way.

"He's going to be okay, right?" Amy's pale face appeared over Rod's shoulder as I mounded pillows beneath Liam's legs and dropped a blanket over his now bare shoulders. "He'll be okay?" Her long black hair was wet and plastered to her face. A line of blood trickled from her temple to her chin. She used to be pretty, but right now, the best word to describe her was "ratchet."

Liam's skin had gone as gray as the sky outside: a nasty unnatural color that said "death" even more clearly than his fast and uneven breathing.

"I'm not sure. There's a lot of blood, but I think the bullet just grazed him," I told her.

Relief washed over Amy's face.

"Okay then. We just need some bandages or something, right?"

"No. It's too deep. He needs stitches," I told her.

Wasserman's single Cyclops eye rotated in his burned face and fixed on Katie. "You got like a needle or something?"

Once again those oversized boots clomped on the wooden planks as the girl/woman scurried to the shelves stuffed with gear. She dragged a huge black bag toward me. It was another medical kit, even more complete than the one Liam had pulled out on the day the bombs killed everyone back home.

"Ain't this it?" Katie asked, sticking a suture kit under my nose. "What you need?"

"Yeah." I shivered, suddenly feeling just how cold and wet I was.

The seven of us had been loaded in a canoe made for four and floating on some pretty deep water. More than once I'd been sure I'd be the one capsize us since, let's face it, I'm no outdoorsman. I was just one of the strongest ones left—strong enough to dip a paddle in the water. In the end, it had been Liam who dumped us, when he realized that Lilly was—

Dead. And if they're counting on you *to save him, that's what Liam's gonna be, too, Nester—dead. Stop fronting. You know Captain Four Eyes can't save the day—*

Nate's voice was so loud and clear that I turned my head to look for him.

"Nester?" One of them was pressing me— waiting for instructions, waiting for me to tell them what to do.

Yeah, Nester, Nate taunted, sounding like he was in the room and not just in my head. *Go ahead. We all want to see this.*

"I—I can't see," I snapped, doing my best to shake my dead brother's voice out of my head. "I need some tape or —"

Marty reached into a lower drawer of the desk, grabbed something and whistled. Katie lifted her arm,

15

snagging a roll of gray duct tape out of the air like she played for the Washington Nationals. She approached me resolutely and pulled my glasses out of my trembling hands. Her fingers were rougher than I expected, but her skin was warm and dry, and her touch was confident. She wound a strip of duct tape deftly around the bridge, wiped the lenses with one of the clean towels and handed my glasses back to me.

The world snapped back into focus. "Thanks," I said, squinting the frames higher up my nose like I always did. I took a deep breath and looked around again.

And there he was.

My dead brother was standing behind me with a candy bar clutched in each of his pudgy hands and an I'm-gonna-tell-on-you grin on his chubby face. He was dressed like he'd been on that last day—green striped Henley, jeans, lime green Jordans—only totally clean, without dirt or blood. He looked as fresh and dapper as a fat kid could. Like he was on his way to school, not the Apocalypse.

Come on now, Nester, he said, licking chocolate off his fingers. *You didn't really think you were going to just wipe me away like that, did you?*

"What the—?" The words burst out of me, yanked like the tablecloth in that old magic trick. The towel I'd been pressing to Liam's side fell out of my hand.

"What's the matter, Nest?" Rod swam into my sight, his forehead tight with concern. His legs twitched and I realized he was trying to get off the floor but couldn't. His spent muscles wouldn't listen to his brain's commands anymore. In the end it was Amy who found enough reserve power to crawl forward, grab the towel and hold it tightly against Liam's side.

"You—you don't see–?" I stammered, swinging my head between Nate and the others so violently drops of the lake water rolled out of my Afro and wet my cheeks. "You didn't hear—? "

16

Rod frowned, peering behind me urgently. "Hear what? See what?"

Yeah, Nest? Nate asked, laughter in his voice. *Hear what? See what?*

"I—I—I thought I heard—" I began, then stopped. There was no way I was telling them that Nate was standing there as large as he'd been in life and eating twice as much. "Man..." I finished instead. The last bit of adrenaline seeped out of my body and I slumped forward, holding my face in my shaking hands. "I'm—I'm losing it. I can't do this. Not now— "

"But Nester, you have to!" Amy's black eyes were pleading, perfect almonds in her face. "You were the one who took care of Rod when he got burned. You bandaged us all up after Lowellstown and you—" her voice dropped to a whisper. "You tried to take care of Lilly—"

"This is different!" I snapped. "Update, girl: this isn't a sprained ankle or a cut. It's not even a burn. He's been *shot*, get me? Even if I weren't—"

Seeing things? Nate offered, completely unhelpfully.

I took as slow a breath as I could manage. "He needs a hospital and doctor—a real one—not some dumb kid who likes to play one—"

"*You're* the one who said we couldn't—we *wouldn't*—lose another one," Amaranth hissed. She had been on the other side of the room, doing her best to comfort Elise, but she uncoiled as suddenly as a cobra and started spitting her unique brand of poison into my face. "But Lilly's gone—Lilly's gone, Nester—"she shuddered like something had walked over her own grave, and more tears sprang into her eyes. "We are *not* going to lose Liam, too. We are *not*—"

"Hospital's thirty miles," Katie interrupted, her gray eyes solemn. "And Mr. David took the truck. You gotta try—"

"Who asked *you*?" Amaranth snatched the suture kit

17

out of Katie's hands and shoved her aside. "None of this would have happened if hadn't been for the two of you—"

"Hey!" Marty darted across the room like a miniature lightning bolt and stationed himself between Amaranth and his sister. He was so small the top of his head only came up to Amaranth's waist, but there was murder in his eyes and a shotgun still in his hand.

"I got it, Marty." Katie's hand grazed his shoulder in gentle restraint, her gray irises like gathering smoke. "Don't put yer hands on me again," she warned Amaranth in a soft voice.

"Or what? You're gonna shoot me, too?" Amaranth's laughter was bitter. Hysterical. "Do you have any idea what we've been through?" she shouted, leaning into the girl like her brother wasn't even there. "Do you have any idea how *awful* it's been just trying to get here? Do you have any idea what we've *lost?*" She was sobbing but she kept talking, leveling the only weapon she had left—her pain — at them. "And we get here—here to where we were supposed to be safe, only for *him*" —she jabbed a finger at Marty— "to try to blow Liam to pieces!"

"I told you: I ain't mean to hurt him," Marty spat back. "You just come running up on us. Just like those others—"

"I don't care—"

"You ought to!" Marty shouted. "Look, I'm sorry for your troubles. And I'm sorry Mr. David's boy got shot. But defending this place ain't been easy, neither—"

"If we wasn't here, you would have run right up to a house full of criminals—and you would have been worse off, let me tell ya—" Katie interjected.

"That's right. So close your mouth, girl." He nodded toward me. "Let the boy with the glasses get on with it or your friend's not gonna make it."

Amaranth stared at the twin siblings like she was trying to figure out which one of them to smack first. The

18

odds weren't good: Amaranth had a good six inches in height on Katie, but the country girl had a scrappy determination about her. Plus she was rested, well-fed and strong. If it came to blows between the two of them, Katie was gonna mop the floor with Amaranth's scrawny butt. No doubt.

And Marty had a shotgun—and he'd already proven he knew how to use it.

"Amaranth." The way Amy pulled Amaranth away from the twins told me she hadn't just been twirling her hair in math class. "I know you're upset, but you've got to calm down, okay? Please—"

But telling Amaranth to do anything is like talking to the weather. She jerked away from Amy and threw the suture kit at me. "Do what you have to do, Nester!"

Do what you have to do, Nester! Nate repeated, taking a place just over her shoulder and imitating her voice and manner almost perfectly. *Do it! What's the matter? Forget your lines? You just gonna let Liam bleed, man? Come on. They're waiting for you. Waiting for you to fix him like a broken coffee cup. All you need is a little super glue, right? Too bad they don't know that you're a chicken.* He put his hands on his hips and started high-stepping, ducking his head and pecking the air. *Bock, bock, bock—*

"Stop that!" I shouted, boiling over with frustration and annoyance. It was just like when he was alive, baiting me and driving me to the point that I just wanted to wrap my hands around his throat and squeeze—

But it was Amaranth standing in front of me, not Nate.

"Do it!" she screamed in my face.

Somewhere, invisibly, Nate laughed again. *She thinks you're talking to her, man. And I know what you're thinking, but you can't kill me, man. I'm already dead, remember?*

19

I stumbled backwards. My hands were trembling like an old man's and my mouth felt like it was stuffed with cotton. I was that kid in the *Sixth Sense*, seeing dead people. And any dude *that* crazy couldn't be trusted to take a needle and stick it into Liam's gaping flesh again and again—

Amaranth's palm stung my face.

OOOHHHH, snap! Nate squealed in my ear. *No she didn't! This is getting good!*

Shock. That was the first thing I felt as her flesh collided with mine. Then the pain of the slap radiated outward, each finger an individual burn that echoed from my cheek down deep inside me, waking something cold, reptilian and nasty.

"Fix it!" I heard her shouting. "Fix it! Fix him! Fix—-" Her voice broke. Shame and regret blossomed in her face.

"Nester. I'm—I'm sorry. I shouldn't have—"

I heard her apology, but it didn't matter. I was too angry— beyond angry. Fury climbed inside me like the mercury in a thermometer left in the desert, exploding out of its glass and congealing on the sand.

"Get out." I'd never heard my voice sound like that before: an octave lower, powerful, a roar of something untamed. "Get out of this room! Now!"

Amaranth hiccupped a sob and barreled out of the room. When the cabin's front door slammed, I exhaled and closed my eyes.

"Nester?" Amy began timidly.

"Shut up."

Nester?

I opened my eyes. Nate again, only he was different now—a younger version of himself, maybe seven or eight years old. He plopped down on the sofa next to Liam, wearing nothing but his underpants.

Don't get mad. I'm here to help you. You're not exactly in good shape, you know. He pulled an old-

20

fashioned clipboard from behind his back and looked it over. *Dehydrated. Starving. Your body is eating muscle now. Chewing on that big brain of yours—*

The brain is not a muscle, you idiot—

Strip him, man. Remember?

I shook my head, trying to erase him.

Strip him, Nate insisted. He stood up and grabbed his briefs like he was going to demonstrate. *Come on, come on. Time's a-wasting,* he said, imitating Marty and Katie's drawl.

"Hey, dude?" Rod had finally managed to recover enough to pull himself to his feet. "Do you—?"

"We need to get Liam out of these dirty clothes," I said. Still in that voice. That other voice—the voice of someone even I would have obeyed. "We need to get him clean—clean as we can. Not just the area around the wound. Everything."

I grabbed Liam's cheap watch and tugged it off his bony wrist. Its face was cracked but the hands were still moving and the calendar still ticked off the days in a little window cut into the center of the dial. Eighteen days. Eighteen days ago, I'd been a normal fifteen-year-old, suburban kid. My biggest concerns had been getting my learner's permit, scoring 160 on the PSAT and making sure Jindal Patel didn't have a better robotics project than me.

Eighteen days.

I lay the watch on Mom's old table, then grabbed the knife hanging from a loop on Liam's belt and handed it to Amy. "Cut him out of the rest if you have to." I turned to Katie, looking down and my own filthy clothes and dirty hands. "I need to wash up, too or I'm just going to make it worse."

"I always got a pot of water heatin' on the cook stove," Katie nodded toward the small room at the back of the house.

Cook stove? What the hell is that? Nate asked.

21

Sheesh, what kind of redneck joint is this—

I folded the *shut up* that rose automatically to my lips back into my brain and focused on Katie. "Great. Show me."

"I'm going upstairs. To the Lookout." Marty sounded like his mouth was full of mush. "Someone's got to be watchin'. Always. And that girl shouldn't be wandering around out there by herself. Ain't safe. Not even here." His eyes met mine, appealing for understanding of why he'd done what he'd done.

Ask someone else, kid. Nester's got a heart of stone. He's like the dude from Star Trek. Vulcan. He made his voice robotic. *That is illogical--*

"Oh will you please just shut up!" I exclaimed. "Just shut—"

When Marty blinked and stumbled away from me, I realized that Marty thought I was talking to him. I opened my mouth to explain that my dead brother was talking *ish* in my head, but he'd already stomped out of the room.

That's great, Nate teased. *You just pissed off the kid with the guns.*

I rubbed my head like I could erase the sound of his voice. "Is there a bathroom? A sink? A place to wash?"

"Sink's in the kitchen. Outhouse outside." Katie's head indicated the door. "You need to pee or just—"

"No, just wash. Rod, help Amy with Liam," I called over my shoulder, and then focused on the table where Lilly lay.

Elise sat in one of the chairs, her knees drawn up to her chin. She rocked herself back and forth, holding Lilly's pale, limp hand in her own dirty brown one, her chest heaving with sobs. I knew how she felt: a mix of rage and fear and guilt that her little body was too small to hold. Everything had been taken from her—from us. It wasn't my fault—or hers—or any of ours. There just wasn't anything we could do about it.

"Elise, I need you," I commanded. "Come with me."

Elise didn't move. I glanced back at the couch. Amy was quickly cutting Liam's jeans off him and we needed to hurry up. I calculated just how many seconds I dared invest before I squatted beside the little Spanish girl's chair.

"Look, Elise..." I began, but that gruff voice coming out of me wasn't exactly reassuring. "Lilly was cool. Brave. She saved our lives, lots of times. I'm gonna miss her, too. But we can't help Lilly now," I said. "We have to help her brother. I *need* you. Please, Elise. Please."

More tears rolled down her face, but Elise didn't answer. She didn't even look at me.

"Elise, please—"

"Let the poor little thing be," Katie said softly. I glanced at her. Before I'd only seen how odd her features were, but now I saw tears forming in the corners of her stormy eyes. "I'll help ya get cleaned up," she continued, nodding at Elise. "After some food and some rest, she'll be better, you'll see. Come on. This way."

I would have rather had Elise—she was familiar—but Katie was probably right: the little girl wasn't much use to me right now. I squeezed Elise's shoulder, then followed Katie through the short hallway crammed with floor-to-ceiling shelves groaning with all kinds of gear, from toilet paper and soap to canned goods. A stockpile. Of course. From what I'd learned about Liam's father, I'd have been disappointed with anything less. Past that was a small room that was clearly the kitchen even though it was nothing like the ones back home.

No microwave. No dishwasher. At the sink there was a single pump instead of a faucet. There were no lights: the room was lit by a window and by two oil-burning lanterns, hung by hooks in the ceiling. A decent-sized butcher block work table filled up most of the wall and an old black coal stove hunkered in the center of the room, radiating heat. A couple of pots rested on its surface and my stomach

23

gurgled at the sight of a half-eaten pan of cold scrambled eggs.

Katie used the pump at the sink to fill another large black pot and heaved it over to the stove. She opened its front grate and added a large scoop of coal from a nearby bin.

"This one's already hot," she muttered, lifting a kettle.

I stripped to the waist while Katie stoppered the sink and poured in half the kettle's contents before spilling the other half into a large bowl she fetched from a shelf on the wall.

The warm water felt like being kissed by angels. I scrubbed, and blood—Nate's blood, bear blood—along with leaves, bits of bark and body scum soon filled the sink. Katie didn't say anything about it and neither did I.

"Take off yer pants." She tugged at the gaping waist of my filthy jeans.

"Hey!"

"Take 'em off," she insisted. She turned away and I thought she was giving me some privacy, but no. As soon as I dropped my pants, she was staring at me again, holding a pair of "tidy whities" and some soft gray sweatpants with a drawstring waist. "These'll have to do. I think you're too tall for the rest." Then she left me for the group at Liam's side.

Once upon a time, BTB—before the bombs—those hokey-looking gray sweatpants would have drawn my scorn, but when I stripped off my soiled and raggedy underwear and slipped into those clean drawers and soft fleece, my eyes welled up.

I pumped at the sink's handle, releasing a stream of clear cold water. I stuck my head under the faucet, filling my mouth, swallowing greedily. Nate was right: I was dehydrated beyond anything a couple of swallows could fix, but when I lifted my head, I felt better.

"Get away from him. All of you. Are there anti-bacterial wipes in that medical kit? And gloves?" I barked when I re-entered the larger room.

"Here." Katie ripped open packages and handed the supplies to me.

I wiped my hands and approached the couch like I knew what I was doing.

"Move," I told Amy.

"Don't you want me to—" Amy began.

"You're filthy. I want you to go away."

"You should take a look at his heel, too. Nasty-looking blister—" Rod began, rising unsteadily. His face was a wreck of seared skin and his left eye was closed for good, peeking sightless out from under the black eye patch he'd found.

"I think we've got more serious things to worry about than a blister right now!" I interrupted.

Amy's mouth opened again but I shut her down. "I said 'no.' None of you can help me. You're all too..." Words flashed through my mind: emotional, weak, tired, useless. "Just get over by the fire. Or better yet. Back there. The kitchen. There's water—" I turned to Katie. "And food, right?"

She nodded. "There's some ready-to-eat stuff on the shelves—"

"Go to the kitchen then," I finished. "I don't need you guys staring at me."

This is going to be hard enough as it is, right? Nate asked.

Katie started toward the kitchen with the others but I snapped my fingers at her. "Except you. Uh, Katie, right?"

"That's right." She stood completely still beside the couch, waiting to be commanded. It was sort of weird. Like having a powered-down android in the room.

As he passed the table, Rod stroked Lilly's face with

25

his good hand. The other one was burned and scarred like his face and hung awkwardly at his side.

"Poor kid," he muttered kissing the dead little girl gently on the forehead. I remembered how he'd made fun of her for the way she talked in the beginning, and how he'd charmed and flirted with her in the end. Even without his good looks, the girls loved him, all of them, little, big, Down's Syndrome, non-English speaking—it didn't seem to matter.

Rod turned to Elise.

"You want to come get some food, *piquena*?"

The little girl just kept rocking herself. Tears ran down her face but she didn't take her eyes off Lilly or answer.

"You're right. We can't leave Lilly alone. I'll bring you something," Rod said as though she had answered. "Then we'll take turns staying with Lilly and remembering her life. Tomorrow, we'll give her to God."

Rod sounded like a *rabbi*. Once, that would have something to tease him about, but those days had gone up in smoke.

Amy slipped her hand into his. The look she gave him wrote a story so much deeper than high school jock and cute cheerleader that the last of my stereotypes about the two of them shattered into a million pieces.

"Let's go see what's cooking," he continued, managing a weak grin at his girlfriend. "Nester's got it. Liam's gonna be fine, right, Nester?"

I didn't know. That was the truth. But Amaranth's fingers colliding with my face made it pretty clear: they weren't interested in the truth. They wanted me to do magic and make Liam all better—and I'm not magic. I'm just plain old Nester Bartlett, a fifteen-year-old dork with a big brain and bad eyes. In the old world, Amaranth Jones would have been mine for cash and pretty Amy Yamamoto might have flirted with me— to get me to do her

26

homework.

"I'll do the best I can," I said impatiently. "Now go."

There was good news and bad news.

Liam was out cold, which was bad news, but I hoped that maybe he wouldn't feel much pain. Katie wrapped a faded pink blanket over his shoulders and covered his legs with a blue one. One of them—Rod?—had covered Liam's junk with a loose pair of clean boxers, which was also good. Without his angry determination to reach this mountain home, without his go-bag on his back and his gun in its holster on his belt, he looked frail and vulnerable. A skinny, starving, busted-up kid.

I closed my eyes. There wasn't any point in asking God—that's like writing a letter to Santa after you've seen your parents wrapping the gifts at the kitchen table—but since I was a ghost whisperer now, there was one other person I hoped might listen.

3

FOR ELISE

"It's okay, sweetie, it's okay."

Nate was eight—and heavy. Even then he'd been about thirty pounds overweight, but Mom scooped him up and carried him into the kitchen, letting him bleed all over her new white skirt before settling him on a chair at the kitchen dinette. Details flooded over me: the lemony scent of the antibacterial soap that my mother washed her hands with; the chill of the air conditioner; the way Nate's brown skin separated into a deep bloody channel; the sound of him wailing like he was dying.

Mom was younger, her hair longer than she wore it now, curving in a sleek black bob at her chin. But the fingers were the same: the color of wet sand, long, thin and a little rough from constantly washing her hands.

"Keep the towel on it, Nester," she called over her shoulder, hurrying into the other room to grab her bag.

She never carried an old-fashioned black doctor's bag like in the movies. She kept all her supplies in a colorful tote that looked more like a beach bag than anything. "Hey, I'm a pediatrician. The kids like it," she explained often. "It's less scary."

She pulled out some kind of liquid antiseptic and

showed it to me.

"We have to clean it," she told Nate. "This might sting, okay?"

It must have burned. Nate whined and flailed and fought her and I stood there, hating his guts for being such a big, fat baby and waiting, waiting for the moment when her patience snapped and she told him to grow a pair. To shut up and take it like a man-—

"No, no, honey," she continued in a sticky-sweet voice. "We have to clean. The fibers from your pants can get in there and make you very, very sick—"

"But it hurts!" Nate wailed. "Why does it hurt so—"

"It's just a little saline." She squirted it into the bloody stripe and let the fluid run out. "I know it hurts but—"

"You got something to clean with? Saline or iodine or hydrogen peroxide? Even water, if that's all we've got."

Katie rummaged through the kit and handed a container to me.

"This will numb it a little." She sprayed a pain killer on to the wound and Nate shrieked like it was poison. "You might not want to watch this," she said, pulling out the suture kit with its curved needle and scissors-like accessory.

Nate scrunched his eyes shut but I watched, mesmerized by the way she rocked the needle gently so it picked up the thread.

I imitated the movement.

Mom pressed the scissors into the furrowed skin with one hand and guided the needle with the other, rocking them toward each other as she pulled the gash back together with the strong black thread.

"That's cool," I muttered in spite of myself.

She frowned at me. "It wouldn't be necessary if you weren't so rough with him! Honestly, Nester. Couldn't you just—"

She kept talking, but I stopped listening, focusing

29

instead on the needle and the way she held it, her wrists making the tiniest movements as the skin rejoined.

"All done, all done." She sang the words, but Nate was still hollering like murder. "And now for a bandage and a Popsicle to put the fluid back in your body—"

The wailing stopped.

"Can I have two Popsicles?" Nate asked.

Mom laughed. "We'll see."

"Can I have one?" I asked.

A knot of annoyance puckered my mother's eyebrows. "Really, Nester? If you hadn't pushed your brother, he wouldn't have needed stitches—"

"But it's my bike!"

"I really don't think you deserve a Popsicle right now," she said firmly. "I'm sick of you fighting him all the time. What are you trying to do? Kill him—"

Kill him...

"Nester? It is 'Nester,' right? What they call ya?"

I frowned. The voice didn't belong in my memory.

Katie stood at my elbow. Up close, her skin was the color of honey clouded with cream. The two puffy pigtails on either side of her cheeks looked more curl than kink.

"What are you exactly?" I asked.

Katie blinked at me. "'Scuse me?"

"Black? Indian? Middle Eastern?"

Her brows knitted with annoyance. "What difference does it make?" She answered, stretching a gauze patch toward me. "Are you ready for it or not?"

I squinted my glasses up. The duct tape holding them together scratched the bridge of my nose painfully enough to snap me out of my racial curiosity.

"Yeah." I felt weird, like I'd been asleep and had just been awakened from a crystal clear, vivid dream. But when I looked down at Liam, the job was done. The stitches were far less precise than my mother's but they were small and

30

close together and I was pretty sure that they wouldn't reopen as soon as he moved.

I just didn't remember doing it.

"You want me ta—" the girl interrupted.

"Yeah, yeah." I stumbled away from Liam, suddenly too tired to stand up another second. My butt found the rocking chair just in time and I sat down hard, closing my eyes.

The worn cushion covering the seat was lumpy in the most comfortable of ways. The chair was the perfect distance from the fire. The warmth from the coals was like a summer's day, but I was shaking like an ice cube in a Slurpee machine. I couldn't stop.

Katie covered my handiwork with a gauze pad and carefully wound a long strip of bandage around Liam's ribcage. He didn't stir, but his breathing seemed to ease a bit. "I'll see if he'll take some water." the girl said.

"Water? Why?"

Once again the girl's eyes snapped to my face. "You said we should give him some water. Sumpthin' about replacing fluid 'cause of all the blood he's lost. Said to use this." She showed me an eye dropper. "Don't you remember?"

No. No, I don't remember that. I don't remember any of it except Nate—

"Oh, yeah. Right."

"You said to keep him warm and wait for him to wake up—"

"I *know* what I said!"

She didn't start or look scared. Instead, she frowned at me like she knew I was a big faker and pulled the blue blanket up to Liam's chin, tucking it carefully around him. When she took the pink one from his shoulders, I thought she was going to give him a second layer, but she surprised me. She came close and wrapped it around my shoulders like I hadn't been bossing her around for the last hour.

"I don't think I could have ever done nothing like that," she said, smoothing the blanket over my chest. "No sir. Not ever." She studied me. "I'll find ya a shirt before I take my turn at the Lookout."

"Yeah...whatever."

"You want some food?" she asked peering into my face like she was looking for something from me.

My stomach rumbled to life at the word. "Yeah, thanks." I was hungry... but mostly, I just wanted her gone so I could *think*.

She turned toward the kitchen, and then stopped again. "He ain't gonna die now, is he?"

I shrugged.

She moved away. Voices floated toward me from the kitchen and then the smell of something cooking filled the air. I could have gotten up and gone in to join them, but I didn't. I didn't want to look at any of them. And I didn't want to think about what we'd have to tell Liam about Lilly when he woke up. Or what I would tell my own mother—if she was alive—about Nate. I just wanted to sit there by the fire and—

I closed my eyes. Dark dreams rose to meet me in shadowy broken pieces. My mother and Nate, my stepfather Irv and Liam's father, our neighborhood and the hallowed ivy-covered buildings of Harvard, the school I'd always dreamed would be my future all of them jumbled together, accompanied by the aroma of macaroni and cheese.

A door slammed and the images faded, except for the smell of cheesy pasta.

I jerked back to alertness as Amaranth stumbled into the room, holding a big bowl.

"Hey!" she exclaimed. Her cheeks were aflame now and her eyes seemed to be bouncing above their shadowed sockets. She lurched across the room and thrust the bowl under my nose. "For you. Rod made it."

She was acting weird, but right then, I didn't care. I grabbed the spoon and started shoveling the food into my mouth like a greedy wolf. It was the boxed kind—my favorite—and the gooey cheese seemed to explode on my tongue, taking me back to the days of video games on the couch, my step-dad on his laptop at the kitchen table working on some death row case, Nate whining for another plate full and Mom on her way home from the pediatric center. As soon as I thought of them, though, the gooey processed cheese curdled on my tongue. I put the bowl down and stared at it, waiting for the sudden rush of nausea that rolled upward from my stomach to pass.

Amaranth giggled, wagging a finger in my face. "Go easy! Or you'll barf like Rod did!" She peered at Liam, her words swimming into each other. "He'sgonnabeallrightnow?" she asked, her voice dropping to a whisper. "Shh..." she hissed at me when I opened my mouth to answer. "Not so *loud!* He's *sleeping*..."

I stared at her. Amaranth Jones wasn't even fifteen yet but in the old world, she was one of *those* girls. The girls people whispered about. I'd heard about her at parties with the seniors, even seen her behind the school with a cigarette and a bottle in a brown bag. And she'd been with *lots* of dudes. Lots of them.

But since the bombs, I'd also seen a completely different side of her. A side that could be compassionate and incredibly strong. The girl I was looking at right now— red-eyed, wild, inappropriate—that was old-style Amaranth Jones, and I couldn't help but wonder what she was doing in our strange new world.

"You're drunk!"

"Not even close," she laughed. "It's a goal, though," she added seriously, pushing a handful of slick hair aside. "Sorry, bad manners." She pulled a half-empty bottle of bourbon with a fancy black label out of her coat pocket and

33

stretched it toward me. "Want some?"

I shook my head. "Where did you get it?"

She lifted the bottle and drank, grimacing a little. "Found it. In the barn. Right there, next to the pitchfork! Just between you and me," she whispered dramatically. "I think Mr. Harper might have a little...tiny...problem..."

"He's not the only one," I said.

"Yeah," she agreed, like I was talking about someone else, then suddenly without warning, spun toward Elise.

The little girl hadn't moved. She still sat in the chair, holding Lilly's hand, but she'd exhausted her tears. Now, she sat dry-eyed, staring bleakly at the body.

"Elise? *Que pasa, chica?* You wanna eat now? *Via a comer ahora?* Please..." She turned to me again. "Been trying to get her to talk to me. To eat something and..." she shook her head. "She won't. She won't talk to me. Not even in Spanish."

Once, Amaranth had been the only one—other than Lilly—Elise would talk to. How many times had I heard them in the Hole, talking together in Spanish, knowing that their conversation was safe from those of us who were lost after *gracias* and *hola.*

"You try, Nester!" Amaranth crooked her fingers at me. "Come on. You try—"

"Amaranth," I sighed. "Just leave her alone—"

"No!" Amaranth's voice rose. "Shh!" she hissed at me like I was the one shouting. "She's got to eat! We went so long without food...Let me try it the way you do it, Nester," She stamped her foot and pointed to a spot beside her. "Come! You! Here!" she barked.

I sighed. I hadn't forgotten the feeling of Amaranth's palm on my cheek and now she was annoying me all over again. Clicking her fingers and calling me like—like I was her dog or something. But then the memory of standing in a church with Nate and Elise swept over me like a bad movie. I saw myself in a rage, overturning the altar while

34

the faithful, Nate and Elise, watched me with silent pity. I remembered the look on Elise's face when Nate died...how hard she cried and the way she fingered the little gold crucifix when she prayed over him.

It was for Elise's sake, not Amaranth's, that I stood up and crossed the room.

"Hey Elise," I said quietly.

She didn't look at me. I didn't take it personally: on a good day I wasn't much to look at—and it had been a long time since I'd had anything close to a "good" day.

"Elise?"

Her eyes were hollow and empty and fixed on Lilly's hand like she believed that if she stared hard enough, her friend would stand up and start trying to reach her father on the radio.

Poor Elise.

Lilly had been her only friend—the only person she knew BTB. Lilly was the person who dragged her out of their second grade class and made her join us in the Hole. Lilly didn't care that she didn't speak much English or that she was so shy that for days and days she'd barely look at the rest of us. I didn't really know Elise's story—who she'd been living with since her mother was deported back to El Salvador or how she'd ended up in MacArthur Elementary's special education class. I didn't even know how she and Lilly had become friends in the first place. But Amaranth probably knew. Those were the stories they shared in Spanish whispers in the dark bunker under Liam's house while the world above of us burned.

I cleared my throat but I couldn't think of a damn thing worthwhile to say. I couldn't think of anything that would make a scared little girl who'd lost her only friend bother to eat a bowl of pasta and artificial cheese flavoring. She had as big a hole inside her as Liam did—maybe a bigger one. One I didn't have any tools to repair.

Amaranth shifted impatiently.

35

"Nester?" she whispered, blowing Kentucky bourbon into my face. "Aren't you going to—"

"Leave her alone." I stalked to the shelves to look for crackers or cereal or cookies—anything to tempt a traumatized little girl.

Those shelves. Those shelves were like opening the door to heaven, man. Stacks on stacks of canned goods, paper products, cereals and snacks filled every inch of space. On the floor, several big white buckets with "freeze-dried" foods in stenciled letters stood in neat rows. Behind them were huge industrial sized sacks of rice, wheat and oats that probably weighed as much as Elise. It would have been close to paradise... if hadn't been for Amaranth.

She grabbed Elise's chair and turned it away from Lilly sharply.

"Now, listen to me," she said, clasping the little girl's shoulders desperately. "It's going to be okay, Elise." She was right: she probably wasn't drunk yet, but the earnest energy of her plea couldn't walk a straight line. "We're all going to miss Lilly. We loved her, all of us. And we all love you, too. We're going to take care of you. We made it to the Mountain Place, right? Now it's going to be okay—"

"Don't listen to her, Elise." I grabbed a roll of crackers and a jar of peanut butter and turned back to them. "She doesn't mean any harm, but we both know it's *not* gonna be okay. It's not *ever* gonna be okay. Never again."

"Nester—" Amaranth shot me a boozy glare, but I ignored her and focused on Elise.

"Lilly's gone. I don't know where your mother is—your family is. Liam's hurt and we're still all alone. Any one of those is a good reason to be scared out of your mind. So if you just want to sit, you just sit. You want to rock, you rock. But you need to eat *this*," I dipped a cracker in the peanut butter. "Not because you're hungry, or because you want to, but because we don't know when we're going to

36

have to run or fight again and you have to be ready for that. You have to eat because we're all too weak and sick to carry you this time, you understand? You have to get strong because this—this moment of peace—it won't last."

"You call that *helping*? You're scaring her even worse!"

"And you call *that* helping—blowing alcohol into her face, telling her lies about how it's going to be okay?"

"Don't listen to him, Elise. Don't listen. We have to have hope. We have to have faith, right?" Amaranth offered in a gentler voice. Instead of touching Elise, she chafed Lilly's pale, motionless fingers with one hand and brushed her hair off her face with the other. "Lilly never gave up hope. She was a good friend. *Una buena amiga, si?*" She frowned. "I don't know how we're going to make it without her. I don't know how Liam—or you—or any of us—will make it without her—"

A huge hunk of Lilly's fragile hair broke off in Amaranth's hands, showing an ugly scarred patch of scalp on Lilly's temple. It made her look even less like the little girl she'd been and more dead than ever. Even more like the skeleton she'd soon become.

Elise shrieked at the sight, her screams echoing through the little cabin like a car alarm.

"It's okay! I'll—I'll—put it back!" Amaranth cried, trying to press Lilly's hair back onto her head. "I—I— was just—"

I scooped Elise out of the chair and carried her away from the corpse. She pressed her face into my chest, still screaming, her fingers knotting around my neck.

Amy scurried in from the kitchen bundled in the coat that Katie had worn. Her hair was wrapped in a towel and her bare legs showed beneath the garment's hem. By the way she held the coat around herself with one hand, I guessed she'd jumped out of the washtub to respond. The pistol that had done Liam so much damage was held

37

tightly in other her hand.

"What is it? What's wrong?" she demanded, glancing from me to Amaranth to Elise.

Katie appeared behind her an instant later with another basin of water in her hands and a mess of pink fabric with the "Hello Kitty" logo and a lot of white lace lining one of the edges. Her stormy eyes darted around the room, like she was trying to figure out which need to satisfy first. Finally, she laid the pink dress—that's what it was, a dress—over the edge of a chair and crossed the room to me, balancing the basin of water carefully.

"It's all right," she said gently to Elise. "Ain't nobody gonna hurt ya."

Elise burrowed more deeply into me but she stopped screaming. I sank back into the rocking chair with the little girl on my lap.

"It's time to get you out of those dirty clothes, okay?"

"She doesn't understand you." Amaranth said nastily. "She doesn't speak English."

Katie ignored her. Instead, her eyes met mine. "I was comin' to get Lilly Harper cleaned up but..." She didn't need to say it aloud but I knew what she meant. The living first, then the dead. "Let's get her out of these wet, dirty things—"

"I'll do it," Amaranth came toward us angrily. "I'll help her—"

Elise yelped, squeezing me like an anaconda.

"No, Amaranth," I commanded. "Go in the kitchen with Amy—" She opened her mouth to protest, but I interrupted her. "Go! Now! Get some coffee—" I glanced at Katie. "Is there coffee?"

"We can make some, yeah. The pot's above the stove. There's some instant, too," she murmured dropping a cloth into the basin and gently wiping the side of Elise's face.

"I'll figure it out." Amy pocketed the gun and reached for Amaranth. "Come on—"

"No!" Amaranth jerked away from her. "I can't believe this! Did you hear what he said? He said—"

"I heard him," Amy snapped, then her eyes at me, blushing slightly. "It's a small cabin. It was impossible not to," she murmured apologetically.

"Well, then!" Amaranth nodded like her point was proved. "What kind of advice is that for a little girl? Why would he say something like *that?*"

"Because it's the truth, Amaranth," Amy said softly. "And when you sober up, you'll remember it."

Amaranth eyes circled the room. At first I thought she was going to challenge me again, and there was a look in her eyes like she might grab Katie by the throat and shove her away from Elise. But just as quickly it faded. Her shoulders seemed to sink in on themselves. Her fingers twitched toward the bottle in her pocket.

Then came the footsteps, loud on the stairs behind us.

"We've got a problem," Rod tumbled into the room, interrupting the tension of the moment. "It's starting to snow." He jerked his head toward the windows. "I hate to say it, but I don't think we can wait. It's time to dig a grave."

4

THE COMING STORM

It was cold. Colder than I remembered it being before—even when we'd been on the water. Something in the air had shifted, and every now and then a stray flake of snow drifted by me. Katie had found me a red sweater: thick and itchy, but I could have used two of them and the coat she'd given me, too, to fight the power of this cold. For like the millionth time, I wished for my smart phone—I could have checked the temperature with the flick of a finger—but I didn't even know where it was. The last time I'd seen it was the first day in the Hole before the light from its screen faded out forever.

How had people anticipated bad weather before there were meteorologists showing us the movements of fronts on big colorful maps days in advance?

The sky was no help: it was the same dull gray color it had been for weeks. But my breath frosted when I exhaled and my hands and ears felt like ice cubes. The earth beneath me was dry and dead and hard as a stone. A single snowflake landed on my lips: it melted, leaving behind something that felt as gritty as sand. Some kind of fallout, I was sure of it. My jacket didn't have a hood, but I managed to work the scratchy red sweater up over my nose.

"So. She says there's a tractor," Wasserman said as if

we'd been having a conversation. He set off ahead of me with his hands jammed into his pockets and his ears tucked close to his collar like a reluctant turtle quitting its shell.

You done good.

That's what Rod—once the smirking high school hunk— had said as Nate lay on the tunnel floor bleeding out, knowing he was dying and terrified of what it meant to cease to exist. *You done good.* Nate's lips had twitched with gratitude. I wished I'd said it. I wished I'd been able to make Nate smile just before he—

I was something of a hero, wasn't I?

Nate appeared as suddenly as lightning, trotting along beside me in a down coat and girl's hat with little pink pom-poms bobbing on the top. He looked ridiculous.

I glanced at Wasserman, but he was staring straight ahead, his mangled lips tight with the burdens of his thoughts.

C'mon, Nest. Give a brother some credit, man!

He was practically running, taking two short fast steps with his chubby legs for every one of mine and holding a bag of Doritos in one hand and his iPhone in the other. *It won't kill you to admit it. I did good. I did good.*

Go away, I thought as hard as I could. *You're dead. Go away. Go away and leave me alone—*

No can do, bro, Nate teased. *Not until you—*

"Did you hear me, Nester?" Wasserman snapped the fingers of his good right hand under my nose.

We stood inside a huge shed filled with all kinds of tools and a few machines...and I had no recollection of how we'd gotten there. Wasserman was staring at me with a strange expression on his face.

"No," I admitted, turning away from him to inspect the place. It was an aluminum building that reminded me of the storage garage where Liam's dad had kept his bug-out bus: a long metal structure with a large rollup door.

41

Some kind of motion-sensitive light came on when we stepped inside, one of those dim florescent lights that uses a battery. The two padlocks that had secured the place lay on the ground in front of us with the keys Katie had given us still inside. Rod must have unlocked the shed and tossed them there.

"I was talking to—I mean, thinking about—something else." I pointed to the tractor. It was a smaller model than the kind I'd seen at construction sites, with a green cab and a small front end loader hanging from one end and a backhoe on the other. "You know how to drive this thing?"

Rod didn't answer. He stood beside me, swaying like a skyscraper in an earthquake.

"Wasserman?"

His knees buckled and he hit the ground, landing hard on his hands and knees, his head hanging loose from his shoulders like it might pop off. His whole body shuddered violently and then he vomited, coughing and lurching like all of his insides had to come out. It looked like agony: his body contracted over and over and over again, each wave more powerful than the last. But as much as his chest heaved and his stomach churned, nothing came up but a thin layer of blood-tinged phlegm.

I knelt by him, waiting for him to recover. It's tough being a dude watching another dude in trouble. I wasn't sure if I should touch him, or if he'd think that was weird. I had just settled on giving his shoulder a thump of support when I saw it.

His pants were so loose that they gapped away from his body, showing me a flash of pale skin. A dark bloody sore interrupted his flesh, bright and angry and out of place, like a bright red bloom on the tundra. I forgot about showing brotherly support and yanked at his coat and sweatshirt, pulling them high.

There were more: a whole line of bloody welts

42

marching up his back. I'd seen those kinds of marks before. On Lilly. Just a few days before she—

Wasserman grabbed his clothes and covered himself. He pushed away from the vomit and turned away from me, resting his back against the tractor's massive front wheel. He looked as bad as Liam: his skin just as ghostly and his eyes just as fevered. He was sweating profusely and I noticed for the first time the spaces where his scalp showed white through what once had been thick brown hair.

I grabbed his wrist; it was clammy and his pulse stuttered faster than I could count before he jerked his hand away.

"Ate too much," he panted. "It's... hard to... go slow."

"There's nothing there, Rod!" I pointed at the slimy pile of upchuck. "No partially digested macaroni. Or bread or anything. There's *nothing*, Rod—"

"I'm okay," he whispered, breathing in heavy gasps as he struggled to recover himself.

"I saw them, man. The lesions on your back—"

"Just bruises," Wasserman muttered, managing to scrunch his lips into a smirk. "We're all pretty banged up. Have you seen your face lately?"

"Look, Rod—" I began. I was going to tell him that those didn't look like bruises. That if they were the same sores—radiation poisoning or reactions to whatever was still hovering over us in the air—he had no business being out here with me. I was going to tell him that I'd figure out a way to dig Lilly's grave but that I didn't want to be digging two of them. But all I said was,

"You're sick."

"I'm okay," he insisted.

"You're not okay."

"So I've got some kind of—stomach bug," he grumbled, looking away from me. "A few days," he shrugged. "I'll be fine."

43

Let it go.

I didn't need Nate to tell me that, but there he was, still wearing that ridiculous girl's hat.

Let it go. I mean, it could be a stomach flu, right? It doesn't have to be radiation poisoning. It could really just be a little stomach bug.

A little stomach bug like dysentery, I thought bleakly.

Sure, like dysentery, Nate agreed enthusiastically. *That's not so bad, right?*

Dysentery doesn't have lesions like that, you idiot. And it can kill you.

So can the stomach flu, stupid, Nate retorted angrily and vanished.

I sighed.

"Go back inside, Rod." I stretched out my hand to pull him to his feet.

"But—"

"We need you healthy. Drink some water and go lie down. At least until it's time to—" I couldn't make myself say it. "Time for Lilly. I'll figure it out. Besides..." I glanced up at the sky. "I don't think this stuff is just snow."

His eyes met mine. I thought he was going to protest, but he grabbed my outstretched hand. Once he'd regained his feet, he moved unsteadily toward the door. He'd only gone a few steps when he stopped. "Do you think he made it? Back to Washington? Back home?" he asked suddenly.

It was sort of random, but there was only one "he" Rod could be talking about: Liam's father. The dude who used to stump around our quiet suburb with "The End Is Near" on a cardboard sign hanging around his neck. Well, not quite *that,* but close enough for everyone to think he was some kind of nutcase.

And he *was* a nutcase... up to the moment he was right.

44

We all would have been dead a long time ago without him and his plans for TEOTWAWKI—the end of the world as we know it. Sometimes—like when we covered Nate with gravel and left him alone on the railroad tracks, and now, when we needed a tractor to dig Lilly's grave—I wondered if that would have been so bad. If maybe survival isn't all it's cracked up to be.

Wasserman was waiting for an answer.

I shrugged. "Don't know, man."

"But if you had to guess," Rod pressed. "Do you think he made it or—"

"Yeah, sure. He made it," I said without conviction. "Go in, man. Ask Katie if there's any protective gear. Gas masks, bio suits. Cover ups. Anything. We're going to need them."

He nodded but still didn't go. "You—you won't say anything, will you?" he asked. "To Amy. Or the others?"

"No. But only because I won't have to, Rod. If it *is* radiation poisoning, they're going to know."

It took half an hour and over a dozen tries, but I figured out the tractor and drove it out of the shed, sputtering across the desolate fields of Liam's family's little farm. The first grains of gritty snow were already sprinkling the ground like sugar when I reached the line of trees that once had been the orchard. Rows of dead branches stretched toward the sky, some still showing black leaves or, here and there, a little shriveled, decaying fruit. Thanks to the stuff I'd learned in Robotics more than any real experience, I figured out how to drive and work the controls for the backhoe pretty quickly. As the claw attacked the cold ground, again and again, opening a trench in the earth, my brain went black-screen. The past opened up in front of me and I fell into it like the next level of a video game.

"Why do you have to fight with him all the time?" Mom demanded, her brows nearly touching with the depth of her frustration.

"Why is he always saying something stupid?" I shot back.

Mom's lips twitched and I knew I was about two seconds from punishment.

"Don't call your little brother 'stupid,' Nester. I don't have any 'stupid' children. He's every bit as smart as you are—"

"He's not my brother. He's my half-brother."

Mom's eyes widened and the anger on her face melted to shock. "What?"

"He's my half-brother. Not my brother. We have different fathers, remember?"

"I'm well aware of that, Nester," Mom said sternly. "But what difference does that make? You live together. You've grown up together. You have the same mother and Irv is the only father you've really ever known so—"

"It makes all the difference," I growled. "It makes all the difference in the world—"

The tractor's motor cut out, snapping me back to the present. I looked down: the hole was big enough for all of us.

5

THE ONION CURE

"Those kids can't stay here," Liam said flatly. "They have to go."

I took a seat in one of the rocking chairs near him. Elise stood beside me, holding my hand tightly, making it pretty clear that this was as "alone" as we were going to get. Her eyes skittered between me and Liam, her brow puckering as she studied him warily.

She had reason, too. He didn't look like himself anymore. It wasn't just the haircut that showed the pale skin above his ears, or the crimp of pain around his eyes. He looked different, like all the feelings inside him were coiled into a tight and unpredictable spring. I was tempted to tell him to lie back—or even better, go back upstairs and rest. But I didn't want to trip the wire and set off a fresh explosion.

"Okay," I said as nonchalantly as I could.

"This is *our* place. My family's. I don't know why my father let them stay here and I don't care," he continued. "And considering that Dwarf Boy shot me—"

"Come on, man," I interrupted. "Don't call him that.

You, of all people, know better."

A pink flush of shame lit Liam's ears and I knew he was remembering the time, in the dark days of the Hole, when Rod had called Lilly a "retard" because of her Down's syndrome.

"Fine," he spat. "Doesn't change the fact that he shot me. Or that they're not supposed to be here. Or that we don't need them nearly as much as you seem to think."

I stared at him.

"Is that it?"

The determination on his face crumpled. He hesitated. "Yeah."

"So, when do you think this should happen? Today? You want me to send them out in the blizzard?"

Liam sighed. "No. I don't think that but—"

"Okay, so later then."

"Yeah. Later, I guess."

"Okay," I stood up. "Let's go check the animals, Elise."

"Okay?" Liam struggled to get up and gave up, holding his side again. "So, that's that? They're going?"

"Of course. Just as soon as you're 100 percent. Which, at the rate you're going, dude, that's going to be..." I pretended to calculate, before continuing, "*Never.* You're right: the kid shot you. So that means you need to rest. Let your body do its thing. Stop dragging yourself around here like there's stuff you need to do." I sighed. "You did your job, man. You got us here. Now—"

"I *didn't* do my job," his voice trembled with emotion, seethed with suppressed fury. "If I'd done my job, Lilly would be *here* instead of out *there*, covered with dirt!"

I crossed the room and yanked up his shirt.

"This is what I mean. " There was blood seeping through the gauze again. "The kid didn't kill you, but you might end up killing yourself. I know how you feel, but you can't—"

48

Hatred, that's what gleamed in Liam's eyes. In that moment, if he'd had the strength to do it, I think he would have grabbed me by the throat and squeezed until my brains came out of my ears.

"You *don't* know how I feel. You're *glad* Nate's dead. You couldn't stand him—"

"Lie still," I pulled at the gauze, probably a little rougher than was strictly necessary. Liam winced but kept talking, hammering at me.

"It's true, isn't it? You're glad. You're glad he's dead—"

Fire burned at the base of my brain, but I focused on the stitches and tried ignore the words. They looked okay: I didn't see the red streakiness that I knew might signal an infection. The skin was cool but not clammy. I redressed it quickly and moved lower to roll down his sock.

"Answer me, Nester. It's true, isn't it?"

I didn't remember doing it, but there was a neat patch of gauze tapped to Liam's heel. I lifted the white tape and...

Holy shit.

It wasn't a white scab like I expected, but a swollen mass of flesh in a host of colors. In the very center, a black dot radiated out to a white sac filled with yellowish green pus. Beyond that, the skin was bright red.

"Answer me! OW!" Liam screamed as I lay just the lightest finger on the hot, red skin.

Elise jumped. I felt her grab my sweater, little fingers like claws in my back. She pressed her face against me, hiding from the noise of Liam's shout.

"How long has this been like this?"

"I don't know," he said irritably. "But leave it alone—"

"Amaranth? Amy? I cried. "Can one of you come in here?"

"No!" Liam shook his head. He backed his voice down to reasonable. "I don't want— she—they already

49

think I'm some kind of invalid, Nester. Don't—"

"Yeah?" Amaranth appeared from the kitchen with a dish towel slung over her shoulder and a frown of concern on her face that told me she'd heard every word we'd said. "Is everything okay?"

Liam eyes were a volume on pleading desperation.

"Yeah..." I lied. "Could you bring me a little water and a clean cloth? I need to clean this blister up."

She nodded and disappeared.

"It's infected," I said quietly. "You know that, right? Normally this would buy you a trip straight to the doctor, if not the ER—"

"It'll be okay. Put some of that antibiotic cream on it. It'll be okay—"

Amaranth came back into the room with two bowls of water.

"I didn't know if you wanted it warm or not, so—" she began.

"Warm," I said, trying to smile at her. "Thanks."

"Sure," she said, her lips turning upward. Not quite enough for a smile, but good enough for her usual tough girl smirk. "Fetching water is women's work. Like the frontier days, right, Liam?"

"Yeah," he muttered without even looking at her.

The word found its mark like an arrow to a bull's eye. Hurt and confusion vibrated in her eyes for just a second before her features rearranged themselves into her usual cool indifference. She flipped a lock of fiery hair off her face and sauntered away from us like Liam hadn't shut her down.

"She was trying to bust my chops a little," I offered, as I wet the cloth in the water and lay it on the hot skin. "You didn't have to—"

"Butt out, Bartlett," he murmured, wincing as the cloth made contact. "She needs to worry about herself, not me."

50

"She cares about you, dude. What's so bad about that?"

"Everything. Especially now that I—" he grunted, shuddering against the pain of my efforts. "That really, really, hurts."

I removed the cloth and inspected the blister again. "I was hoping the warm water would pop it, but..." I shook my head. "I don't think antibiotic cream is going to do much good now. It's already gone further than that. I don't suppose your old man stockpiled any drugs anywhere?"

It was a fair question. While my parents finished the basement and updated the kitchen, old man Harper had sunk his money into MREs, ammunition and bunkers. It didn't seem impossible that he'd found some way to store medicine, too.

Liam shook his head.

"That's really hard to do," he said.

"Yeah, I know," I agreed. "Insurance companies, regulations and all that." I'd heard my mom rant about that stuff a thousand times. "Okay, there's got to be something else we can do. I mean, people got infections before there were drugs." I lay a hand on his forehead to check for fever.

"Cut it out, man! What are you, my mother?" he demanded, slapping it away.

"You wish."

I wasn't expecting it, but a genuine chuckle escaped from his lips. "You're right," he said softly. "I wish that more—almost more—than anything in this world." He lifted an arm over his face as the laughter degraded. He choked back a sob and turned away from me. To give him a minute to get himself together, I got up and moved toward the bookshelf.

Elise shadowed me, but I was getting used to that now. Her hand was still knotted onto the back of my sweater, and she moved with me like we were conjoined twins.

51

The title that had jumped out at me the first time I contemplated the bookcases evaded me now that I wanted it. I scanned the rows of books left to right and front to back, but somehow it got lost. Or maybe it was that I couldn't help hearing the soft gasps of Liam's tears.

He's right. They all know it. Nate grabbed the other arm of my sweater. *You didn't like me.*

"What difference does that make now?" I asked the ghost and for once, Nate shut up and faded without another word.

Elise shifted behind me.

"Don't mind me, Elise," I said, turning to her. "I'm *loco.* Just... *loco.*"

She stared at me like this wasn't exactly news.

"There was a book," I continued, turning back to the bookcase. "With a blue spine." I wrinkled my brain to remember Freshman Spanish, but languages—hell, even English—aren't my thing. "*Un libro...uh... con un ...*" I didn't know the word for spine, but it didn't matter. Elise lifted a finger and pointed.

"That's it. Good job, Elise."

Survival Medicine, the cover read in big black letters and in a smaller subtitle *Everything You Need to Know to Survive When the SHTF.* I knew the acronym now: SHTF meant "shit hits the fan" and it was survivalist code for life without the comforts of the modern world.

I flipped to the index, then to the section on infections.

"It says you're hosed, man," I said over my shoulder, jokingly. "No, it says that a broad spectrum antibiotic is the best treatment, but we already knew that. We've got to ride it out, keep you hydrated and hope it doesn't get any worse and..."I turned the page. "There are some herbs that might help. Potions and poultices—"

I heard Marty before I saw him. He ambled into the room lugging a bucket of coal that had to weigh almost as much as he did and stopped, staring at us, his mouth slack like he belonged in the slow class, but his eyes were alert and shrewd. Liam glared at him through red-rimmed eyes. Mutual distrust wafted through the room like smoke.

"Seen Katie?" Marty said at last, directing the question toward the fireplace.

I shook my head. "Thought she was in the Lookout."

"Rod is up there now."

"Maybe she made a trip to the outhouse," I offered after it stayed quiet a few seconds too long. "Or out to check on the animals."

"Yeah, that's probably it." Marty wouldn't look Liam in the face, but he couldn't miss his bare foot, sticking up on the arm of the old sofa like a beacon. "That don't look so good," he said after another uncomfortable pause.

"It's fine," Liam muttered, moving his foot out of the kid's line of sight.

"Not quite 'fine'," I corrected. "It's infected, I think," I pointed to the book. "This says we could make a poultice that might help. Calendula flowers," I read. "Raw honey—"

Marty frowned. "Never heard of calendula. But—"

The girls' voices rose in the kitchen.

"I was going to do it!" Amaranth shouted. "I just forgot, okay? If you'd just—"

"There's stuff you can't forget!" Katie retorted angrily. "Them animals help to keep us alive and that means we got to keep *them* alive—"

Amaranth's reply was sarcastic and too quiet to hear. Katie stomped into the room a moment later, her cheeks red and mouth clamped tight. The look she and Marty exchanged told me they'd had a conversation about getting rid of *us*, too. Then her eyes swept the room and landed hard on me.

"What did you do to yourself?" she gasped. "All your pretty hair!" She covered her mouth with both her hands like she was trying to hold it in and then gave up and just laughed at me. "Oh my!"

Katie giggled and kept giggling until I started to get annoyed. But it must have been contagious because suddenly, Elise laughed, too.

It only lasted a second and she swallowed it back almost as soon as the sound escaped, but not before we all heard it. Even Liam was distracted by it. His eyes widened in astonishment and a genuine grin eased across his face.

"I look pretty bad, huh, Elise?" I squatted in front of her and stared hard into her face. There was a glimmer in her eyes that hadn't been there before. "I look pretty silly, huh?"

"You look like a naked mole rat," Liam offered.

"With eyeglasses!" Katie exclaimed, trying—and failing—to suppress another round of giggles.

"Good one," Liam chuckled in spite of himself. "Yeah, that's exactly what he looks like: a naked mole rat with glasses."

Elise smiled.

"Is that what I look like, Elise?" I asked. The description wasn't flattering, and I'd be lying if I didn't say I wished Amy Yamamato chin hair and back fat for cutting my hair down to the skin. But if Elise would talk—or even just laugh again—being a bespectacled mole rat might be worth it.

"Is that what I look like?" I asked again.

The little girl nodded.

"Good girl!" A stinging feeling burned my eyes and I blinked a few times to clear the sudden tears that escaped lockdown. I grabbed her into a hard, quick hug, but it was a brief victory: almost immediately her smile faded, and her face went blank again. Her fingers dug into mine, insistent and terrified.

"Good girl, Elise," I repeated. "You're coming back to us. You're coming back, I know it."

When I looked up, the others were staring. Katie's

anger had evaporated and Marty looked a little less suspicious. Even Liam's simmering resentment had been knocked back a notch.

But Nate was standing in the center of the braided rug with tears rolling down his face and his fingers curled into tight brown fists.

"What?" I asked.

Why her, Nester? Why not me? Why not me? Why couldn't you love me? Why—

"Nothin'," Katie replied. "Just nice to see you got a soft side." She wrinkled her nose. "You been kinda hard—"

Why? Can't you answer? Even now? When I'm dead and it doesn't even matter anymore—

"I don't know what you want from me," I snapped. "Just let it go, all right?"

Katie's mouth closed. She and Marty swapped another of their secret glances. Even Liam glared at me.

"He wasn't always this much of a jerk," he muttered to the other two. "No, wait. I take that back. I guess he was always a jerk. The kind of friend who'd leave you hanging."

"Come on, man," I began as embarrassment burned my naked scalp. I knew what he was talking about—his first day at JFK High School after years of being homeschooled. His father had showed up in full survival mode, wearing Army green and driving a camouflage-painted bus. The whole school saw it. Who could blame me for backing away from that situation? "That was a lifetime ago and—" I nodded at Katie and Marty. "I didn't mean that the way it sounded. I just don't understand why you're all so surprised. I've got feelings, too."

And I'm being haunted by Nate. Isn't that an excuse? I wanted to say it, but didn't dare. There was enough going on in this claustrophobic little cabin without me admitting to going mental.

"Right," Liam said. He closed his eyes and a heavy sigh escaped from his lips. Katie's frown returned.

55

"Katie, have we got"— I consulted the book again— "garlic, honey and Calendula leaves?"

The girl squinted at me. "You making a poultice?"

I nodded. "For the blister on Liam's heel."

The odd twins stepped forward together, moving in tandem without touching. Liam had moved his foot off the couch, but clearly it hurt too much to rest on the floor, so he held it up in a way that looked far from comfortable.

"Once, when we was shimmying through a wire fence—" Marty began.

"Down near the government offices in Benson—" Katie interrupted.

"Got a cut on my leg. Didn't think nothing of it at first—"

"Just looked like your average scratch. Not too deep, not even all that long," Katie continued, coming close enough to Liam to peer at the blistered foot. "Nothing special—"

"And for a few days it was fine. Then after about three days—"

"Turned bright red. Got all full of pus—"

"Was running an awful fever—" Marty continued.

"I covered it with a poultice. No raw honey, though. Used onions—"

"It split wide open. Felt better after that."

Katie looked up at me. "We got some onions in the cellar. You want me to make you some?"

"Yeah, but can you teach me? I'd like to learn how to do it, if that's okay."

She considered me and consulted her brother silently before she nodded. "I'll get what we need."

As Katie left the room, Amaranth appeared at the edge of it. If I hadn't been flipping the pages of that medical book like a madman, I might have spoken to her, but she wasn't interested in me. Her eyes were for Liam only— and his eyes were closed.

56

I checked the book and cross-referenced every synonym for "mental illness" I could think of, but the survival medical book didn't have a single entry. Apparently, at the end of the world, "crazy" didn't even merit a mention.

6

NESTER'S GIRLS

I couldn't sleep.

The bedrooms were decorated a lot like the cots in The Hole: two twin beds in each of the rooms, covered with colorful quilts that somebody's grandmother probably made a long, long time ago. Each room had chest of drawers made of unpainted pine and another small chest at the foot of each bed, all of which looked like Mr. Harper had made them himself. Resting on the chest of drawers was a plastic basin filled with water, and under every bed was another empty one meant to cut down on trips to the outhouse.

I had taken Elise up and laid her down on an empty bed in the room where Katie slept in her clothes, her body curled into a tight ball. I sat on the edge of the bed, rubbing her back gently like I'd been doing it all my life, until she was deeply asleep. I knew I should probably lay down beside her—I was supposed to pull a shift up at the Lookout soon—but I knew I'd only lay there, staring up at the ceiling, thinking about the world that used to be.

Instead, I stood up and left the room.

Rod and Amy lay intertwined on a single bed in the room across the hall. His arms were draped around her shoulders and her head was on his chest, but there wasn't anything else going on. They both wore their clothes—right down to the shoes. Amy's backpack of supplies rested at the foot of the bed, and her guns were looped around the bedpost within easy grasp.

Aren't they cute? Nate hovered in the doorway. Literally. He floated a few inches off the ground, looking more ghostly than he ever had before. I figured he'd given up spooking me with his "aliveness" and was trying to spook me with his "deadness," so I just ignored him.

If he dies, that could be you, cuddling on Amy.

"Shut up," I whispered.

Marty lay on the other bed. From the looks of things, he slept restlessly: he'd kicked off the quilt and now lay with his arms wrapped tightly around his body like he was cold. I stepped into the room and picked the coverlet up, dropping it around him. Asleep, he looked peaceful and harmless. Just a very small boy, not a soldier of the apocalypse.

Oh, so you can be nice to him, too, huh? Nice to Elise. Nice to Marty. Nice to everyone but me, Nate hissed in my ear.

Yeah, I replied. *Everyone but you.*

As I turned to leave the small room, I caught a glimpse of my own face in the mirror.

I looked like a naked mole rat...with glasses. Awful. I'd never thought I was good-looking, but I didn't think I was ugly, either. Now, I could add "my hair" to the list of things I'd lost, along with my family, my future, and my mind.

When I looked again, Nate stared back at me in the place where my own face should have been.

Hi there, handsome.

"Man, you are *not* real. You're not real..."

59

I hissed the words over and over like the old Bloody Mary rhyme that scared us all back in elementary school. You'd say "Bloody Mary" over and over to the mirror when you woke up in the middle of the night to pee and this old witch was supposed to appear, covered in blood. She might tell you your future... and she might scratch your eyes out.

"You are not real," I told the spirit of my dead brother. "You are not—"

Of course I'm real, Nate answered, rolling his eyes. *I'm just dead.*

"Go away."

I'm here to help you, Nest. I'm like Casper, man. Totally friendly.

"Go away—"

Nester—

"Go away!" I managed to keep from shouting, but across the hall, Katie stirred. I hurried down the back stairs to the kitchen before she could sit up and start asking me questions I didn't want to answer.

I'd left my shoes in the mudroom and the thick pair of white gym socks protecting my feet from the cold wood floors made my steps relatively quiet. I paused in the kitchen just long enough to understand that there was nothing in there that I wanted, and then headed to the living area. I didn't exactly have a plan, but there were some books on the shelf that had potential. Or I could tinker with the radio, or maybe—

"I just don't know what to do."

I stopped when I heard the voice, peering into the room.

Amaranth sat on the edge of the couch, bending over Liam, who lay stretched out across it. At first, I thought they were having a private conversation and I sure as hell didn't want to get in the middle of *that*— until I realized that Liam's eyes were closed.

60

Amaranth stood up suddenly and paced away from him.

"It doesn't make any sense, Liam," she said in a low voice. "It doesn't make any sense that I'm still here, and those—" her voice broke. "Those *good* people like Mrs. Cantwell and her family are dead."

Liam didn't answer. His chest rose and fell, slowly and deeply, but other than that, no part of his body moved. I crept the tiniest bit closer so I could see his face; he was asleep.

"I—I told you about her remember?" Amaranth continued. "At least, kind of. She—she was my foster mother for a while. A really good person. Religious. But not in that fake way most people are. She really tried to live it, you know. She..." Amaranth stopped and when she spoke again there were tears rolling down her face. "She really loved me," she continued in a whisper. "Even after the state made me live somewhere else, I knew...there was one person who really loved me. And now... she's dead."

She buried her face in her hands and for a long time, she didn't say anything else. I watched her, feeling helpless, wondering if I should make my presence known or if that would somehow make it worse.

"I just don't understand..." she moaned at last. "Why would God take a good person like that and leave a person like me here? Why—"

The plank floor beneath my feet creaked.

Amaranth spun around, her face hardening into its usual toughness.

"What?" she demanded, smearing her tears off her face like they were a mistake.

"Nothing... only, I thought you were supposed to be watching."

"Yeah, I'm going up now," she said quickly. "I was just checking on Liam, that's all. He really should have gone upstairs to bed. It gets so cold down here—"

61

"It's cool, Amaranth," I said in a low voice, nodding toward the sofa. "If you want, I'll switch with you. You can stay with him a while longer, and I'll go up. You can relieve me in a few hours."

"It's no big deal," she said casually with a shrug. "I'll go now. I'm all ready." She gestured to the fresh protective suit and mask draped over the nearest rocking chair. "Besides, it's not like we're having a conversation or anything. He's asleep."

She grabbed her gear and headed for the stairs. The only things that gave her away were her red eyes and the pink patches of emotion on her face. She was gone before I could comment on either of them.

But I was unnerved by what I'd heard. I crossed to the bookshelf and grabbed the first novel that came to my hands, without even looking at the title and collapsed into the rocking chair without even opening it. I sat there for a while, thinking about Amy and Rod with their arms around each other, and the way Amaranth looked at Liam when he wasn't watching. An old familiar feeling of frustration mixed with jealousy pounded in my brain. I imagined myself, years from now, wildly successful for having invented something truly life-saving, dating a gorgeous beauty queen who loved me for *me*.

None of that would happen now. I'd been cheated of a hot girlfriend on top of everything else.

I gave up on reading and crept out of the room.

I found Katie in the kitchen, adding coal to the stove.

"What are you doing up?" I asked.

She shrugged. "Thought I heard something," she answered. "People talking."

"Oh."

She filled the teapot with water and set it on the stove. "You want some?"

I slumped forward, rubbing my forehead. I was bone tired but my brain was hyper, jumping from thought to

62

thought, unable to find rest. When I didn't answer, Katie got two mugs anyway. "Chamomile is nice," she said quietly. "Sort of soothing." She sat down across from me. "I see how it is now."

"What?"

"Well, it's Amy and Rod. They're a couple. But that weren't too hard to figure out. They act like it. Bickering and stuff, but also..." she ducked her head like she was embarrassed to say the words. "Well, sleeping together and all."

"I don't think it's like *that*—" I stopped because I realized I really didn't know what Rod and Amy did, especially BTB. "At least not now."

"And it's Liam and the other one. Amaranth," she said the girl's name like it was a bug in her mouth. "Though I don't see why," she added under her breath.

"She's not that bad."

Katie let the doubt in her face reply. "Guess Mama was right. Opposites attract."

I could see why she might say that: on the surface, Amaranth and Liam probably seemed about as different as two people could be. But only on the skin. Once you'd peeled them both back a layer or two, though, it wasn't so simple. And if you'd seen them scrambling to survive, being stubborn, trying to keep anyone from touching their sore spots— they had a lot more in common. I was about to say something like that when Katie threw me a curve ball.

"Did your girlfriend die?" she asked gently, as if she'd been reading my mind.

"Girlfriend? Who me? No, I—" But the kettle whistled and the girl jumped up to silence it.

"Sorry, if it ain't nothing you want to talk about," she said quickly, pouring the water. "I just figured...a boy like you. Who knows so much stuff and..."she shrugged. "Takes care of people so good and all. Makes sense that you have...had... you know... someone," she managed with her

63

cheeks the color of sunrise.

She likes you, dude.

Nate sang the words in my ear.

She likes you. Got a big fat crush on the naked mole rat...

"Yeah," I said, suddenly feeling as awkward and uncomfortable as she looked. Something in her eyes when she said all that made me want to get up and run for the door. "I mean, no."

"Oh." She spoke like she understood, then frowned like she didn't. She didn't look at me again and I tried not to look at her, either. We both waited for something to happen, but nothing did, so I drank my tea so quickly I burned my tongue and then stood up, stretching.

"I guess I should catch a few hours of sleep." I tried to yawn, but it probably looked as fake as Amaranth's ID.

"Yeah," she said. "Me, too. I'm gonna check on Liam first." She hesitated. "You take the empty bed. I like the rocker—"

"No, that's okay—"

"Really," she said, blushing again. "It's okay."

She left the room quickly, without looking at me again. But before I climbed the stairs, I heard her say, "You're up."

"Yeah," Liam answered.

"You need anything? Want some tea?"

"No, I'm good."

I couldn't stop myself from peeking into the other room. The two of them were just sitting there in silence, Liam lying on the couch and Katie in her chair, tilting back and forth a little.

"Stove's low," she said and stood up to tend it. I watched Liam watch her, wondering if he thought she was pretty or if he still hated her too much to notice anything like that.

She finished at the fire, pausing to pull the blanket

64

higher around Liam's shoulders like she'd been tending him all her life.

"Thanks," Liam muttered. He turned his head and watched her tuck herself into the chair again.

"'Night," she said, closing her eyes.

"'Night."

As I turned for the staircase, I wished for that thing that Rod and Liam both had. A gift I hadn't been granted and wondered if I'd ever obtain. The thing that made girls put their heads on your shoulders and wrap their arms around you. The thing that made girls smile when you noticed them and cry when you didn't. The words and the way of acting that made them come close instead of run away.

7

AMARANTH LOOKS OUT

I dreamed of dark vinyl booths and Roman landmarks painted on the walls. Of the low lighting and the menu that never changed, and the owner, Antonio, who always greeted me by saying "I'd grown so big" like I was still ten years old.

Cappy's Italian Ristorante: my family's regular Friday night haunt. Nate's favorite place.

Nate sat across from me in the red vinyl booth; Mom's arm draped his shoulders in an embrace that wasn't quite a hug, but close all the same. Either he didn't notice or he took it for granted because he ignored her, face deep in his iPad. I was squeezed in beside Irv, my stepdad.

"It looks like I'm headed to Alabama at the middle of the month," he said. He had started balding a few years ago and his solution was to shave his head. That was when I started growing mine, but people still thought he was my real father.

"So the Justice Project has decided to take him on." Mom looked tired—there were dark half-crescents under her eyes and her brown skin looked as dull and washed out as old chocolate milk. But she managed a smile.

"Yeah. It was a tough one," Irv said. "We get so many requests. They pour in every month. Most of them aren't right for us—"

"You mean most of them are guilty," I interrupted just to mess with him.

"It isn't so much about guilt or innocence, Nester," Irv corrected. "It's about what kind of people we want to be. It's about whether we respond to violence with more violence or with—"

The waitress set a basket of bread and a dish of garlic butter on the table. I reached for it, but Nate tore his attention away from his game and snatched the whole basket, dragging it towards him before I could get a single slice.

"Hey!" I cried.

"—residual effects of generations of being second class citizens in this country. Black men—and women—but especially men—" Irv continued like nothing happened.

"They know, dear," Mom said quietly, touching his hand to stop Rant Number 3.

She failed.

Irv ranted on: about young black men being sentenced to death while their white counterparts got jail time for the same offenses. About how people would always judge us by the color of skin first and that's why we needed to get good grades and make something of ourselves so we wouldn't live up to the negative stereotypes. About how racism was alive and well and walking to school with us every day—

"My friends aren't that way."

Irv quirked a glance at Mom, and she smiled into her plate.

"They're not!" I insisted.

Irv chuckled and Mom tried to hide in her shoulder, but in the end, she gave up and laughed, too.

"I'm sorry, baby," she said. "But you're far from Mr. Popularity. And that's okay," she added quickly. "You get good grades and keep up with all your schoolwork. But friends? Who are you talking about? That odd kid you used

67

to play chess with on Saturdays?"

"Muhamet's not weird. He's just really focused."

"Or our crazy neighbor's son?" Irv always called Mr. Harper 'Our Crazy Neighbor.' "Liam? Haven't seen him in a while. Guess he's been out on that farm his old man bought—"

"Why anyone would want to live way out in the mountains is beyond me," Mom shook her head in bewilderment.

They geared up to trash-talk the Harpers. There was plenty to talk about: that ancient truck that looked like it should have been in the junkyard when Eisenhower was President. The huge grocery trips, financed with coupons. The odd-shaped UPS packages. Snippets of arguments between Mr. and Mrs. Harper in the driveway or on the front lawn. But on the occasions when I'd been in their home, it seemed normal enough to me. True, Mr. Harper made us cookies, which was unexpected from a guy wearing a T-shirt that said "Army Proud." And he was always really interested in what I carried in my backpack. But other than that, he didn't seem much weirder than Irv, who could drop a lesson on "oppression" and the "legacies of white supremacy" faster than most people could look the words up on the Internet.

"How's he adjusting to regular school?" Irv asked, but before I could answer, Mom said,

"I heard he got in big trouble a couple of weeks ago. At back to school night." Mom locked eyes on me. "You know anything about that?"

"No," I lied. The whole story had gone around the school as fast as naked pictures, but it didn't feel right to tell them that— especially after my parents had pronounced me friendless and unfriendworthy.

"It was pretty serious, as I understand it." Mom eyed me like she knew I was lying. "I think it would be better if you stayed away from him. You're judged by who you

68

associate with. I'd hate for that kid's influence to get you into the kind of trouble that would cost you a place at one of the Ivy League schools—"

"I agree," Irv said. "Unless, of course, the end really does come!" He laughed. "Then you get your brown behind over to Harper and beg him to let you in!"

I opened my mouth to say something—defend or condemn— but thunder crushed out my words. Lightning flashed outside the dark window, growing bright and closer until the sky was on fire. Irv started shrieking as he burst into flame. I scrambled away from him, knocking over the fake red leather booth and hiding behind it as the heat seared my skin and the noise filled my ears and the smell of frying flesh hit my nose. Katie was already there, her face shining and fearless.

"No!" I screamed over the explosion. "No, no—"

"Yes, yes, yes!" she said calmly, smiling at me. "That's all gone. Welcome home—"

I sat up, my brow wet, my heart thumping, adrenaline coursing through my body.

Elise was awake and staring at me somberly. Without a word, she stood up, slipped on her boots and gathered our coats. Her movements were as powerful as any words. *There's nothing you can do about it now*, her dark eyes seemed to say. *So get up and get to work, Nester.*

"You're right, Elise," I muttered, putting my size 14s down on the cold wood floor again. "It's our turn to watch."

There was a trick to reaching the Lookout, a hidden spinning door just like the ones in every *Scooby Doo* cartoon ever written. You flipped a switch inside the gun cabinet—you had to know the digital combination to get it open— and the whole wall spun, dumping you into a dark alcove. Then you climbed a short staircase, opened a hatch cut in the ceiling—a hatch that could be locked from up on

69

the Lookout—and climbed the last few steps into the daylight. It was the most impressive and complicated system in the house—especially given the size of the gun cabinet. The thing was massive: nearly tall enough for me to stand up in, at least four feet deep and holding rack after rack of weapons. The setup was ingenious, really. In the event of an intruder, you could escape to the Lookout with all of your weapons secured inside with you.

I lifted the hatch and Elise preceded me up into the daylight. If it *was* daylight. The sky was dark gray—but it always was since we'd seen that flash of light and the big mushroom cloud light up in the southeastern sky. According to Liam's watch, it was early morning, maybe an hour after the sun should have risen.

The Lookout itself was pretty small—I could walk the entire circle in ten long steps— but the view would have been killer if it hadn't been obliterated by swirling snow. On a clear day, you could probably see down to the lake, but we hadn't had any clear days yet. Instead, the snow made it tough to see more a few hundred yards, even with the night vision goggles and the binoculars Mr. Harper had thoughtfully left in a storage cubby built into the center wall. The ground was invisible under the white dust and, except for the places where we'd worn tracks to the barn and the outhouse, the whiteness was pristine and undisturbed and deep. The cupola's round roof offered a little protection from the worst of the snow, but not from the wind or the bitter cold. That was okay by me. Comfort was the enemy of the wary.

"Amaranth?" I called, circling the narrow space. "It's me and Elise—"

The tip of my boot touched something and it rolled, clinking musically until it met an obstruction. I followed the sound.

Amaranth sat on the floor of the Lookout with the night vision goggles covering her face and her feet splayed

70

wide. Snow had dusted over her clothes, nearly covering her. I thought she was hurt—had collapsed or something—until it registered that the sound I'd heard was an empty bottle.

An empty alcohol bottle. Gin, this time.

"Amaranth!" I shook her.

She jerked her head in my direction. "I'm awake..." she murmured, drunkenly. "I'm awake...."

With difficulty she got her legs under her body and stood.

"What—what are you doing here?" she asked in confusion.

"Relieving you. From your watch. Which you pretty clearly weren't doing."

"I was, too," she hiccupped. "Why else would I be *up* here, Nester? Duhhhh..."

"Then what's this?" I shook the gin bottle at her.

"*That* is a bottle of gin. An *empty* bottle of gin." She was joking with me, playing. "It has kept me nice and warm, while I watched the snow fall."

"You can't drink until you pass out when you're supposed to be watching—"

"Passed out?" Amaranth shook her head violently. "Me? No. I wasn't passed out. Relaxed, maybe," she waved her forefinger at me, "But definitely *not* 'passed out.' And as for 'watching'— she opened her arms wide and spun in a slow 360 degrees. "Just what did you expect to see? There's snow. Just snow. Just snow and more snow!" She made another circle like a dancer in an odd ballet. "Snow, snow, snow," she sang. "Snow, snow, go away! Come again another day! It's really sort of stupid, if you ask me. If you're out in this, I'm not gonna have to shoot you. The cold is going to kill you first. So you're dead anyway!" She chortled. "Isn't that funny, Elise?" she asked leaning toward the little girl. "Isn't that—?"

Elise shrank from her like she was contagious.

"What did I do, Elise?" Amaranth asked, suddenly serious. "We're supposed to be family—"

"Maybe she's not thrilled about having a 'sister' who's a lush," I grumbled.

"Yeah, she prefers a 'brother' who wanders around having conversations with people who aren't there!" She shot back. "What's the matter, Nester?" She asked in a voice that wore sarcasm for a coat. "Did you think that was a— a—" she couldn't remember the word *secret*. "A 'shh' thing? Did you think no one had noticed?" She jabbed her chest, continuing in a rush of drunken words. "*I* noticed, Nester. *I* noticed. I notice lots of things that no one else notices. You know why? Because that's how I *survive*. Or how I survived..." she stopped, frowning. "Survived. Yeah, survived I think—"

"You're not making any sense."

"Nothing makes sense, Nester. You were right."

I quirked an eyebrow at her. "Right? About what?"

"Our situation," Amaranth pronounced. "Think about it: we're here, trying so hard to stay alive when we're all gonna end up like Rod anyway—"

"Shut up," I hissed. "You want them all to hear you?"

"What difference does it make? You think they don't know?" Amaranth shook her head dramatically. "I always thought you were smart, Nester, but if you think there's a single person in this house who doesn't know that Rod—"

"I wasn't right," I interrupted in exasperation. "I was just mad, Amaranth." I took her by the arm and guided her toward the hatch. "You're drunk and you don't know what you're talking about, so just go in. Go to bed. Go to the kitchen. Go to the barn. Go check on Liam. Just go somewhere and sober up." I threw open the door and jerked my head toward the stairs. "Please."

For two long, cold hours Elise and I paced the Lookout, shivering and stamping our feet to stay warm, staring out into the swirling dark snow. Amaranth was right: I couldn't see much, but I did see her stagger toward the outhouse. She stayed out there a long time, then finally emerged and made her way to cabin with her head down like a kid who knew she was going to get grounded as soon as she crossed the threshold. Later, we saw Katie slog through the deep snow to the barn holding an empty pail. She emerged several minutes later, lugging a full one. Milk from the cow, I guessed. I wondered who was on KP—kitchen patrol—and if there'd be hot food in a few hours. From time to time, Elise warmed her hands in my pockets, but other than that, she walked the parapet as steadily as I did, staring at the horizon, the night vision goggles perched on her head like giant goo-goo eyes. I would have loved to send her inside to wait for me, but I knew she wouldn't have gone.

Nate was a no-show.

When Rod finally lifted the hatch to relieve us, I felt like a six-foot Popsicle. I wanted nothing more than to find a mug of hot cocoa waiting for me downstairs, but that was unlikely. I hadn't seen any kind of chocolate in the pantry, for one, and if I did find some, it sure wouldn't be ready and waiting for me. I'd have to make it myself.

Amaranth sat at the table in the kitchen with a mug of something steaming in front of her and a sullen, I-dare-you-to-say-anything-to-me look on her face. Liam hopped on one foot between the pantry and a large box resting on the butcher block table, his face set with grim determination. The odor of a fresh batch of Katie's onion poultice overwhelmed the room.

"What are you doing, man?" I asked.

He ignored me and stretched himself up toward the pantry's top shelf. He lost his balance and automatically put his weight on his bad foot in the effort to right himself. He winced, an involuntary gasp of pain escaping from his lips, but he was undeterred. A moment later, he pulled a glass

73

liquor bottle down and then hopped toward the box. I heard the clang of the bottle connecting with others like it.

"I told you: you don't have to—" Amaranth said petulantly. She didn't sound drunk anymore, just irritated.

"Yes, I do."

"I think you're overreacting," she grumbled. "It's really not that big of a deal—"

"What are you doing?" I asked again.

"Getting this stuff out of here."

"What are you going to do with it?"

Liam shrugged. "You're going to hide it."

"Where?" I asked, looking around.

"You're the big brain, not me," Liam muttered. "Anywhere *she* can't find it."

Amaranth's face colored. A nasty mix of shame, embarrassment and anger combined in her eyes.

"Fine," she muttered, grabbing her coat. "I'm gonna go feed the animals—"

"Take your gun," Liam muttered without looking at her.

"I know."

"Do you?" Liam's voice was ugly.

"Yeah, I do. But I think I'll to go see Lilly first," she retorted. She waited until Liam's shoulders contracted with grief, then slammed the door.

If I hadn't needed that hot tea so bad, I would have turned around right then and retreated as far from the drama as the small cabin would allow, but instead I pumped some water into the kettle and set it on one of the burners. Elise slid close to me, as wary of Liam's simmering anger as she was of Amaranth's drunken rampage.

I stared at Liam for a minute. "How's the foot?" I asked after a minute.

"What do you think?" he muttered.

"Stuff sure smells bad enough. Maybe I should take a look—"

"Katie already did all that," he said impatiently. "Take this booze out to the root cellar and hide it somewhere," he commanded.

Pissed. That's what I was. Lately, it was always "Nester do this, Nester do that" from everybody. I was only the dude left strong enough to do the heavy work—and heavy work hadn't been in my life's game plan. It made me want to start screaming. Start on one of Irv's slavery rants. Or one of his modern-day analogies: *People equate brown skin with labor. They see 'brown' and think you're the maintenance man, not the manager.* But thinking of Irv was the only thing that kept me from popping off. I didn't want to be like him, so I took a deep breath.

"Look, man. I get you. And we have to do something. But the key to the root cellar stays on that hook," I said pointing. "Amaranth can just—"

"That's why I asked you to hide it, Nester!"

"Liam," I began cautiously. "This *is* Amaranth we're talking about. Amaranth's not stupid. If she's decided drinking's her thing, she's gonna have more than one stash by now, man. And I think..." I was speaking on tiptoes, but it had to be said. "I think she's found a few of your dad's hiding place—"

"Then you find them, too!" Liam snapped.

My resentment must have shown on my face.

Liam sighed. He hopped close to me, his voice pleading instead of angry. "Look, she talks to me sometimes. When she thinks I'm asleep and—she's really messed up, Nester. More than I thought." His eyes locked on mine. "Just hide the alcohol. Please. I—I don't—I can't let anything happen to her," he said blinking fast. "Will you help me, Nester?"

I just stared at him. To tell the truth, getting in the middle of Amaranth and Liam was the last thing I wanted to do. I just couldn't figure out a way to refuse him.

"You know what I think? I think you ought to spend

a whole less time worrying about Amaranth Jones and a lot more time worrying about yourself," I muttered, sinking into the chair and rubbing my bald head.

Liam grimaced, but I wasn't sure if that was because of my words or because he was in pain. "Nester..."

"Oh all right. I'll do the best I can."

"Thanks," Liam said. Relief seemed to steal something from him and he deflated suddenly. I noticed for the first time that he looked sort of sweaty. Feverish, maybe. I was about to comment when he said, "I—I'm kinda tired. Going up for a bit."

"Yeah, sure. Good idea."

I watched him hop the stairs one at a time, wondering if I should follow him. Insist on checking him out. When I turned around, Amaranth was standing behind me, watching both of us. From the intensity of her gaze as she followed Liam's slow progress up the stairs, I knew she'd heard every word.

8

THE ANIMAL IN THE BARN

I waited until the snow had died down to random flakes that floated around like they couldn't figure out where to land. Then, Elise and I suited up again and headed to the cellar with the box of bottles.

The cellar was part root cellar, part storm shelter, located in the woods about 50 yards from the main house. The entrance was camouflaged to blend into the landscape. Once inside, the door locked with a bolt and heavy steel latch, and you descended a 9-rung ladder into the safety of the space. It was about the size of my bedroom back home—maybe 17 feet by 15 feet. There was a second exit somewhere behind the stored gear that Katie said led to a tunnel below ground. That tunnel dumped you out on the path that led to the lake.

In the center of the room, two cots were bolted to the cement floor. The space beneath them had been packed with all kinds of duffels and boxes. The four walls were lined with utility shelves brimming with Mason jars filled with every kind of fruit and vegetable you could want, along with more canned goods and some big plastic jugs that at first I mistook for kitty litter until I realized they were all filled with freeze-dried food. And of course, there was water stored in several 40-gallon drums. A heavy strip of tarp hung in the corner; I knew without investigating that behind it was the toilet bucket. It smelled a little, but not nearly as bad as the Hole had smelled before we left it. There was an old metal cabinet against the far wall, its door hanging open enough for me to see more weapons nestled inside.

We hid the liquor the best we could by dispersing the bottles randomly amongst the jars of pickles and preserves. When we were done, Elise tugged on my arm, pointing to the barn,

"You want to see the animals?"

She nodded and I sighed. If I'm a hundred percent honest, I really don't like animals, but Elise liked to let the goat nibble her fingers and I wasn't in a big hurry to go back in the house. I let her lead me, following Amaranth's footprints in the fresh snow. They led right up to the barn, and then veered away. At first I thought she'd gone around the side for the muck cart, but no. They kept going, compacting the deep snow in the direction of the orchard, back over the fields toward Lilly's grave.

The barn was open...and it wasn't supposed to be. The padlock was missing and the board that secured the two doors like a large old-fashioned latch was lifted.

"You think Amaranth did this before she went to see Lilly?" I asked, staring toward the orchard, but of course she was too far away to see or call. For just a moment, I was nervous. But then I talked myself out of it.

"There are no other tracks but hers and ours," I told Elise, but I was really talking to myself. I turned up to the Lookout. "Who's on duty, Elise? Rod, right? I think it's okay," I told my little shadow and pulled the doors open.

We'd been at the Mountain Place a week—seven long, dark and mostly snowy days and it seemed like the work never ended. I missed electricity. I missed running water. I missed supermarkets. I missed being stupid and clueless about where food came from and how much work it took to get it. Even with all of us doing a share, the work was everlasting, mindless and sweaty: mucking out the

78

barn, feeding the animals, clearing snow from the roofs, pumping and lugging water, composting our trash, cleaning and maintaining weapons, washing and mending clothes, cooking and cleaning and keeping an eye on the state of our supplies. And always—always—keeping watch.

Before our life at the Mountain Place, I'd been in a barn exactly once: on a kindergarten field trip ten years ago. I didn't like it at all. Animals are pretty and interesting in nature specials and in cartoons, but in real life, they are loud and demanding and smell like crap. This barn smelled like the barn in my memory and was organized much the same way: on the left, a few stalls that held a massive sow, a goat and a single cow, all of them staring at us with the same listless stupidity. To the right, a wall lined with hand tools and farm equipment. A short ladder ascended to a dark loft full of browning hay.

As soon as she saw us, the cow swung her head at me and lowed, probably expecting to be milked again, but that was a job for Katie or Marty. Just thinking about grabbing the beast by the udders revolted me and made me wish for supermarket plastic containers that I could just open, and forget about where the white stuff came from. The hens squawked and shook their feathers. Blind in the darkness, I reached along the barn's inside wall, groping like you do for a light switch in an unfamiliar room, until my fingers closed on the lantern and matches. I lit it quickly, and then hung it carefully from a hook on the beam above me. Then I closed the barn door behind us, shutting out the cold howl of the windswept snow.

"We don't have the basket for the eggs, Elise," I said, wrinkling my nose against the strong smell of animal poop. "See anything we can use?"

She stared at me silently like she always did. I glanced around. Under the glimmer of the single lantern, the barn was creepy. The loft hung over us like heavy black wings.

"Well, we'll take what we can fit in our pockets. If there's any more than that, Amaranth will get them when she comes back. Besides," I handed her one of the smaller shovels from the tools on the wall, "the first thing we gotta do is scoop."

Nothing. No change in expression from the little girl, but when I took a deep breath and dug in with my shovel, she joined me. We moved together through the barn, scooping poop and dumping it into the muck cart under the lantern's steady flame. It seemed more than usual, much of it wet and pungent, like some kind of animal diarrhea.

As I worked, I imagined constructing a robot that could do this job. It would need a pitchfork attachment and probably a shovel, too. A bin in its bottom half for the poop and soiled hay and an ejector to dump that mess when the bin was full. It would have to be wider than it was tall: low to the ground so it would be sturdy enough not to get tipped over by kicking animals, maybe treads instead of wheels...

Did it need a face? Would that make the animals more comfortable or did it matter?

By the time we reached the chicken coop, I was sweating and out of breath. The coop was nothing special: a simple frame of wooden beams stuffed with hay that looked like Liam knocked it together in a quarter of an hour without supervision. There were only four chickens, but it stank like a factory full of them. I held my breath and reached in, pulling out a single brown egg, covered in poop and feathers. I handed it to Elise, who brushed off the yuck and dropped it gently into her pocket. Half a dozen eggs later, I rolled the wheelbarrow close and pitched in some fresh hay. My body moved mechanically while the memory of Marty showing me how to do it all played like a silent movie in my mind.

"Mwaaah!!" The goat bleated like a car alarm, but as

Elise stretched her fingers out to it, her little face lost its anxiety. The thing licked at her clothes with its determined pink tongue, protesting with more bleats when it realized her glove was inedible. Elise smiled.

"Calm down," I muttered at it. "Hay first, food second."

But the hay bin was low. I turned toward the dark loft above us. Up there, there was bale after bale of it, corded and stacked in neat rows and more piled up in soft, loose stacks. A time would come when it would be gone, but that was another day. The worry for now was that I'd have to go up there into the darkness—since carrying a lit flame into a hayloft is a shit-for-brains idea—and pitch some of it down into the bin.

I hesitated.

What's the matter? Nate teased. *Scared?*

I sighed. Nate sat at the edge of the hayloft, swinging his legs back and forth.

Are you ever going to go away?

"Elise, I gotta go up there," I pointed to the ladder and the loft. "You wait right here, okay?" I stuck out my hand, just to prove I didn't mind the creature. "Hold the light up for me and play with the—"

A big red sore puckered the goats' muzzle.

"What the..."

I dropped to my knees and grabbed the beast by the forelock, my dislike of animals forgotten. A line of lesions, partially hidden by its fur marched down its throat. I felt its belly: another line ranged down the skin on its abdomen.

More sores. The same kind of lesions Rod had—the same ones that covered Lilly's body as we traveled from our home to the mountains. Elise watched me with scared eyes as I raced frantically to the cow, jumping over the door to share her pen, ignoring her snort of protest and the nervous stamping of her hooves.

"Crap," I muttered as I ran my hand along the cow's

hide and felt the lesions rise up like barnacles.

I climbed cautiously into the sow's pen. She was huge—the size of a hot water heater laying on its side—and I thought she might charge at me or something for entering her space, but she just let out a weak grunt. I circled her carefully and she watched me but didn't move until I was close enough to touch her. Then she lumbered wearily to her feet and dropped again, rolling to the other side like she knew she needed help.

Sores. All over her belly like an ugly red crust. She grunted at me again.

"I don't know," I told her. "I wish I did."

Elise approached the pen, searching the evidence with somber eyes.

"Crack one of those eggs in your pockets, Elise."

She blinked at me, frozen with fear. I climbed out of the pen and reached into the deep front pocket of her protective coveralls. I squeezed one of the eggs open clumsily. Instead of the sunny shade of yellow I had expected, the yolk that dripped off my glove was a slimy green. And the smell! My stomach lurched.

"Maybe it's just one, right?" I smeared the nasty egg off my hands and reached for another one...and then another.

Green, all of them.

"Man," I muttered. My legs slipped out from under me and I landed on my butt in front of the little Spanish girl. "Man. We just... can't catch a break, you know that, Elise?" Tears stung at my eyes. "We can't catch a break," I repeated softly, looking around the barn at the animals, then back at the little girl. "They're all dying. They're all... I don't know why I'm surprised. This barn isn't any protection, not really. The question now is do we dare slaughter them and eat them or—"

A sudden noise the loft over our heads interrupted me. A creaking shifting sound, but not the gentle creak of

82

wood settling or a mouse moving under the dried alfalfa. This sounded loud and heavy. Like the weight of a man, turning under the hay.

Elise's eyes widened. I signaled for her to be quiet—though I guess that wasn't necessary—and pulled myself off the ground, peering up into the dark loft.

"Come on, Elise. Let's go tell the others," I said loudly, moving quickly as I aimed us both for the door. "Lock this place up and get back to the house—"

Another sound—louder than before—rose in the darkness from the loft. A noise like a growl or a groan and the sound of something moving, groping its way through the hay—

I yanked the door open and pushed Elise out ahead of me. "Run!" I yelled, extinguishing the light as I reached for my firearm. "Run!"

Something yowled in the darkness behind me. I grabbed the barn door, hoping to barricade the thing—whatever it was—inside. But it took the door at a run, barreling against it with all of its weight and knocking me backwards into the snow. I scrambled away in panic, my hands shaking as a huge, brown, furry form panted in front of me.

A bear.

The bear.

The bear that killed Nate.

But that was impossible.

That animal was dead, butchered and skinned, partly by my own hands. I remembered the stringy taste of its meat. But the creature that stood up on its hind legs was the same animal—but different. Dead, I realized. Dead like Nate. I blinked at it, paralyzed, struggling to make sense of what my eyes were seeing—if my eyes were seeing anything at all. For a second, I thought I was hallucinating—after all, Nate kept popping up and I knew damn well there was no way he was really there. But did I have to be haunted by the bear that killed him, too?

Shoot it! Shoot it now!

In another blink, memory caught me by the throat and the snow and the barn disappeared. I was back in the tunnel and Nate was screaming, screaming in pain, screaming while claws as long as knives ripped into his chest.

Shoot it! Shoot it now!

I raised the gun.

The thing clawed at my ankles, growling something that sounded like human words, demanding food and water, shelter. Then, it suddenly dropped to its knees in front of me, coughing raggedly, struggling for breath while I propelled myself to my feet.

A gunshot exploded and a bullet struck the barn door with a *zing* sound that made both me and the bear flinch.

"Don't move!" Rod cried from the Lookout.

Footsteps, running behind me. Then Amy was there, without any protective gear except her mask, her weapon trained on the bear-man. Elise stood at the cabin door, panting and flushed.

The bear raised his paws again, and this time the fur slipped away. I saw a bare human forearm scarred with tattoos. More fur slid off him and a shaved head appeared, also covered with tattoos. Even his face was inked. Beneath his bloody bear-skinned cloak, the man wore a jumpsuit that had once been a bright, prison-orange and now was amber with dried blood and dirt. There was no mistaking the pistol in a belt on his hip. He was probably a white guy, but it was hard to tell: everything I could see was inked, like the character in that old Ray Bradbury sci-fi story, *The Illustrated Man.* There were whorls of blues and grays and blacks on the bit of chest that showed out of the neck of the jumpsuit, on his arms and scalp. You couldn't tell what any of the images were anymore because of the awful ridges of lesions that competed with the tats for skin space. Around his eyes he'd submitted to a black-socketed effect that made him look like something undead—only the eyes that stared out at me were human-looking enough. Once, he'd been a muscle dude—the kind with no neck and 'roid rage—but from the way his jumpsuit hung loose off his shoulders, I guessed that it had been a long while since he'd eaten. His lips were cracked and bleeding and he looked about a thousand years old, sitting in the snow, coughing onto a dead bear with a filthy once-white pillowcase clutched in one fist. There was something in it—I saw lumps—but not much. It looked as sad and depleted and nearly empty as the man himself.

"I wasn't gonna hurt ya!" The bear-man coughed, spitting more blood on the ground. "I wasn't going to do nothing. Just wanted to ask for maybe a scrap of food. Anything—anything—'cause I'm about to starve to death and I got to get to Kinder. Gotta find my kids—" The sentence was consumed by more noises and I understood that the coughing wasn't coughing but vomiting and nothing was coming but blood. Tumbling down the loft after us had used the last of his strength.

I grabbed his shoulder and leaned toward him. The odors of sweat, piss, crap, old blood and vomit assaulted me.

"What are you doing, Nester!" Amy cried.

I divested the dude of his gun—some kind of pistol— and handed it to her. When I released him, the man collapsed forward and lay on the cold ground, whimpering and shivering.

"Empty," Amy said, checking the pistol quickly. "That's probably the only reason he didn't come out shooting. How long have you been in there?"

"Don't know." The man told the ground. "Came in... blizzard... out of... cold... few hours ago. It's not much further, is it? Little town called Kinder—"

85

Amaranth came jogging up at that moment. Her eyes and cheeks were bright red. A bottle poked out of the pocket of her coat before she stuffed it hastily back inside. "What happened?" she asked.

"He was in the barn. *Someone* must have fallen asleep on their watch," Amy muttered, glaring at her in a way that let everyone know she'd seen the gin.

The pink in Amaranth's skin deepened.

"I—I—" she stammered.

A sound behind us interrupted her as Katie and Marty emerged from the house with their guns ready. In the doorway, coatless and leaning hard on the door jamb I saw Liam, his eyes hot and bright above his mask and his revolver steady in his hand.

"Who else is with you?" Katie yelled.

'Where are they?"

"Where did you get the bear skin?"

"What's in the sack?"

"What happened at the prison? Are there more of you coming?"

Questions rose from all around.

The man struggled to his knees again. "Can I... can I have..."

"Answer first," Amy hissed, easing the safety off her gun. "Or I *will* shoot you."

The man assessed her. "Do it." He grinned at her, a ghostly remnant of a threat on his face. "I'm dead anyway. Go ahead little girl. Go—"

Amy raised the weapon higher and I closed my eyes, expecting to hear the gun bark and to open my eyes to splattered brains.

"Wait!" Amaranth cried. "We need to at least find out if there others—"

"You think he's going to tell us the truth?" Amy shook her head but didn't lower the gun even a millimeter. "Assume there are others. Assume the whole damn prison

86

is skulking toward us—"

"Where did you get the bear skin?" My voice was soft, but commanding. I felt all their eyes shift to me, but I didn't care. It was the only question I needed an answer to.

"Found it," the man answered simply. His ancient sick eyes met mine and I knew the rest of the story—that he was with the group that had scared us away from Nate's grave. He was one of them, one of the group that had stolen the bear carcass and eaten its meat and hunted us, hoping for more. He was the reason we'd had leave Nate, right after we'd buried him. The reason we'd been running, pursued until, in desperation, we'd jumped into the cold water to escape.

I hated him for all that.

"Others?" I asked.

He shrugged. "Got too sick to keep walking. Left 'em. Probably dead now."

We considered each other silently. Snow eddied around us, whipped by a bitter wind.

"Okay," I said quietly.

Amy raised the gun again.

"Not here," I said. "Not in front of Elise. We'll take him out in the field. In the woods out there. Less mess."

"Yeah, that's a better plan." Amy's face beneath the respirator was hard and determined. "Get up," she ordered the man.

"No," I barked. "I'll do it. I'll take Marty or Katie—"

"I'll go," Amaranth said softly. "This is probably my fault—"

"Probably?" Amy's eyebrows shot up. "I thought *you* were supposed to be taking care of the animals, not Nester and Elise. That's what's on the chore chart."

Amaranth's eyes slid off our faces. I didn't have to turn to know she was looking at Liam. "I just went for a walk. I thought—I thought it might help clear my head."

Only the wind answered her. In the long pause that

followed, Amy's lips crunched together.

"Go in, Amaranth," she said at last. "We need to talk." Her eyes flicked to me. "Are you sure, Nester?" She kept her rifle trained on the man, but leaned toward me, lowering her voice so that only I could hear. "Are you sure you can do it? Are you sure you can kill him?"

I stared at the man, but all I could see was the dried blood of the bear carcass, striping his skull like war paint.

"Yeah," I answered. "Yeah, I can."

9

MERCY KILLINGS

He lurched along, still draped in the bear's skin as we led him away from the cabin and the farm buildings on a death march of our own making. Katie and Marty and I followed the man as he shuffled along, prodded by our commands and our guns. Every seven or eight steps, another shuddering wave of vomiting brought him to his knees.

"This is far enough," I said, when he fell headlong into the snow and didn't get up. We were within a few yards of the shed where the tractor and other larger tools were protected from the elements. "Agreed?"

Marty nodded. Katie stared down at the man, chewing on her bottom lip. Just before he passed out, he'd coughed up another thick chunk of blood. It spread through the snow like a rose opening on time lapse.

"What happened? Is he dead?" Katie asked.

I shook my head. "He's still alive, but barely."

"Playing possum probably," Marty said. "Trying to figure out a way to get out of this—"

"I don't think so. The radiation's got him. It's been almost a month since the bombs. If he's been exposed the whole time, especially in the beginning when it was strongest..." I shook my head. "Whether we shoot him or not, it won't be too much longer."

Marty stepped forward. "Then let's just do it and get

it over with," he said grimly, stretching out his revolver.

I tried to think of the man as an animal—the kind of animal who could wrap himself in the skin of something recently dead. The kind of animal who'd gotten himself a jail sentence so long he'd chosen to pass the time covering his body with tattoos. I tried to transfer the fury I felt over Nate and my parents and the loss of my dreams of college and success and returning to high school no longer as a nerd but as "nerd who made good" onto him so that I could pull the trigger.

But all I saw was a cold, weak, suffering lump. Once he might have been something to fear, but at that moment, he was too pathetic for me to shoot in the back for the crime of crawling into the barn in the hopes of surviving another day or two. Irv's voice echoed in my head: *It's about what kind of people we want to be. It's about whether we respond to violence with more violence or with compassion...*

Marty leveled his weapon at the base of the motionless man's skull. "You say he's dyin'?"

"I think so, yeah."

"How long's he got?" Katie's voice was little more than a whisper.

"I don't know for sure. But if we leave him out in the elements like this? Not long. He'll freeze to death within a few hours."

The twins considered that possibility. So did I.

"We can't just leave him out here, though. Ain't right," Katie said at last. "I wouldn't do that to a dog—"

"He's lower than a dog, Katie," Marty said, anger snaking through his words. "He's come from the prison. We don't know what he's done. Or would do, if he could—"

"Look at him. He ain't barely breathin'—"

"But he *is* breathing. That's the point. Just a few minutes ago he was strong enough to come at Nester—"

"Well, yeah," I interrupted. "He surprised me. But

90

then he just fell down and started throwing up. Kinda like that," I added, nodding at his prone back. "And then I realized he was just begging for food and talking about how he needed to get to Kinder. To find his kids."

The wind whistled through the silence between us. I shivered like somewhere, someone had stepped on my own grave.

"We can't stay out here much longer or we'll be frozen, too." Marty adjusted the revolver like he was getting into position, but once again, didn't fire.

"You're right, but—" Katie shook her head. "It just don't seem right, killing in cold blood. We've shot at folks before, trying to defend the Mountain Place. Killed for all I know. But we ain't never done nothing like this. This is like an execution or something—"

"No it ain't. We're still defending ourselves, Katie," Marty insisted. "And if there's others of 'em out there, we're letting them know: we may be kids, but we got guns and we ain't scared to use them. We need to stop thinking about it and just do it."

But he still didn't fire. Instead, he stared at me like he was waiting for a signal. My brain was alight, flashing me decision trees and images of possible outcomes.

"In a way," I said at last. "It would be mercy to kill him. He's suffering pretty bad."

Katie's eyes met mine, seizing on this rationale. "Ya think?"

"Yeah. And..." I pulled out my gun. "And we could do it together. All of us. Like a—"

"Firing squad?"

"Yeah." I inhaled, preparing myself. Katie levelled her rifle at the man's back. Marty took aim anew at the man's skull and I—

I'd held guns on our awful journey through the woods trying to reach the Mountain Place. Liam had explained a lot about them to me as we walked those many, many miles. I'd patrolled with one on the Lookout. I'd carried one around the grounds of the Mountain Place, according to the protocol we'd devised. But I'd never actually fired one. On the road to the Mountain Place, firing practice shots would have been like lighting a flare, announcing our location to all kinds of threats and mayhem. And the bad weather so far had made target practice impractical. And then, there was the other stuff. The stuff my parents believed about weapons and the people who owned them. I could almost hear my stepdad Irv winding up for dinner time rant number 9: the gun control lecture. *"The second Amendment gives Americans the right to bear arms, that's true, but it's been extended far beyond its original intention. The Constitution is time-bound, people. It spoke to the concerns of the tyranny of the British monarchy, not to our modern problems. Remember, this is the same document that considered slaves to be 3/5 of a person!"* It went on from there, rising in passion until his forehead was sweaty and spittle flew from the corners of his mouth. How could he have known I'd end up living in a time when not knowing how to use a gun was a bigger handicap than being black?

I aimed for the man's general chest area, concentrating hard on keeping both arms locked in front of me like I'd been taught, being careful of my grip to avoid the unfortunate accident that would make me the Four Fingered Man. "On three," I said with a conviction I didn't feel. "One...two..." I closed my eyes. "Three!"

I expected hear the POW of the others' guns and I squeezed my eyes tight against the sound of the blast. But my own finger slipped on the trigger. I hadn't taken off the safety.

I opened my eyes. The others were staring at me.

"Why didn't you fire?" Marty demanded.

"Why didn't you?"

"He didn't fire for the same reason you didn't," Katie

shot back. "Because it's wrong, and we all know it. This man is weak and sick. He can't hurt us. If he was threatening us, I wouldn't have no problem with it. But as it is..." Her head wagged in the negative again. "I can't do it. And I don't want you to do it either, Marty."

She peered at me over her respirator. "If you feel like you need to do it—'cause of what happened with your brother—"

"A bear killed my brother," I said quietly, lowering my gun and hoping the others didn't see how badly my hands shook. Relief flooded me like a tsunami. "For what it's worth, I believe him, about the others. He might have been in a group before, but now, he's alone."

Marty shook his curly head from side to side but he let his revolver drop. "So you just want to leave him here? To die in the snow?"

Katie frowned.

"Maybe... maybe we could put him in the shed. At least he won't be in the cold—"

"No," Marty said. "We aren't locking some criminal in our shed!"

"We can lock the door from the outside!"

"There's all kinds of tools in there, Katie. He can take the door right off its hinges if he's got a mind to."

"But he can't, can he, Nester?"

I sighed. Amy Yamamato screamed, "Pull the trigger now!" in my head. But it was too late.

"No. He can't. At least, I don't think so."

"Can we at least tie him up?" Marty sounded completely aggravated.

I leaned over and pressed my fingers to the man's neck. His pulse was so weak, I wondered briefly if perhaps a bullet really would have been the kinder thing to do.

"I suppose," I answered instead.

Katie smiled at me under her mask. "If he's gonna die, at least he can die warm and quiet. That's the human

93

thing to do—"

"Humane."

"Huh?"

"The word you want. It's humane. Not human."

Katie frowned at me, a lecture about useful and useless information shining in her clear gray eyes. I immediately wished I hadn't said anything, but before I could apologize, she dismissed me and turned to her brother. "Me and Nester will drag him. You go open the doors, Marty."

Even as starved and skinny as he was, he had to be at least 150 pounds of slack weight. By the time we situated him in the shed and tied his arms behind his back and his ankles together, we were sweating. The walk back to the cabin would feel even colder when the wind chilled my wet skin.

The man hadn't regained consciousness. From the gray color of his skin and the labored sound of his ragged breathing, I doubted he ever would. The feeling of doing the wrong thing for the right reason tickled the back of my brain, but I couldn't change my mind and shoot him now.

"Get the bear skin, Marty!" Katie said.

"What you gonna do?" Marty snapped in exasperation. "Tuck him in?"

"I'll get it," I said, eager to be out of that room, away from the bickering twins and alone in my own head.

The bear skin lay where we'd left it, a few yards from the shed. The pelt was matted with dirt and snow on the outside and thick with dried blood on the inside. My stomach flipped at the sight of it, opening a window to the ugly moment that Nate had left this life.

I'm scared, Nester...

That was the last thing my brother had said to me.

I yanked at the bear's skin, preparing to drag it toward the shed when my eye fell on the pillowcase. I

94

scooped it up and peered inside. There was as little there as I expected: a couple of pieces of wet paper in a faded envelope, an empty lighter and a few crumpled cigarette wrappers, a torn triple X magazine. A woman with the biggest boobs I'd ever seen offered herself to me on the cover. I flipped through it quickly soaking my brain in the images until finally, overwhelmed, I stuffed it back inside the pillowcase and took it and the skin back to the others.

"What's in there?" Marty asked as his sister wrapped the man in his bearish burial shroud.

I handed him the pillowcase. "Nothing," I replied and promptly forgot about it.

"What are we going to say to the others?" he asked.

"We're going to tell him he's dead." I said. "Because for all practical purposes, that's the truth."

I expected Amy to bombard me with questions as soon as I stripped out of my gear. But when we entered the cabin, I could tell I'd missed something. Amaranth sat at the table with her face determined and immovable like she was under torture but would not be broken. Amy stood nearby with her arms folded over her chest like an interrogator, her expression stern. Liam leaned against the butcher block table, standing on his good foot. He glanced at me quickly when I stepped into the room, and then looked away, staring grimly out of the window like there was something important happening out there.

"You do it?" Amy asked me.

I nodded curtly, but offered no details. Elise came to my side and slipped her warm fingers into my cold ones. "I guess you know about the animals."

"Yeah," she said. "Think we can salvage anything there?"

"Why are you asking him? Nester's never even had a *dog*. Everything he knows about slaughtering animals for meat is what I taught him," Liam muttered.

95

He was right, but it pissed me off anyway.

"She's asking me because *I'm* the one who's going to have to do it. Me or Marty or Katie," I couldn't stop myself from adding.

Liam glared at me, ready to launch his retort, but just then Amaranth stood up so suddenly her chair scraped the floor.

"If the disciplinary hearing is over," she sneered, "I'm going out."

"Where?" Amy asked.

"The john." She leveled eyes full of resentment at each one of us. "Do I need an escort or am I safe to go alone?" she asked nastily.

Liam. Amy and I looked at each other.

"Let me know when you figure out my fate," Amaranth snapped, moving toward the mudroom. "Right now, if you'll excuse me, I've got to pee."

She strode of the room. We heard the cabin's rear door bang shut.

Liam exhaled, his shoulders sagging.

"What did you say to her?" I said, sliding a chair in his direction. He collapsed into it and rubbed his forehead, squinting like his brain hurt.

"She's on probation," Amy replied. "One more drink and—"

"And what?"

Amy   sighed.   "I   don't   know."

"We'll come up with a penalty if it happens again," Liam said, then turned accusing eyes on me. "Did you find her   other   stash   yet?"

"Just when was I supposed to do that, huh, Liam?" I said, throwing my hands up in frustration. "Cut me some slack, man! Between the work in this cabin and in the barn and my watches and managing intruders and trying to have a little time to sleep and eat—"

"It's important!" Liam interrupted and when he

96

looked at me there was a different kind of pain in his face, a pain that reminded me of when we'd found Amaranth alive and well after we'd all thought she'd drowned. I remembered the way Liam had run to her and the way Amaranth's arms wound around him and the look they gave each other just before they kissed right in front of us. I'd felt incredibly happy for them and deeply jealous of them at the same time.

"I'd do it myself if I could, Nester," Liam said tightly.

I sighed and stood up again. "All right. It's got to be out by Lilly's grave—"

Elise moved for her coat.

"No, Elise—" Amy began, but the little girl ignored her.

"It's okay," I said wearily. "She can come. Maybe she can help, right Elise?"

Liam hopped toward me, the odor of the onion poultice reaching me before he did. He pounded my shoulder gently. "She's... just a little messed up right now," he said quietly.

"Yeah."

"It's for her own good, right?" he continued. "And in a couple more days, my foot will be better and I'll be able to do more, right?"

I glanced down at his foot. It seemed to be even more swollen than ever, stretching the fabric of the gym sock. But then, that was probably just the layer of onion wrapped bandages, adding mass, pulling at the cotton.

"Yeah," I repeated.

He nodded at me and then hopped out of the room, groaning as he sank into one of the rocking chairs. I heard the sound of the radio's static as he searched the channels, listening for a signal that had yet to come.

Amy stopped me just before I headed back to the mudroom to don my mask and suit again.

"You really killed him? The convict. He's dead?"

"Yeah," I answered, staring her straight in the face. "He's dead."

10

A KISS IN THE SNOW

I hadn't been to Lilly's grave since the day I covered it with dirt.

The crude cross of two tied sticks stuck out of the snow-covered mound, marking the spot. Elise's fingers tightened around mine and when I looked down I saw that her brown face was streaked with tears.

"Go talk to Lilly, Elise," I told her, my voice distorted by my mask. "I'll be right over there." I pointed to the black trees at the edge of the orchard. She didn't respond, but her fingers uncurled from mine and she trudged away from me, stopping near her friend's grave with her head bowed. I couldn't see her lips moving, but I hoped with all of my heart she'd found the words to pray again. Someone needed to pray—for us all.

We'd followed footprints in the deep snow—Amaranth's, I assumed—right up to the edge of the grave. Then they veered off, continuing into the trees. I struck out in that direction. Once, in a life that had gone up in smoke, "tracking" for me had been about the key strokes on my computer. Now it was following prints in the snow, looking for liquor.

Half an hour ago, I'd been sent out to kill a man. *Which you didn't do.*

Nate trudged beside me, still in his parka and girly pom-pom hat. For once, he didn't sound like he was making fun of me.

"No."

Do you think you should have?

"I honestly don't know."

Amaranth's footprints ended behind a tree only a few yards into the orchard's shadows. I didn't have to be genius to start pushing aside the snow with my hands. In a matter of seconds, the effort was rewarded: I pulled up another bottle of bourbon and two more bottles of gin.

I grabbed them. I was able to stuff two into the deep pockets of my protective suit. The third one I held like an orphan in my hands.

When I turned around, she was coming toward me.

Amaranth.

She moved quickly across the field, hurrying, wearing neither her mask nor her gloves. Her cheeks were chapped with cold.

"This is ridiculous, Nester, and you know it," she said angrily.

"Yep," I agreed. "So why don't you just cut it out? You don't need this stuff, Amaranth."

"You're right. I don't. I keep telling them that they're overreacting but—"

"After what happened in the Lookout, I'm not so sure about that."

"Okay, that was a screw up. I admit that. But you've been up there, in the cold and snow. You know it's hard to see anything—"

"That's why it's even more important to be clear-headed."

She sighed. The wind grabbed a loose hair blew it over her face, concealing her eyes for a second. She lifted a bare, shaking hand and swept it away.

"You're right," she said in defeat. "Of course you're

100

right, Nester." She hung her head. "It's just...I've been having such a hard time sleeping. I close my eyes and it's all there, all over again. The fireball and the Hole. Richter. Nate. But you understand that. I know you do," she told the toe of her boot. "It's like you said, we're all...hurting. Just trying to survive."

"Yeah."

"Only..." she jammed her hands into her pockets and shivered a little. "I can't figure out *how.* How to survive. How to push all that back far enough to—to keep going."

She took a few steps closer to me, peering into my face like she was looking for me to offer her something, some kind of answer or a survival skill or clue to how to forget the past and accept our new world. But she had the wrong dude for that. I wanted to say so—that I didn't have a clue, that every time I closed my eyes I dreamed of the world I'd lost, that Nate was standing over her shoulder right now reminding me of what a fuck-up I *really* was, no matter how many jobs they gave me back at the cabin—

But I couldn't. Just like when I was sitting with Katie in the kitchen, the words dammed in my throat. I stood there, staring at her like a big dumb rock, feeling my weaknesses, swaddled in pain and empathy, desperate for connection but terrified of it, too.

When I didn't say anything, Amaranth came closer still to me and lowered her voice.

"And then I look at Liam, still suffering after everything he's already been through and it's all so *unfair!*" she roared into the silence.

Unfair.

The word seemed to echo around us. My hand curled into a fist of silent agreement.

"Especially for you," Amaranth continued. "I don't think anyone's given you credit," she continued in a soft voice. "You've lost as much as anyone. More. And you're right: you're doing everything. Most of the hard work.

Keeping us organized. Holding us all together..."

She smiled suddenly and I caught a glimpse of what Liam saw in her: a quirky prettiness as unusual as her name. She laid a chapped, cold hand on my arm. "It's a raw deal, Nest. First and worst, you've got me." Another ragged smile slanted across her face. "These days all Liam does is yell at everyone. Amy's turned into some kind of Nazi. Rod does the best he can but—"

She stroked my arm, gently like she was warming her hands on the fabric of my coat, then settled it on my shoulder. It wasn't quite a hug, but the closeness made the wind seem not quite as sharp. Her face was near—close enough for me to see the beige sprinkling of freckles around her nose like cinnamon in whipped cream.

"I can only imagine how hard this has been for you, Nester," she said in that mesmerizing and gentle voice. "You've been like wallpaper, you know? People don't even see you anymore. Everyone's so wrapped up in themselves that they've forgotten about Nate and how we had to just *leave* him there."

She tilted her face up to me and touched my cheek. Her fingers were cold, but the spot where they touched me went warm. Then she wrapped her arms around me and pressed her head against my chest.

Amaranth's pretty tall, but I'm 6'1" and still growing. Back in the old world people used to ask me if I played basketball all the time. I'd say, "No, but I'm president of the robotics club" and watch their stereotypes explode on their faces.

Good times.

Now, the top of Amaranth's head was just below my chin. She held me tightly, her slender body pressed tightly against me. Even through our coats, I felt the bumps of her breasts and her fingertips, gently massaging the base of my spine. The giant boobies of the convict's dirty magazine and the images of girls in spike heels with their legs spread wide rose invitingly in my mind.

"I haven't forgotten. And I want you to know that I appreciate how you've stepped up. In spite of your own losses. You're taking care of everyone. Liam. Elise. Rod. Even me." Amaranth murmured, lifting her face toward mine again. "Thanks, Nester."

When she lifted her head, I thought she was going to move away from me, but instead, she reached up and laid her hands on either side of my face, pulling down the respirator.

Watch yourself, bro, Nate warned. *She's gonna—*

Amaranth pressed her lips against mine. They were cold and soft and a moment later, I felt her warm tongue dip into my mouth.

I'd never been kissed. Never—not even a peck. My body reacted before my brain could process what was happening, and for a second I was lost in the sensation. I was warm from the inside out, on fire, raging for physical connection, plugged in, in a way that made me hungry for more. I forgot her name, forgot she was my friend's girl, forgot everything but the feeling of her body close to mine and her lips. It might have stopped then—I might have recovered myself and remembered—but she slipped a cold hand down to the front of my jeans and tugged at my zipper, pushing aside the hard denim and the soft cotton, cupping my junk with urgent fingers.

My brain powered down and as my body lit up like a new motherboard and I grabbed her, grinding against her until her back was against the tree she'd stashed her liquor against. Her face was lost to me—all I could see was those dirty girls from the magazine—but her fingers knew me. She didn't stop and I didn't stop her. Neither one of us said a word until finally, I groaned, spurted and shrank.

We stood still for a moment in silence. Then Amaranth stepped away and I turned, jamming my zipper up quickly, shame already steeping my cheeks. When I turned around Amaranth's back was to me.

"Look, Amaranth..." I began, but then I saw what she was looking at.

Or rather... who.

Elise stood watching us with wide eyes.

"*Que pasa, chica?*" Amaranth whispered. Her voice shook. "*Esta bien—*"

"Hey, Elise—" I called, but the little girl turned and walked away from us both, her head down as she moved along the desolate fields.

"Oh crap," I muttered. "This is bad. Did she see all of that?"

Amaranth swung toward me. To my surprise, she held a bottle of gin in her hand like she'd forgotten about it. I touched my pocket: sure enough, one of the bottles I'd stowed there was gone. She'd slipped it loose while I was... swept away.

She'd played me—worked me up as a distraction so she could take the bottle.

"I can't believe you, Amaranth," I hissed, swiping the bottle out of her hands. "Is this"—I shook the bottles at her—"That important? What happened to you? Did you really think you could just—?"

"I'm sorry Nester." She stretched her hand toward me. "I shouldn't have—"

"Get away from me," I warned. "Don't you ever touch me again! Ever! I mean it—"

Tears welled up in Amaranth's eyes. "I just got—I don't know—"

"Come off it. You knew *exactly* what you were doing! Don't stand there and lie! I'm not gonna let you jerk my chain any way you want. I don't play that. You can run your game on Liam, but that crap isn't gonna work on me, so save it!"

The words detonated on her face one by one. Her arms dropped to her sides and she stared at me for a long

104

second, her green eyes wide. Finally, her mouth crimped and I knew by the way she flipped her hair out of her eyes that she was about to lay waste to me. That she would make it my fault and then give me a map for the fastest route to hell.

"So what are you going to do? Tell him?" she demanded, glaring at me. "You're going to tell Liam what we just did? Because if you tell him, you're telling on yourself. You liked it. You were into it, you know you were. If it weren't so damn cold, you'd have had me on the ground—"

"No, I'm not going to tell him," I interrupted. I didn't want to hear her say the words we both knew were true. Anger and shame and embarrassment and guilt got all mixed up inside me. I'd given anything to go back and erase the whole nasty encounter, but I couldn't. "I'm not going to tell him," I repeated. "But not because of you. Or me. I'm not going to tell him because he's got enough on his plate just trying to get well. I'm not going to tell him, because, God help him, he actually *loves* you...and trusts me. But this drinking binge ends. *Now.* I know this stuff is valuable but I swear I'll dump it all if I have to. Do you understand?"

Amaranth's face was hard and remote. The tough girl's survival face. But she nodded once before turning away from me, her hands—the same hands that only minutes ago had worked me out of my good sense—jammed tight into her pockets. "Okay, okay," she said softy. "Okay. But what about Elise?" she asked. "Do you think she'll tell?"

There was a part of me that hoped that Elise was running back to the cabin to blab the whole nasty thing. That her first words in over a week would be to tell Liam that his girlfriend and his best friend had been... whatever. I sighed. I didn't even have a word for what had just happened, other than "wrong." All wrong.

105

But in my heart I knew that Elise wouldn't say a word. She'd just file it away, somewhere deep in the silence inside her. Another sad moment of hurt and distrust, dealt by the people who were supposed to protect her.

I hated myself—and Amaranth—even more for that.

"I hope she does," I muttered and strode past her toward home.

I thought I'd gotten my wish when Amy came running toward us as soon as the cabin came into view. Her long dark hair flew out behind her respirator and her dark eyes burned with fury.

"You lied, Nester Bartlett!" she shouted.

Lied?

"You didn't kill that man!"

The man? My brain was in another place and it took me a second to cast back to what she was talking about. Finally, the fact of the convict we'd tied up in the shed shoved aside the memory of Amaranth's tongue and fingers.

"No, but—"

"Why? We agreed—"

"Look, Amy. That dude was dying—"

"Dying!"

"From exposure and radiation sickness. He was pretty far gone, so we decided—"

"You decided! You and Katie and Marty?"

"Yeah. We decided it was more human—I mean, humane— to let him die naturally. So we tied him up in the shed and Katie covered him with the bear skin and—"

"Gave him some warm milk and a kiss goodnight?" Amy exploded. "I can't believe you, Nester. I can't believe after everything we've been through you fell for that. I can't believe *Marty* fell for that!"

The same uncomfortable feeling I'd had just before we decided to drag the convict into the shed jiggled in the

106

back of my brain.

"We didn't see the harm—"

"You didn't see the harm?" Amy' shook her head so violently all the firearms strapped to her body trembled, reminding me of the heroine in those futurist novels, only she was Asian and her weapon of choice was an assault rifle, not a bow and arrow. "I'll tell you the harm: he's gone and so's the tractor! He drove it right through the shed walls!"

"*What?* But how—"

"He wasn't dying, that's how! At least not yet."

"There wasn't much gas in the tractor. He couldn't have gotten far."

"You're missing the point," Amy hissed. "The point is you had a job to do and you didn't do it. The point is we had something—something valuable— and now we don't!" Her voice got loud and shrill. "The point is you've put all of us at risk because I just know—I *know*— he wasn't alone. And the others will be coming. And coming soon!" She got right up in my face like she was going to strike. "Why didn't you   just   kill   him,   Nester–"

"You think it's so easy—to just snuff someone out?" I shot back. "Who have *you* killed, huh?"

"No one, but—"

"Then stop yelling at me!" I shouted, suddenly sick of always being 'the one'. The one everyone counted on. The one everyone expected to know what to do. The one to do the work and to take the brunt of everyone else's crazy. The raw shame of what Amaranth and I had done hit me like a brick in the face and Amy's accusations were just the last straw.

"It's not like on TV, Amy. It's not like the movies. It came down to could we shoot an unconscious, unarmed man in the back! And I couldn't do it. If you were standing there, I bet you couldn't have done it either," I screamed. "Back off up me!"

107

Amy's face hardened into an older, more world-weary mask. "You're wrong. I think I could have shot him. In the back. Unconscious. Whatever. I think I could. And you know why, Nester?" She didn't wait for me to ask, but continued, wound up on her own trip of anger and fear. "Because I don't ever, *ever* want to be as scared as I was on the trip up here. I don't ever want to be at anyone's mercy—not ever again. From now on, it's shoot first, ask questions later—"

"Like Marty?" Amaranth asked quietly. I knew she was behind me, but I couldn't look at her, not even when she stepped into the space at my elbow. "When he shot Liam?"

Amy's pale skin flushed pink.

"We need to go see if we can fix the shed. Right now there's a tractor-sized hole in the side of it," Amy continued without answering her. "And we need to try to set some booby traps around the cabin's perimeter—"

"Knock yourself out," I snapped. I was done with the Mountain Place and everyone inside it. "I've barely slept and I've had nothing to eat. You're not working me to death, Amy. Go give Rod your 'honey do' list and see how well it gets done." I know it was mean, but I'd had it and couldn't stop myself. "Or see if Marty or Katie will help you. Amaranth's standing there, ask her. What? Burned all your bridges? Boo hoo for you. I'm done, okay? This brother's going inside."

Then I marched past her into the cabin and I didn't stop until I was alone in one of the upstairs bedrooms, where I could close the door and shut them all out.

//

PILLOWCASE TALK

"I think we're done."

I jumped, surprised by the voice. I'd been so completely lost in my own world that I'd forgotten I wasn't alone.

Marty stood behind me, a bloody knife in his hand. His protective suit was like mine, slick with blood from the entrails of the goat. Nate stood beside him, wearing a white protective suit that strained his girth like it was two sizes too small. As usual, he was completely unwelcome.

"Take a break, and then we'll quarter it."

It had been two days since the convict escaped from the shed: two days of frenzied activity and Amy's recriminations. Two days since Amaranth and I had done what'd we'd done. Two days of waiting for the other shoe to drop.

A day ago, Marty and I had found the tractor—less than 500 yards from the shed. The man had barely made it down to the edge of the lake in the thing before having to abandon it. We found it with its tank dry and its cab empty. Reporting those facts didn't do a thing to get us back into anyone's good graces and a part of me didn't care. All of them stayed away from me: Amy because of the convict, Amaranth and Elise because of what happened in the woods, and Liam and Rod because they knew I was sick of doing all the grunt work they weren't able to do. That left

Katie and Marty. More and more, those two country kids were my best and only friends.

I got pretty friendly with my own guilt and doubts, too.

Amy's words kept circling in my brain: about not wanting to be at anyone's mercy. About shooting first and asking questions later. Much as I wanted to dismiss her as wrong, I wasn't sure any more.

I'd been so certain the man was dying...but apparently I'd been wrong. And deep down, I knew the truth was that I hadn't wanted to shoot him. I wasn't sure I could have.

Think of it like a video game, Nate suggested. *Sort of real. But not.*

Thank you for that totally unhelpful suggestion, you idiot.

Days had gone by without Nate's appearance—like he, too, was ashamed of me and couldn't bear to be in my presence. I'd begun to hope he'd finally gone to the light.

But no. For some reason, he was back again, wagging his head at me in an *I Know What You Did Last Summer* kind of way. He bothered me, but Elise's abandonment bothered me the most. As hard as it had been to get my work done with her constantly at my heels, I'd gotten kind of used to her. And she'd seemed to be getting better, slowly. Now she'd relapsed back to not responding, barely eating, barely sleeping and of course, not speaking.

That she didn't trust me anymore hurt almost as much as the weight of guilt I felt standing between me and Liam.

"Did you find it?" he had asked me as soon as I set foot in the cabin.

I opened my coat like a dude selling watches on a New York City street corner and Liam exhaled like he'd been holding his breath since I'd left to search.

110

"Does she know you've got it?"

I nodded.

"What did she say?"

The memory of Amaranth's touch flowed back over me. My ears lit up like he'd put a flame to some wick inside me.

"What can she say?" I said, turning away from him. "Your father has an awful lot of this stuff."

Liam didn't answer. When I got my face under control and turned back to look at him, he was frowning into the pages of the book on his lap.

"I think I've got a perfect hiding place," I said, but he didn't answer.

I mounted the stairs and found Nate's old backpack crumpled in the pile of stuff that belonged to me. I loaded the bottles into it and dropped the backpack into the cedar chest at the foot of the cot. I was covering it with some of my clothes, when Elise came in.

"Shh," I said, trying to smile. "I found a good hiding place, Elise."

She climbed on the bed and turned her face to the wall, shutting me down so completely my heart sank.

Of course, she doesn't trust you. She saw you getting down with your boy Liam's girl. And him all busted up and everything. That's low, man—

Nate's head wagged back and forth like he was a man of the world and not some dumb twelve year old with even less experience than I had. But I found myself arguing, justifying myself anyway.

It wasn't my fault. You saw what happened. She just—just—

Looked to me like you weren't minding it so much.

"Enough," I said aloud, bringing the barn and the present back to life. Marty shrugged like I was talking to him.

"Well, we got to finish it," he said. "But you're right. We need a break."

It was only the second time I'd skinned an animal and while I didn't feel like I was any better at it, this time I didn't throw up when we pulled out the entrails. Without the head or the skin, it didn't look like a goat anymore: just hunks of bloody muscle. I walked around the goat's carcass, inspecting it. Evidence of the lesions we'd seen on the animal's skin showed in the muscle. I took my knife and sawed deep, to the bone.

"I'm not sure we're going to be able to eat this," I said with a sigh. "Look."

Marty barely reached my elbow, but he tilted his head and peered at the slice I'd taken from the animal's hide. The flesh looked warped and smelled diseased. He ran his hand along the goat's flank. "Maybe we can butcher around those parts? And we can salt cure it. Brine it good. Then, maybe?"

"I don't know. All of us have already been exposed..." I didn't finish the sentence. I didn't know how. If we were all dying anyway, what difference would eating the meat of an irradiated goat make?

Marty sat down heavily, leaning his back against the cow's stall. The animal was alive but only barely, now almost completely overtaken by the symptoms of radiation poisoning. It lay on its side, huffing out giant breaths and lowing weakly. There probably wasn't any point in slaughtering it now; it was too far gone. The sow had died already, blood oozing out of every orifice, its skin peeling away from its body in loose pus-filled strips. It had taken all of us who were able to drag it out of the barn. After much debate about burying or burning, we surrendered it to nature and went back inside.

"Dammit," Marty pulled back the hood of his suit and lifted his respirator to take a sip from our water bottle.

There were shadows under his eyes.

"You all right?" I asked folding myself down in the hay beside him. My whole body ached; it was a feeling I was getting too used to, along with being about eight hours short on sleep. But at least today when we went back up to the cabin, there would be food and warmth. Rod was cooking the midday meal: beans and rice mixed with one of our remaining cans of soup to give it some flavor. He'd perfected dumplings made with flour and some lard we'd found in the root cellar and those would be sprinkled into the mixture, too. We'd each get a tablespoon of sweet peach preserves on a bit of yesterday's bread for dessert. Once, I would have turned up my nose at such a meal, but now, my stomach grumbled at the thought of it. I'd eat as much as I could, especially since I knew that supper would more than likely be inedible. Amaranth was supposed to cook it and everything she made ended up tasting like an overcooked hockey puck.

Amaranth...

She'd spent the last two days wandering around with dark hollows under her eyes, a ghost floating from room to room. I knew she hadn't had a drink in days...but she hadn't slept, either. I didn't know if it was nightmares or guilt or something else. I didn't ask. I stayed as far from her as I could, but the insomnia was going to be as big a problem for us as the drinking if it didn't let up soon.

"Ain't been sleepin' so good," Marty said, adding his insomnia to hers. "Keep thinking about that man." His granite gray eyes fixed on mine. "You still think we done right?"

"We did what we did," I said, reaching for the water bottle after him. "Can't undo it now."

Nate stuck out his hand to be next for the canteen and I almost handed it to him, until I remembered he wasn't really there.

"You still think he's dead out there somewhere?"

113

"Yeah," I answered, realizing that was true. "I do."

"But your friend—Amy— she don't think so."

I sighed. "Amy's working through some stuff. Some stuff that happened on our way here. And..." I hesitated, but Marty was smart. He had to have already guessed at the truth. "She's worried about Rod."

"He's got what the animals got." It was a statement, not a question. "What the man had."

I nodded.

"Is he gonna die, too?"

I didn't know how to answer that. Rod looked so bad it was like he was already dead, his body just didn't know it yet. The haircut Amy had given him couldn't conceal that his hair was falling out in clumps and the depth of the shadows under his eyes gave him a perpetually haunted look. Little red sores covered his face and arms. He looked like an ancient old man with a bad case of zits. And every day he was a little weaker. He avoided me like the plague. Like he was afraid I'd tell him something he didn't want to hear.

"I—I guess so," I said and felt the same twisted braid of rage and grief that I'd felt digging Lilly's grave.

"But you're good with the medical stuff," Marty pressed. "There ain't nothing you can do?"

I shook my head. "I wish there was. I really... wish..." I stopped. For a long time, I didn't, couldn't say anything. Nate and Marty sat one on either side of me, waiting for me to get myself together.

"See, after—after my brother got killed, we all made a promise to each other. That we wouldn't lose another one of us. That we'd take care of each other. Like a family."

Marty nodded. "They was telling the story. Rod and Amaranth, a few nights back. About the stuff that happened to y'all, trying to get here. About the bear." He paused. "Don't know what that must have felt like, seeing that man wearing the skin."

114

How did it feel, Nester?

For once, Nate didn't sound like he was mocking me. He sounded genuine, like he really wanted to know.

"Felt like a punch in the gut. Reminded me... of all the things I wish I'd done and didn't—couldn't— do. " The words tumbled out my mouth before I could stop them. It wasn't something I could have said to any of the others. But Marty didn't know Nate. Never had. And he didn't know me—or at least not the person I'd been before—either. The goat's blood dripped steadily on the hay, making an odd background noise for the true confessions of a teenaged brother.

"And it was my fault, anyway," I told the kid. "It was my fault that bear got him."

"Don't see how," Marty grumbled. "Way I heard it, Liam was the one who was supposed to be watching—"

"Yeah," I sighed. "He fell asleep. But I can't be mad at him for that. You—you—" My voice got crackly like a cell phone in a dead zone. "You don't know tough it was. He—all of us—we were so hungry and so exhausted—"

"Been hungry. Been tired." Marty's eyes bored into mine, telling a story I didn't really want to hear. But there wasn't any judgment in them, just the weird kinship of bad tales.

"Yeah, I guess you have," I said. "So Liam fell asleep. Doesn't matter. It was me who did it. I was the one who hitched a ride to his school as soon as the fire alarms went off. I was the one who said we should go to Liam's. Who took my stepdad's joke about begging the Harpers to let us in literally. If I could go back—" I stopped. Marty waited while I sorted through my feelings and translated them into words. "If I could go back, when I heard the bombs were coming, I'd have still have gotten him from school. But then, I'd have stood in the center of my street—and I'd have made him stand with me—and I'd have spread my arms open wide and let the heat wave do its thing."

115

Marty considered that for a moment. Then he reached under the elastic leg of his coverall and pulled out a scrap of fabric.

"That's from the convict's pillowcase."

"Yeah."

"How—" I furrowed my brow trying to remember.

"You said there weren't nothing in it. Tossed most of it away. But, I found this."

He unwound the strip of fabric to reveal an old piece of notebook paper that had been folded and refolded so many times its edges were torn and stained.

"What is it?"

Marty nodded to the paper. "Open it."

Not that you care, but you're a father. There's two of 'em. The boy almost didn't make it and they say he ain't never gonna grow right. But like I said, what do you care? You ain't gonna be no kind of father to 'em no how. By the time they let you out, they'll be grown and won't need you. I don't need you now, you sonofabitch. But here's the life your sorry ass missed out on the day you got the idea robbing banks was an easier way to get money than getting a goddamned job and supporting your family.

A picture fell out of the fold. Of two kids—a girl and a boy—sitting together on a threadbare quilt. The girl looked like she was about six or eight months old. She was dressed in someone's idea of fancy: a fuchsia onesie with a big flowered headband around her bald head. Her skin was the color of honey and at the moment the picture was snapped, she was either laughing or crying; it was hard to tell which one. Her little fist was clenched tightly around

116

the boy's wrist. This baby was much smaller and not sitting up but lying on his tummy, scowling at the camera like it had done him wrong. They both had eyes of gray steel.

"These are you and Katie!" I exclaimed. "Then that means the kids he was trying to get to were—"

"Don't mean nothing," Marty said.

"But—"

"Don't mean nothing," he repeated stridently. "He could have gotten that letter from someone else. Stolen it. Lifted off a dead inmate—"

I frowned. "Do you really think—"

"Don't mean nothing," Marty repeated. "Not now." He took the letter and the photo out of my hands and before I could appeal, ripped them into tiny fragments the goat would have found delicious. But even then he wasn't satisfied. He grabbed the lantern and fed each of the scraps to the flame.

"But what about Katie? Has she seen it? Did you tell her? Does she know—"

"She don't need to know nothing about that. It'll only cause her more hurt." His voice dropped to a low growl. "I may be small, but I'm always gonna protect her, best I can, for as long as I can. Just like what you did with your brother."

"Me?" I shook my head. "It's not the same at all."

"Don't matter that you didn't like him much. You knew that taking him to that Hole was the safest thing. You protected him. Long as you could. Otherwise, you'd have done the other thing. Stood out there. Let the fire get ya. Or just left him at his school. With strangers."

He fell silent, letting me chew on that for a second.

"Family's about what you *do*, not the stuff you say. Mr. David used to say that all the time. It's what you do for the people you care about. To protect them, even if it ain't always pretty or nice. Even when they hate you for it." He hesitated, and then continued in a calm, level voice. A killer's voice. "If that convict comes back, Nester, I'm taking him down, no matter who he could have been. Too late for him to be anything but an intruder to me now."

He pulled himself up and started for the barn door.

"I'm gonna get a sack of salt from the cellar. We can use one of them barrels with the lids."

"Okay," I heard myself say but I didn't even look at him. Instead, I turned to finally say something directly to Nate's ghost. But of course, just like in life, when I wanted him, he wasn't there.

I stood up, ignoring the protest of my knees and back, grabbed the meat saw and began the work of cutting the goat's carcass into two halves. The Nester Bartlett who had been president of the Robotics Club, 4.0 student, Harvard-bound—he was gone. Gone like Nate and my parents and the hope that the remaining members of our little Doomsday kids family would all survive to see the sun again. The goat's sinewy body was as good an outlet for my rage and grief and pain as anything—and I attacked, wondering if, when the situation presented itself again, I could channel those feelings into my finger and pull a trigger.

The barn doors swung wide and I turned, expecting to see Marty, but instead, Amaranth stood behind me. She looked awful: worn, pale and exhausted. But of course, when she saw me, even her fatigue was covered by a cool mask of indifference dropped over her features, like being in my presence was no big deal.

"Oh, Nester," she said, sniffling like she had a cold or something. "I didn't know you were still out here."

I turned away from her. A million words raced through my head all of them coated with acid and flame, guaranteed to melt the flesh off her bones. If I let them out, there was no way to predict where I'd stop—if I could stop at all. So instead, I sawed at the goat, splitting bone and separating flesh.

She stood behind me, watching, waiting, wiping her face and snuffling, weighing her words. When I was out of breath, I stopped and gave her a side-eye.

"Stop trying to work the angles and just spit it out, Amaranth. Whatever it is."

A slight flush hit her cheeks like a fresh burn. She swiped her hair out of her eyes and said, "Fine," in the breeziest of tones. "Remember those people? The ones we met in the forest? Samir and his parents and all the others?"

Of course I remembered. If it hadn't been for Samir and the others, we might have had ammunition when the bear invaded our camp. We might have been able to shoot it sooner and maybe, just maybe, Nate would be more than a figment.

"Do you think they made it? To Kentucky or wherever?"

I shrugged. "Not if they ran into this weather. They probably had to take shelter at least for a while. Funny."

"What?"

"Rod asked me the same thing—or close to it. He asked about Liam's father. Whether I thought he could have made it back to Washington, D.C."

"And do you?"

Once, I might have measured it simply in miles or meters. But I'd learned a bit about other yardsticks, like a man who'd been in jail for over a decade walking home to find children he'd never even met. Like me: I didn't even like Nate and I'd have gladly walked backwards home—me, who couldn't even start a fire without matches— if I thought it would bring him back.

"Yeah," I said. "I think he did. And you know what else I think? I think—"

Katie pushed into the barn, nearly knocking Amaranth over in her haste. One look at her and I knew something—something *else*— was wrong.

"Nester—" she began urgently.

"We were having a conversation!" Amaranth snapped irritably. "Can't you... knock or something?"

Katie's stormy eyes locked on me. "He's gonna be mad at me, but I don't care. Right is right." She lifted her chin at me and I caught a glimpse of what she'd look like in a few more years, when the awkwardness of her body filled out and her face lost its roundness. She'd be really pretty— if she got the chance to grow up.

"Who? What happened?"

"It's Liam. He's running a fever. Has been since yesterday. First noticed it while you and Marty were out looking for the tractor. He didn't want to tell you. Said it was nothing, but—" she shook her head. "It's getting worse and—" she glanced at Amaranth. "I'm scared. He's in a bad way—"

Amaranth glanced at me. In an unguarded fraction of a second, I saw her whole heart: the shame and sorrow, the love and care, the faithfulness and haunted humiliation. Then she spun around and raced out of the barn ahead of us.

12

HEY DUDE, THAT'S MY FOOT

The digital thermometer read 101.6.

"It's no big deal," Liam kept repeating the words, growing more and more belligerent with every round. "She shouldn't have told you." His eyes glittered in a way that didn't look right. "I'll be fine in the morning, Nester. You'll see."

I checked the wound in his side just to be sure, but I knew it wasn't the problem. When I rolled off the sock, though, Liam yowled. The room reeled for a moment and I fought down the urge to vomit.

The flesh was a rainbow of colors radiating from a central pus-filled wound the size of a silver dollar. I wasn't sure if it was the lingering odor of the onions or his foot itself but something smelled putrid: like decay. When I touched just the arch of his foot—far from the damaged yellow green wounds, Liam jerked himself away from me, wincing.

Holy crap! That's what I wanted to say, but I managed to keep that in my head.

"The poultice hasn't done anything." I tried not to sound like his foot wasn't gross enough to have its own

YouTube channel. "It hurts...here?" My fingers hovered over the thing—calling it a "blister" now was an insult to its size and seriousness. Beyond the pus-filled center, the reds and purples, greens and yellows spread from the heel down the sole of his foot and over the arch.

"Yeah, there," Liam agreed. "But it hurts all over. Worse than here," he indicated his side. "Though that still hurts, too."

I stared at the wound, fascinated and horrified at the same time. "I'm not sure what to do. I gotta check the book, Liam."

I'd made Amaranth and Katie leave, but I knew they weren't far away, listening. Hell, the whole cabin was listening: it was unavoidable in a place this small. But they made themselves scarce, to give us at least the appearance of privacy. Only Elise stayed close, perched in the rocking chair, quietly rocking, her eyes fixed on the fire. But to my surprise, at the mention of the survival medicine book, she stood up and brought my old friend from its spot on the corner of the desk. She didn't reply when I thanked her and retreated to the furthest edge of room when she was done, dissing me hard.

"What did you do?" Liam wondered. "To piss off Elise?"

I shrugged and buried my face in the pages of the book.

"Must have been pretty bad," he continued. "She's been like your shadow for a week—"

"Okay," I said, loudly. Too loudly. I cleared my throat and forced my voice back down to a range that didn't betray me for the slime I was. "It says *that* is an abscess. Katie and Marty were right: a warm cloth filled with a natural antibiotic is supposed to naturally pop it. Drain the pus from the infection. But it doesn't look like that was enough. So we need to take the next step which might hurt a bit. I'm going to have to pop it like a big old zit."

"Okay, do it."

"Elise—" I began, but Amaranth appeared from the alcove with the medical kit, Katie treading at her heels. Both girls looked terrified.

Liam turned his head, refusing to look at either one of them. I studied the contents of the kit like it was urgent that I account for everything inside.

"Do you need any help?" Amaranth asked.

I shook my head. "Got it. Thanks."

"Hot water?" Katie followed. "I can fetch some—"

"No. We're good."

The girls hesitated long enough for me to finally look over at them. But neither of them was paying me any attention. Liam had their eyes, even though he didn't want them.

I cleared my throat.

"What are you standing there for? He said he doesn't need any help," Amaranth hissed at Katie, shoving her slightly.

Katie glared at her, but simply turned around and left the room without a word. Amaranth shot me a look that seemed part apology and part appeal, and then followed her.

I slipped on a pair of latex gloves. The kit was expansive, but we'd been using like it could magically refill itself. The truth was, it would run out and soon. The gauze was already low. So was the antibiotic cream. There weren't many more pre-sterilized implements. Katie was right: soon we'd be bandaging ourselves up with scraps and rags.

I found a small, unopened scalpel in its sterile plastic wrap and popped it open.

"You want a drink?" I joked, gallows-style. "That's the only reason we didn't pour it out: moments like these."

Liam shook his head. He closed his eyes and steeled himself against the coming pain. "Just do it."

I glanced back at the book, and then made the cut

as quickly as I could. Blood and pus gushed out of the slit skin like water out of a busted dam. I tried to contain it with a cotton ball, then gave up and reached for one of the last gauze pads. Liam bit back the worst of his scream, but a little whimper of pain escaped in spite of his best effort to He-Man his way through it. When I squeezed his heel, a spot of blood appeared on his lip in the shape of his front teeth.

"Sorry," I muttered, inspecting the result, comparing it to the drawings in the book. It didn't look the same, but I wasn't sure if that was just the difference between a real wound and an illustrated one. Not for the first time, I wished for the Internet. Just by typing the word, I could have had a million results— a million images— of every kind of abscess imaginable.

One thing the picture didn't have, though, was the blackened edges of skin. I read the text again. "It says the black stuff is dead. 'Non-viable' material. It says it might come off on its own but it's better to cut it." I looked up at him. "Can you handle some more?"

Liam grimaced. "Do what you got to do... just do it quick. That..." The first wan smile I'd seen from him since my haircut cracked his lips. "That really, really hurt."

My knife hovered over the damaged skin. "You ready?"

To my surprise, Liam giggled. "You know what I just thought of? Remember that day? During that big storm and you were out of school and we were bored with playing in the snow. My dad let me go over to your house and we sat in the basement and watched a marathon of that dumb cartoon? Remember the one where the guy was—the guy was all like—" He imitated the character's voice. "'That's my foot, dude—'"

"Yeah, man," I said, grinning at him. "And the other guy goes—" I mimicked the voice the best I could. "'I'm the one who's got to smell it! Just drink your juice!'"

And we both laughed, we laughed like that was the funniest thing ever, that dumb old cartoon that we watched back in middle school. Before the bombs and dead siblings and girls. Elise's head shot up like she thought we'd both lost our marbles—and that made me laugh, too. For a few precious seconds, I forgot about the dead man in the shed, dead animals in the barn and the sad members of our traumatized dysfunctional family. Anyone listening to us cackling over his swollen, infected foot should have called the guys with the white coats.

"Only there aren't any guys with white coats anymore," Liam countered when I told him. And that set both of us off again.

"Do it, Nester," Liam said mid-chuckle. "Do it now—"

I steadied myself and made a tiny cut on the black skin.

Liam's chuckled escalated into high-pitched shriek. An ugly sweat popped out on his face. "Keep going," he panted. "Cut it out. Fast—"

Elise slapped her hands to her ears and started rocking violently, terror etched into every pore of her little face. I closed my eyes. He'd been unconscious when I'd done the stitches—but now he was wide awake and every move I made was causing him intense pain. *You can do this, Nester.* I told myself. *You can do this—*

I cut more aggressively, slicing a thick hunk of blackened skin from the edge of the abscessed heel. Liam grunted and groaned, but managed to keep from shrieking again.

"You got it, right?" he hissed through his clenched teeth. "That's it?"

I'd cut deep—the bone gleamed whitely back at me—but it was surrounded in more black tissue on either side. I lay down the knife, whipped off the gloves and grabbed the book again.

"What?"

125

My first result sent me to another entry and another. I read quickly, dragging my finger under the words and then comparing the images to my real life example. But when I turned the page and saw the graphic images drawn there, the room went cold. I swallowed down a hard lump of pure fear and lifted the book high so Liam couldn't see the picture or read the words.

"What?" he demanded suspiciously. "What?"

"This could be bad. Really, really bad—"

He struggled upward, reaching for the book. "What?"

I sighed. "It's more than just a little dead skin at the edges, Liam. It—it might be gangrene."

Liam's bark of laughter was like slap.

"Gangrene?" he chuckled hoarsely. "Be serious. That's like—like from the Civil War or something!"

"In case you hadn't noticed, the life we're living is straight out of 1864," I muttered, nodding at the page. "This book is the truth. Pictures and everything. Listen: 'Gangrene is caused by a severe wound that stops blood from flowing to the affected area. Bacteria invade the tissue. There is pain, swelling, blistering and a foul odor.' " I paused and looked over at Liam. "Check, check and check."

"The smell is those damn onions," Liam insisted, shaking his head. "Go on."

"'Wet gangrene...'" I began, and then wished I hadn't. "'Can be fatal, causing sepsis or blood poisoning. It is difficult to treat in survival situations since it requires antibiotics and other medicines typically only available in hospitals. If caught early, however, gangrene is treated by surgical removal of the dead skin in a process called debridement. More serious cases are treated by—'"

"Amputation," Liam finished. "You're not the only one who has studied the Civil War. I know how they used to treat gangrene and I'm telling you right now, there's no way I'm letting you chop off my foot, Nester."

126

"Man, I wouldn't know how, anyway. This a good book with some nice pictures, but that's some heavy stuff, you know?" I tried to laugh, but that moment had passed and couldn't be recaptured.

"You need to keep cutting—"

"I'm not sure—"

"Cut it out!" He shouted, angrily. " You need to keep cutting!"

"Listen to me, man. I'll cut, okay? I'll cut all the black I see. But I'm carving up your muscles now. And that isn't going to just heal over and you're good as new. Even if it goes well, it's never going to be the same—"

"I know that, Nester. But if you think it's gangrene, then do what you have to do. I am *not* going to lose my foot—"

"Listen to what I'm trying to tell you, man: you might lose it anyway. You think I know what I'm doing, but I got a big news flash for you: I don't. Not a freaking clue. I'm slicing away here and for all I know, I'm—I'm—maiming you for life. Or re-infecting it. If this fever you've spiked means the infection is in your blood stream—"

"I know. I'll die."

I sighed. "All this time, I was worried about the bullet wound. I thought maybe *it* would get infected. Or that I was wrong and that there was some internal damage." I shook my head. "I never even thought about a stupid blister. There's a lot of dead tissue there, Liam. A lot of it. Down near the bone, beneath the skin. It could already have spread through most of your foot. The top layers just aren't showing it yet." I lowered my voice. "This might come down to the whole foot. And if it's a choice of your foot or your life–"

"Then it's my life."

"Liam. Don't be—"

"That stuff Marty was talking about," Liam interrupted in a low, determined voice that shook as he

127

spoke. "About my dad teaching him things and—and all that," he continued hurriedly, to keep the bubble of emotion from bursting on his lips. "I remember that guy. That version of my dad. That's the way he was with me. Once. Before—" he stopped and I knew he was talking about the war and the amputations David Harper had endured. "He changed after that—at least with us. With me. I guess... you have to change when people knew you *before*. As a whole person. And every time they look at you, you can see in their eyes that they remember. They remember who you were before. I don't want that. I don't— I can't—after failing Lilly—"

"You didn't fail her, man—"

"She's dead, isn't she?"

I had no follow up for that.

"It's hard enough, watching all of you work for our survival. Laying here like a lump of useless nothing. Seeing the looks in everyone's faces: concern. Pity. I've seen those looks before. I've seen my mom look at my dad that way. And then, in time, she'd look at him another way. With just the tiniest bit of resentment—"

"That was different. Your folks, they had their issues, but they were cool with each other," I cleared my throat so I could say the word the situation demanded. "Loved each other—"

"She'd asked him for a divorce," Liam said quietly. "That's why he was up here. So far from us on the day when the shit hit the fan. She said she was done. That he'd changed and she couldn't take it anymore. And..." his voice trembled but he forced the words out. "The look on her face. All that: the pity, the concern and the resentment. All mixed together. If Amaranth—" he stopped himself, but her name was already out, hanging in the air between us. "If anyone," he corrected himself, "If anyone ever looked at me like that, I don't think I could stand it." He fixed his feverish eyes on my face. "I'd rather die, man. I'd rather die."

128

I leaned close to him. "Look, forget Amaranth, man." My voice was urgent, meant for him and him alone. "She's not the only girl in the world—"

"She is to me," Liam shot back. "I know you don't like her—"

My whole bald head lit up like it was under a heat lamp and sweat rolled down my temples.

"No, no," I said quickly. "It's not that. It's just—"

"You don't. And I get it. She's trouble. Does all kinds of crazy things. But that's all bullshit. Protection. Because in here..." he touched his chest. "There's something really decent about her. Sweet."

I thought about Amaranth, unzipping my jeans and sticking her cold hand inside. *Sweet* wasn't a word I'd have picked to describe a girl who could do that for a bottle of gin.

"Promise me, Nester. If this doesn't work. If it gets worse, promise me you won't cut it off. Promise me—"

"Okay, okay, man" I said. "If it's your foot or your life, it's your life—but only because it's not gonna happen anyway. Now just calm down. I need to finish cutting and then we need to figure out what we can do about that fever."

13

IN HIS BLOOD

"I think we've got a real problem," I said as softly as I could.

We sat around the long table: me and Amaranth, Rod and Amy, Marty. I'd helped Liam up the stairs to bed. Elise followed us, but I wasn't completely sure why.

"It's probably just some kind of bug," Liam said over and over. "A flu or something..."

"Sure, man, sure." I said. There was a big part of me that wanted to point out that even the flu could be fatal, but I told myself to "shut up."

"My heel feels better already. It's just some kind of bug. I'll be better in the morning."

"Sure."

But I wasn't sure. The blackened flesh of his heel scared me. I'd cut plenty—too much. More than once I scraped bone and Liam had screamed with pain. I doubted it would ever heal right no matter what we did. There had been no point in binding it: the back of his foot had a huge gouge in the center like someone had taken a bite out of him. Liam cursed and shuddered while I treated the skin with hydrogen peroxide and then, when it was done, cursed and shuddered some more as he tried to erase the sensation from his memory. I put a loose cloth over it, held in place by a single strip of adhesive. There was no need to tell him to stay off of it; he couldn't have put weight on it under any circumstances. If we had to run, unless we could carry him, he was screwed.

The other thing I didn't tell him was that for all the cutting, the battle was lost. There was more black, dead tissue than I could bear to slice away. The infection was spreading.

"Keep an eye on him, Elise," I told the little girl after I'd gotten them both settled. I left one of the utility candles burning since I knew Elise didn't like complete darkness, but she didn't even look at me.

"I told you, you're over-reacting," Liam murmured, but he already sounded dreamy and half-asleep. "Remember what you promised..." he reminded me with the last of his consciousness. "Remember."

"Are you sure that's what it is?" Amy's forehead was puckered with doubt.

"No," I admitted. "I'm not sure. I'm going on something I saw in a movie once, if you want to know the truth." I pointed to the page. "But all the symptoms are there. The coloring, the dead skin. The pus. And the smell. If it's gangrene, that's bad. But I'm much more worried about the fever. If the infection spreads to his blood..." I shook my head and let them write the end of the sentence in their own minds.

Amy gripped the survival medicine book tightly between her two hands. "Listen," she commanded. "'Rapid breathing or a change in mental status may be signs that sepsis—" she looked up at us. "That's the medical term for a blood infection, sepsis— is starting,'" she continued. "'Other common symptoms include fever, shaking, chills, vomiting, diarrhea, rapid breathing—'"

"Geez. Maybe that's what I've got. And all this time, I thought it was puberty," Rod wisecracked.

No one laughed.

"It doesn't say what the treatment is," Amy continued, frowning into the book.

"There isn't any. Not out here in the middle of nowhere—"

"But there has to be something!" Amaranth interjected. "We can't just—"

"Whoa, whoa," Amy's voice rode above hers. "It's not sepsis. At least not yet, is it Nester?"

I shook my head. "I think..." I began but stopped. It felt like a betrayal just saying the words. "I think it may be gangrene. Which is treatable in a couple of ways. The first involves massive doses of antibiotics. The second is amputation, which he really, really doesn't want—"

"Of course not," Amaranth said softly, voicing what we were all thinking. "Of course he doesn't. Not after all the stuff with his father. It—it just wouldn't be fair. For him to have to go through the same thing."

Sweet. That's what Liam had said about her. I stared at her, looking for evidence. When she felt my eyes, I looked away.

Amy flipped to the dog-eared entry on gangrene, her lips moving slightly as she sped through the words. Rod hoisted himself slowly out of his chair and stood, swaying for a moment before he righted himself and moved quickly and deliberately out of the room. We all watched him go, listening to the creak of the pump at the kitchen sink, the splash of water, and another coughing splash that didn't sound like water at all.

"Okay, wait. It could be lymphangitis. It's an infection, too. Gets confused with sepsis all the time. Same symptoms—" Amy read, and then stopped. "But the treatment is the same. Hospital. Antibiotics." She closed the book and stopped talking before the urge to point out that the heel wasn't near any major lymph node compelled me to correct her and make her look stupid.

Instead, silence ruled the room as we all processed the situation. Finally, Amaranth stood up. She moved deliberately to the storage shelves and started searching, moving items around with purpose. A few minutes later, she emerged with her old backpack stuffed full and her coat on her back. One of the respirators rested on her forehead like a pair of oversized sunglasses, holding back the fire of her hair. Rod stood behind her, also wearing his coat, his shotgun slung over his shoulder. His skin was waxy-looking and his lips were cracked gashes in his face. He steadied himself on the back of Amy's chair.

"We're going to get antibiotics," Amaranth announced, her eyes locking on Marty. "Where's the nearest hospital?"

The boy opened his mouth, but paused as footsteps echoed down the wooden stairs. Katie appeared. She'd stripped off her protective suit but she still wore her coat and the night vision goggles hung around her neck and her gun was in her hand. Instead of the two ponytails on either side of her face, her wild curls were smoothed into a neat bun that made her look older and prettier. Or it would have if she hadn't been cold and tired and pissed off after two hours alone in the Lookout, peering out at the snow.

"Nester, your turn," she said wearily. Her eyes swept the room. "Is he worse?"

"Liam needs an antibiotic or he might die," Amaranth said tersely. "Where's the hospital?"

"In Benson," Marty drawled, frowning dislike at her. "'Bout 30 miles away. But—"

"Amy," Amaranth said calmly—like she was going over to the mall for earrings instead of planning a suicide mission over 30 miles of unknown territory, hoping to find a functioning hospital. "Do we still have the map?"

Amy opened her mouth, but it was Marty who answered.

"There's a few of 'em in the desk," he said. "And an

133

atlas, too. On the shelf there, but—"

Amaranth crossed the room, opening drawers and slamming them closed again until she found a stack of highway maps. Amy considered her silently for a moment, and then calculated—correctly, in my estimation—that she'd have better luck talking to Rod.

"There's at least two feet of snow out there," she began. "Think about this a minute: it will take you days just to get there. And in that kind of time—"

"He could die, anyway." I finished flatly.

No one looked at me. Amy kept her eyes on Rod; Marty studied the floor. Amaranth bent over the maps like she could will time and space to contract and in a blink we'd find ourselves in an ER back home.

"Well, what do you propose: that we stand here and watch him do it?" Rod asked simply when the silence had stretched to breaking.

"No." Amy turned away from him. There were tears welling up in her eyes, but when she continued, her voice was even and calm and didn't give anything away. "No. I don't think any of us can take that. Watching another one of us die..."

Rod put his arm around her. "Then we've got to try, babe," he said. "Let's be honest. I'm not much use here," he added.

"There has to be a better plan than the two of you just—just setting off on hope, Rod!"

It was almost like they were the only two people in the room. Or like we were watching characters on TV.

"Even when you get there—if you get there—what makes you think the hospital will be open? Or that they'll just—just give you drugs and let you walk away with them!" Amy continued. "Every time we've been in a town—or had to deal with other people—it's gone bad for us. If the woods are scary, the towns are worse. You know I'm right, Rod."

Everyone—well, I don't know about Katie and Marty— but the rest of us knew what she was talking about. We remembered the terrible road trip. How we'd hoped to find adults who would help us, care for us. But instead, we'd been stolen from, assaulted, nearly killed. We'd learned to stay off the roads, out of sight. We'd learn to run at even the *sounds* of other humans. We might have even killed a few—or at least Liam and Lilly might have. Back in Lowellstown where we'd been surrounded by guns; where Amaranth had gotten beaten up pretty badly and Nate had turned the tables and saved the day.

The convict's tattoo-scarred and radiation-ravaged face swam before my eyes, a reminder of threats eliminated... and not eliminated.

Killing him would have been different. He was unarmed. He was alone. He was defeated, I told myself.

Would it? Nate asked. I heard him in my mind, but he stayed out of sight. *What kind of society do you want to be?*

But that's just it. There isn't any society. *Not anymore.*

"Nester," Rod stretched his ruined face at me in appeal. "Tell her we have to go."

I shook my head. "I don't see the point of it, Rod. I don't believe you'll find any help there. Not anymore. That world is dead."

"He's right. Don't know about Benson, but last time we were in Kinder..." Marty's little head wagged from side to side. "Weren't like it was before. Kinder was like one of them Wild West ghost towns. No people. Shops closed. Abandoned cars. But there might be another way—"

"If he's going to start on some story about another potion or poultice that made him 'right as rain' I'm going to scream!" Amaranth interrupted, her voice rising with her frustration. She swung to face Marty. "Did you hear what she read? Even in a hospital, a person could die! I don't

135

want to hear anything about any country remedy! I want to know where the *hospital* is—"

Katie bounded across the room. Before I could guess her purpose, she slapped Amaranth's face so hard her head rocked on her neck. Amaranth's eyes widened in shock, but only for a millisecond. She went for Katie with her fingers extended like claws and tackled her in a single leap.

"*Fight! Fight! Fight!*"

Nate. In my head and that's all. No one else was cheering for this grudge match. Marty dove toward Amaranth with murder on his face, but I picked him up and set him behind me before grabbing Amaranth by her waist and dragging her off Katie. Amy straddled Katie's chest, preventing her from a fresh attack.

"Come on! Come on!" Amaranth shrieked over and over.

"Had enough of you!" Katie spat. "Had enough of havin' to redo your chores after you do 'em. Had enough of your excuses and your wanderin' around here like some kind of zombie. Like we're all supposed to feel sorry for you or somethin'—"

"That's *enough*!" I roared. "Both of you!"

"She started it!" Amaranth struggled in my arms. "You saw her—"

"Somebody needed to slap your face a long time ago, girl! Comin' in here, like you got some rights to this place. Nose in the air, swilling down all the liquor and bossing us around—get off me!" She hollered, throwing her arms at Amy, flailing beneath her weight.

"Cut it out, both of you!" I yelled. "We've got to figure out what to do about Liam—"

"That's what Marty was trying to tell you if you'd had the good sense to listen to him, you witch!" Katie screamed from the floor. "That we don't gotta go all the way to Benson to find someone who might be able to help Liam!"

I let Amaranth go and hurried over to release Katie

from Amy's restraint. There were scratches along her cheekbones where Amaranth's nails had raked her face. She stroked shaking fingers against them, checking for blood.

"Why not?" I demanded. "Is there a clinic or something closer?"

"No—" she began.

"There's a doctor living next door," Marty finished.

"Old Man Watson is a doctor?"

Marty shook his head. "Old Man Watson's dead. Been dead forever. Years before we ever came here. That's just what they call the land—"

"But his wife still lives there," Katie muttered, glaring at Amaranth like she wanted another round. "She is—was— an animal doctor—"

"A veterinarian," I nodded, relief washing over me. "Okay. Now we've got a plan. If she's got any kind of antibiotic for horses or cows or even dogs, it'll work. Maybe we can convince her to come back here. Take a look at him." I started moving. "I'll go—"

"I'm going with you," Amaranth declared, lifting a face full of determination at me. There was a red spot on her cheek in the shape of Katie's index finger. "To Old Man Watson's—or old lady Watson or whatever. I'm going with you, Nester. I can't—I won't—stay here."

"Fine," I said. Truth was, as long as she and Katie were separated, it didn't matter to me how the barrier was created. "Marty, could you come with us? To lead the way?"

Neither Katie nor Marty moved. Their eyes locked on each other in a way that I'd learned meant trouble.

"What?" I asked in exasperation.

"Well..." Marty began.

"About old lady Watson," Katie continued.

"What?"

"She's..."

"What?" I demanded. Amaranth had a point: sometimes these twins' way of talking was frustrating.

137

"Crazy," Marty said simply.

"Nuts," Katie added. "She was shooting at people who came near her house *before* the end of the world—"

"And wandering around talkin' to herself—"

"No, not to herself. To Old Man Watson," Katie shuddered. "Like he's still alive. It's creepy—"

I burst out laughing and even though they gawked at me like I was old lady Watson, I couldn't stop. Here we were: Amy corseted in ammo like a comic book character and Amaranth sleepless and coming on to nerds for gin. Liam, who'd walked 200 miles to die from a blister, and Rod who had walked all those miles too, when his mom, if she was alive, had been just 12 miles in the opposite direction. And when you added me without my towering Afro, with Nate standing behind me pointing and giggling like the dorky kid he'd been in life—well, I felt sorry for old lady Watson. She could be as crazy as she wanted to be; she wasn't anything for me to afraid of—not anymore.

14

DON'T TALK TO STRANGERS

"What's up between you and Amaranth?"

Amy stood in front of me with her arms crossed over her chest. Her waist length dark hair was braided into a long ponytail and her dark eyes glittered. Even with the penetrating glare and pointed questioning, she was pretty enough to make me a little nervous. With the questions, my anxiety kicked up a dozen notches. I hid my face in the effort of packing my gear.

"Nothing."

"There's something," she pressed. "Since you went to find her stash—"

"Well, I took her drug," I said, showing her my shoulder and not my face. "She was pissed. We argued. Whatever."

Amy's eyes narrowed and she wrinkled her nose like she could smell the lie. I pushed past her and headed up the stairs for the last thing I needed to pack.

The team was going to be me, Amaranth and Marty... but at the last minute, Marty weirded out on us.

"Rather stay," he said, flatly. "Defend the cabin, just in case..." he didn't finish the sentence, but I knew who he was thinking of. "Kind of shorthanded here, you know."

"He don't wanna go because—" Katie stopped short,

exchanging a glance with her brother. Secret twin communiqués, I'd nicknamed them in my head. "I'm not so good with shooting at folks." Katie continued, lowering her head. "If you think we got trouble headin' this way, he'll be better to have around than me—"

"That's an understatement," Amaranth grumbled. "We all know how good a shot he is—"

"How many times does he gotta say he's sorry?" Katie hissed, coming out of her seat again and leaning toward Amaranth like she was ready for a second round.

"He's never going to be sorry enough, if you ask me!" Amaranth muttered. "We wouldn't be in this situation if it hadn't been for—"

"That's enough!" I interrupted. "I don't want to hear this crap anymore. What happened happened. While the gunshot wound hasn't helped anything, what we're dealing with now doesn't have anything to do with it, okay?"

The girls glared at each other, but they both closed their mouths. Marty stared at the table, his young-old face harder to read than any player in the World Series of Poker.

"I'd rather Katie go," he repeated.

Rod raised his single eyebrow.

"I think I'm a better choice than having Katie and Amaranth go together, man," he quipped. "I'm slow, but at least you won't have to mediate a cat fight."

"Shut up, Rod," Amaranth hissed.

"Sober up, Amaranth," Rod shot back.

Amaranth popped out of her chair like a cobra about to strike.

"Sit down, Amaranth," I said, pulling on her sweatshirt. She landed hard in her seat. "Thanks, Rod." I didn't want to tell him he'd be more of a hindrance than a help, so I just kept talking. "Look, I don't care *who* goes—" It wasn't true: I'd given anything to think of a reason not to travel with Amaranth, but there wasn't any way to say that without answering a bunch of questions that would land me in a nasty mess of quicksand. "I don't care, but I'm telling you right now, I'm not listening to any more of this bickering. What else can you remember about old lady Watson?"

"Not a lot," Marty said after a pause. "Ain't never really talked to her. Like I said, went to her property once. Didn't go back again."

"We need to take something," Katie said. "To trade. To pay for her services—"

"Take the liquor," Amaranth suggested immediately.

For a long moment we all stared at her. The suggestion had come too quickly, too suspiciously.

"She's right," Marty said at last. "Rumor was she liked to drink. That's why she ain't a vet no more. After Old Man Watson passed, they say she started up with it. Made some mistakes. Livestock died—"

"And she had to close down," Katie had finished. "Or at least that's what people around town used to say. All this happened years ago. Before we was born."

Gin. Just the thought of it, brought the memory of Amaranth's tongue in my mouth back to me and set my cheeks aflame. I couldn't look at her—at any of them—so I focused my attention on the center of the table.

"Okay. I'll get it out of its hiding place."

Amy stood up with me. "I'll come with you."

Elise sat up as soon as we stepped into the small room.

"Hey, Elise," I said softly. "How's he doing?"

She didn't answer, but Liam opened his eyes. For a moment, his brown irises communicated nothing but dazed confusion. Then he offered us a lopsided grin.

"Hey, dude," I said. "Didn't mean to wake you. Just getting some stuff," I explained, opening the cedar chest and pushing aside the clothes until I found Nate's backpack. "How's it going?"

"Been better." His lips twitched like he was trying to be funny. "But you know how it is."

"Yeah, I know how it is." I set the bottles on the floor and moved to the bed. "While I'm up here, let me get a reading. Open up, man." I grabbed the thermometer resting beside the ewer and slid it under his tongue.

"You want anything, Liam?" Amy asked.

"Sunlight, a cheeseburger and oh, I don't know, my old life back," he quipped around the instrument.

Amy's grim face broke into a good-old-days smile. "Me, too."

"Me, three," I chimed in. "Now be quiet."

We waited in silence for the reading.

"It's better, right?" Liam said. His eyes roved past me, to Amy in the doorway, then up to the ceiling, then closed heavily like the effort of focusing them was more than he could manage.

"No. About the same," I lied. The truth was it was higher: 103.3. I moved, lifting the quilt to inspect his foot.

"So... you're going in search of drugs, then," he asked. His eyes didn't open but his eyebrows lifted. "To the farm next door? Yeah, I couldn't hear it all, but I heard—ouch!"

I wasn't sure if it was my imagination or if his foot looked that much worse. Amy gasped and turned her head.

"Yeah, I think it's worth a shot," I said as calmly as I could, inspecting the spreading black tissue.

"Well then, good luck. Try not to get yourself killed out there." He blinked his fevered eyes at me and shivered a little, even though the room was warm. "Don't get a big head about it, but we kinda need you around here..." His voice was thick, skimming the border of delirium.

"Right, but I think we need you more," I began but his eyes had closed again. His chest lifted in a heavy gasp.

142

Amy shot me a look of alarm.

I tiptoed away from him, gathering those stupid bottles of liquor into my arms. They clanged together, a musical reminder of guilt. I stuffed them into my backpack as quickly as I could, while Amy stared me down.

There was one more thing I needed to do.

I shouldered the backpack knelt beside Elise's cot.

"Look, I know you're upset with me," I whispered. Amy probably heard, but there wasn't anything I could do about that. "I—I know I let you down. But I hope you can forgive me. Try to help Amy until I get back, okay?"

She just stared at me—I hadn't expected much else—but just before I stood up to go, she reached for my hand. A feeling I'd never had before swept through me as our fingers intertwined. There wasn't a single word for it: faith, gratitude, forgiveness, protectiveness and hope got all mashed together when she held me with her sad, black eyes.

"I'm sorry," I said again.

She let me go.

"You'd better get going," Amy's voice was the perfect tonic for the moment. When I stood up and faced her, she was staring at me again, her brows drawn tight together. Before she could ask me just how I'd let Elise down, I started talking.

"Try to manage the fever. Cool cloths, fluids, the Ibuprofen in the medical kit—"

"Yeah. You'd better go," she repeated turning into the hallway. As we moved down the stairs, her eyes locked on mine. "If we had to do it—to amputate, could you?"

"He doesn't want it."

"That's not what I asked you." Amy shrugged like Liam's wishes were irrelevant. "If it was the only way to save his life. Could you?"

It was a question I'd asked myself as I studied the drawings in the survival medicine book over and over

143

again.

"I don't know," I said.

She sighed like I'd just failed another test in her mind. "Then you need to come back with some serious help." She paused. "Do you—do you think she might be able to do anything for Rod?"

I doubt it, I thought. The images from a show I'd seen once about the bombings of those Japanese cities at the end of World War II played in my mind. Radiation sickness was deadly, its cures limited. Amy knew that from her grandmother's stories about being a girl in Kashima—a little town not far from Nagasaki—right after the nukes dropped at the end of the Second World War Her question didn't even make sense—I almost said so—but then I saw the faint glimmer of tears in her eyes.

"Maybe so," I said and patted her shoulder in my best imitation of how Rod would have done it.

I tumbled down the stairs and donned a fresh protective suit.

"Nester!" Amy's voice was like razor wire, flaying my back. I tried not to let her see my sigh of annoyance and turned around.

"Aren't you forgetting something?"

I patted myself, unzipped my go-bag and peered inside. "I don't think so..."

Amy rolled her eyes. "You're going to get yourself killed."

"All right, Amy. What am I forgetting?"

She handed me the assault rifle hanging from a strap over her back.

"Um..." I didn't want to take it. The revolver was one thing—I didn't like it either, but I appreciated the control and practice it would take to learn to use it well... even if I'd had neither. The assault rifle was something else. Just looking at it made my stepfather's voice start playing like a bad commercial jingle in my head: *There's only one purpose for a gun like that: to kill people. Lots of them.*

"Look, Amy, we're going there to ask her to help us, not for some kind of shootout—"

"Amaranth's got a shotgun and Katie's got a pistol so you're pretty well covered for defense at different ranges," Amy continued unloading half a dozen heavy boxes of ammunition into my other palm. "It's loaded," she said. "These are extras. You heard Marty: the crazy old bat likes to shoot at people—"

"Are you listening to me? We don't want to shoot back. We need her *help*—"

"I know that, Nester. But it might take more persuasion than just booze." She grabbed my arm and spun me around, jamming the boxes of rounds into my backpack. The weight of the ammo added to the liquor bent my back. "Besides, she can just kill you and take the bottles off your cold dead bodies... if Amaranth doesn't drink it first," she added under her breath. "Check your revolver."

"Amy, if this is payback for the convict I—"

"Check it, Nester!"

I sighed and opened the revolver's loading gate.

"At the floor, Nester," Amy chastised. "Never at a person...unless you intend to fire it. But I suppose in your case *that* will never happen." She grabbed the revolver out of my hands. "Like this."

I was annoyed, but I was also impressed. She handled the weapon with smooth efficiency and absolute confidence. It was kinda hot, watching her little hands at work on the pistol's dark barrel.

"How do you know how to do all this?" I asked.

"My grandfather," she said calmly. "Scary guy. Very military. Very strict. He insisted that all of us grandkids learn to shoot. I didn't want to, but I was too scared to say

145

'no'. Even my mom is—was—scared of him—" she tried to laugh, but the loss of her mother was too recent for the memory to be bittersweet. "She wanted to tell him 'no' but she didn't dare. The weird thing was I started to like it. I was pretty good and Gramps started entering me in competitions and stuff. I won a few," she continued. "Turns out, Gramps wasn't so scary. He just distrusted most people. Thought the easiest way to keep them away was by being an asshole." She looked me dead in the face. "And he was right."

She handed my revolver back to me, the delicate bones of her fingers closing over mine. I stared at her for a moment, seeing her as the petite beauty she'd been walking the halls of JFK High in her cheerleading skirt, remembering how many times I'd watched her and thought she was the hottest girl in the tenth grade—

But then she started *talking* and ruined it.

"You're a straight-up guy, Nester. You don't bullshit people and I figure I owe you the same." She stepped closer to me and lowered her voice. "I *will* protect this place and the people inside it. I *will.* So if you come back with a threat on your heels, I'll do what I have to do. If you or the others get in the way..." She didn't finish the sentence, but her jaw tightened and her eyes narrowed, glinting with the fever of her own personal PTSD.

I was scared of her—scared *for* her. Once she'd been the kind of girl who drew a tight circle around her friends and laughed at the people on the outside of it. And that had been bad enough. But the losses and terrors she'd lived through had twisted that circle into a noose. I felt like I should do something, say something to erase the blackness I could hear in her voice, but right then Katie stuck her face between the door and the jamb.

"You ready?"

"Yeah," I muttered and left the cabin for the snow.

****

It was only a couple of miles, but it was a tough walk. We'd decided against the road in favor of a trek through the woods that we hoped would be safer. But that was debatable, I realized, almost as soon as we reached the lake and left the paths of the Mountain Place for the trail-less woods, following Katie deeper into the trees. The snow disguised the slopes and hazards of the terrain, and more than once, we fell or waded through snow up to our armpits. Cold seeped through the thin plastic of my protective suit.

The suits turned out to be an advantage, though. If they'd been bright orange or even Army green instead of white, we'd have been bright as Christmas lights in a winter wonderland. But the fabric worked with us, not against us. We moved nearly invisibly, if not exactly comfortably, through the snow. It was the longest I'd been out in it since the day we'd arrived at the Mountain Place, and whatever else the suits might be doing, they weren't much for keeping out the wind that raced down the mountains and cut through us like a broadsword. The longer we walked, the itchier and hotter the respirator got on my face and the smell of my own breath gagged me. I wanted to rip it off and take deep gulps of the icy air, but I didn't dare.

Katie stopped several times, staring around her like she was unsure.

"Do you even know where we're going?" Amaranth muttered after we'd been walking awhile. Her face was chapped and irritation shone in her eyes.

"Ain't never walked it in this much snow."

"Great," Amaranth sighed. "We're lost in the woods."

"We ain't lost," Katie said, glaring at her. "I'm looking for..." she turned around and around in the snow. "It should be..."

"What?" Amaranth demanded. She walked as far

147

from me as she could, and avoided looking at me as steadfastly as I avoided her. "Why are we just standing here—?"

"Hush up!" Katie hissed.

Amaranth rolled her eyes but she closed her mouth. We stood, motionless in the snow, waiting and listening. Katie closed her eyes and it seemed to me almost like she was praying for Divine guidance to reveal the route through the trees.

"Wait here a sec," she said tramping off a few feet ahead of us in the snow.

I wanted to give her the benefit of the doubt, but we stood motionless for so long that I was beginning to think Amaranth was right: we were lost already. I eased the heavy backpack off my shoulders and sank to the ground, unzipping the front pocket for the compass.

"I don't know why she's here," Amaranth muttered into the air beside me. "She's completely lost."

"You're just mad because she told you about yourself."

Amaranth glared at me. "Thanks for your support, Nester."

I shrugged. "I don't know what you expect from me." I lowered my voice to be sure it didn't carry to Katie. "Why, Amaranth?" I asked. My voice shook, but I had to know. "Why did you do—that—with me?"

"It's what I do." Her voice was brittle, hard-edged, and poisonous.

"I don't buy it. Look, I'm guilty too. I know it. I could have stopped you. I didn't. But I just want to know—"

"What's taking this girl so long?" Amaranth paced away from me, kicking up snow impatiently. "We never should have trusted such a dim-witted—"

"Ease up," I snapped. "As much as you have in common, you really ought to get along better with her."

"Have in common!" Amaranth snorted. "What on

148

earth do we have in common?"

"Well no parents, for one."

"They had a mother."

"But their father's in jail. Has been all their lives. I don't know what he did exactly, something about bank robbery and murder—"

"Are you serious?" Amaranth's eyes met mine for the first time in days. "How do you know?"

I laid out everything I knew about the twins, including the letter we'd found in the convict's bag. "I'm only telling you this so you'll cut it out, okay? She's right: you need to suck it up. You're not the only one who's had it tough. At this point, all of us are candidates—"

Something moved in the trees.

I didn't need to signal—we were already crouched low—but we immediately went silent and still. Voices floated toward us, echoing under the dark branches.

"...have to keep moving, you know that."

"But it's so cold," the voice was of a child, maybe Elise's age, but I couldn't tell if it belonged to a girl or boy. "Why couldn't we stay—?"

"You know why. There's no more food there. Now that the snow has stopped we have to keep moving. We'll find another place. Or someone to help us. It'll be all right—"

They passed us, a straggling line of dark forms moving slowly through the woods. I counted seven of them: a couple of older boys and a girl around the same age—maybe a little younger than me—and then some smaller kids. I saw rifles and backpacks. I saw one of the kids carrying a younger kid on his back. A girl held hands with another little kid. A boy in a blue parka wearing a nerdy pair of black glasses led the group, picking his way warily through the trees.

"They're just a bunch of kids!" Amaranth whispered, amazement shining in her eyes. "They're just like us!"

149

Before I could answer, she was on her feet.

"What are you doing?"

"I'm going to talk to them—"

"No!" I yanked her back onto her belly beside me. The group of kids in front of us stopped short. .

"There's someone here." The kid with the glasses lifted his weapon. "Who's there?" he yelled. At his signal, the others moved as quickly as possible away from us until they were invisible in the snow. "Who's there? Show yourself or I'll—" he racked the shotgun and aimed it blindly in our direction.

Amaranth's eyes pled with me but I made my face stone and held my breath and her arm, locking her in place.

The kid paused a long time, staring into the woods like he could melt the snow and discover us. Then at last, he turned and hurried to catch up to his friends. From time to time, he peered back through the dark trees hesitantly. At last, he gave up and disappeared into the forest.

We stood up slowly, shaking snow from our suits.

"Why couldn't we have talked to them? Maybe they have some information. Maybe they came from Benson or Kinder or some other town. They might know where we could find some help—"

"If there was help where they came from they'd still be there." Katie popped up from where she'd hidden and started walking with confidence again. I followed.

"We could at least find out where they came from. Where they're going—"

"And then what?" I asked. "You saw them. They looked just like *us* before we got to the Mountain Place—"

"Exactly," Amaranth said urgently. "That was why I wanted to talk to them—"

"And then you'd have wanted to help them," I said quietly. "Which we can't afford to do. We're already running through the resources at the Mountain Place—and that's with Rod and Liam both too sick to eat much. Can you

150

imagine if we added seven *more* hungry kids—?"

"But if we don't help them, they'll die."

"If we help them, we won't have enough to get through this winter—"

"It's always going to be winter, Nester!" A sudden wet sheen glowed in Amaranth's green eyes. "You know that, I know that, we all know that. There's never going to be a spring—"

"Then we can't afford to share."

Amaranth glared at me. "You sound like *her*. Like Amy."

She meant it as an insult. Before I could respond, Katie cried,

"There it is!"

She pointed to a little clearing. A small shack sat in the center of it. It was dark, old and nearly falling in on itself, its black windows like watching eyes.

Katie marched up to the door and kicked it open.

"If there's anybody in here, you need to come on out!" she hollered, aiming her pistol into the darkness of the shack. "Ain't nothing in here worth havin' no way."

Nothing happened. There wasn't a sound from inside and nothing rushed out at us, either.

"Where are we? This isn't Old Man Watson's, is it?" Amaranth frowned. "I was expecting something...more."

"We're on Watson's land now. This was our place before Mr. David told us to come up to the cabin."

It was one room, about the size of a backyard shed. An empty lantern sat in the center of the floor. An ancient chest that looked like it had come over on the *Nina*, the *Pinta* or the *Santa Maria* was partly open, showing some scratched plastic tumblers and assorted dishes. I didn't see a fireplace or a coal stove or any other heat source. Four walls and a roof— and that was about it. It made the Mountain Place look like a palace.

"Those kids been using it. There was a little food—

151

nothing special, some canned beans and stuff we put up from last summer's garden— but it's gone," she announced. "Had some kerosene, a lantern, some tools and a few blankets. They's gone, too. But if they went up to the farmhouse, that's bad for us. Means the old lady's gonna be all worked up. First shot might not be a warnin'," she added grimly. "Get yourselves ready. It ain't far now."

15

THE HOARD

"Get down. Right here." Katie dropped to the ground at the edge of a cluster of black trees. "The house is up ahead, but she'll know we're here."

Muffled by the respirator, her voice sounded like she was talking through a tin can. She pointed. "There's a kind of path through there. Leads right to the front door."

A small cottage sat in the middle of a junkyard. Seriously. A junkyard. Rusty snow-covered vehicles, old containers, all kinds of unrecognizable objects in metal, glass and plastic covered the hundred yards between us and the house. Some of it was in towers as tall as I was. Katie said there was a path, but I couldn't see it—or the farmhouse either. All I saw was a solid wall of trash.

"Looks like junk, yeah, but some of the stuff she's got is still useful. Make stuff out of, if you like to tinker with things. That's why me and Marty came up here: looking for some stuff to use. Didn't get to touch none of it, though. The dogs came running and she fired on us 'fore we even saw her—"

"Dogs?" I swung my head toward her.

She nodded, her face a beige oval in the white hood of her suit. "She's got at least a dozen of 'em. Maybe more—"

"A *dozen* dogs?" I cried. "You didn't say anything about that! How could you leave that out? How are we going avoid a dozen dogs? Why didn't you tell us?"

"I couldn't. Not without shamin' Marty—"

"Marty?" Amaranth rolled her eyes. "Now what? What does Marty have to do with this—?"

"He's afraid of 'em. Dogs. Her dogs. Some of them are big. Nearly as big as he is. I couldn't say nothin' about 'em without making him feel bad."

"Oh, we wouldn't want Marty to feel *bad*—" Amaranth grumbled.

"Okay, okay," I said. "We just have to regroup. We have to think of a way to—"

Amaranth stood up. Before I could stop her she left the protection of the trees and started walking deliberately toward the little house, balancing on that thin line between what some people would call "brave" and other people would call outright "stupid."

She'd gone less than ten feet when the barking started. Out of nowhere, half a dozen dogs of all sizes and breeds emerged from the trash piles barking, their teeth bared. They raced toward her with violent intent. Amaranth stopped with her hands out in front of her like she was trying to pet them or something.

"That girl is crazy," Katie muttered.

"Yeah," I agreed, but I stood up, lifting the revolver, targeting one of the moving canine blurs. I wasn't sure I could have hit it if it was standing still, but I couldn't just stand there and let Amaranth get mauled to death—

A gun's report cracked the sky. I looked down at my weapon in surprise, but I hadn't fired it. The dogs circled and raced away from Amaranth disappearing back into the junk, still braying and barking their warnings.

"Mrs. Watson!" Amaranth yelled. "Please don't shoot again! I just want to talk to you!" She shrugged the shotgun off her shoulder and laid it on the ground. "Please, Mrs.

154

Watson!" She wriggled a bit more and set her backpack on the snow in front of her. "I brought you some new stuff, too. Please. I just want to—"

"Make them others come out!" A female voice shouted. "Yeah, I see 'em. Tell 'em to come on out or I'll—"

A second shot zinged off something metal, and a tottering pile of mismatched and broken objects quivered like an avalanche before settling.

"That girl don't got good sense," Katie added like a footnote to her earlier diagnosis. "She's gonna get us all killed. How we gonna help Liam then?"

"I don't know, but there's no turning back now. Come on."

We shuffled forward, maneuvering through the piles toward Amaranth. A rusted Volkswagen's bug-like headlights peeked out from one pile, an old TV console with a shattered screen from another. I thought I saw an old baby stroller and the curve of a guitar, but it was hard to tell for sure under the drifts of white snow.

"Stop right there!" the old woman yelled when we were just a step behind Amaranth. "And put your stuff down. All of it!"

Katie and I obeyed.

"A new plan would have been nice," I grumbled in Amaranth's direction. "A few minutes to figure out some kind of defense—"

"Stop talking!" The woman shouted, still invisible to us. "Now turn around and go. Leave the stuff and the guns and get off my property. Now! Before I change my mind!"

"No!" Amaranth yelled back. "You can have the guns. You can have the stuff! All of it! We brought it for you. As a peace offering. A gift! But we won't go until we talk to you—"

"She's right!" I stepped forward, my hands up. "We have to—"

Nate appeared suddenly in the snow. A Hawaiian

155

shirt covered his broad torso and he wore flip flops and sunglasses. He perched on the hood of the Volkswagen, munching on a slice of watermelon.

Take off your glasses, man.

"We have to—to talk to you—" I repeated, groaning inwardly. *You got to go away. You have got to go away!* I thought desperately. *Please, Nate. Just—*

Don't be a hater, man, Nate insisted. *For once in your life, just do what I say. Take. Off. Your. Glasses*—and he lifted the sunglasses and showed me his empty eye sockets.

They were crawling with squirming maggots.

"Shit!" I screamed, yanking the mask off my face, my stomach rolling in horror. "What the—"

"What's wrong? What happened?" Amaranth swung toward me, her eyebrows high over the respirator, her body poised to assist.

"It's nothing," I replied shakily, wiping slick sweat off my mouth and forehead. "I thought—it felt—like something was eating at me—"

The sound of crunching snow stopped me from having to explain any further. A figure stood about fifty feet away from us, holding a shotgun high on its shoulder. It could have been the old lady—or an old man—or anyone else. It was impossible to make out any kind of detail other than the figure was large around the middle and wearing a heavy coat of some kind of shaggy fabric, a black fedora and boots.

"Is that her?" I asked Katie without moving my lips.

She nodded, but the look in her eyes said she was strongly considering abandoning us and diving for the cover of the junk.

The figure moved warily toward us, one careful step at a time.

My respirator hung abandoned in my hand, but toxic air doesn't matter when you're about to get your head

156

blown off by a shotgun at close range. And that was what I was pretty sure was going to happen as she kept coming toward us, the snow crunching under her boots, the shotgun still leveled at us. We stood there, as frozen as the ground, paralyzed by both her steady advance and our uncertainty. Finally, she got close enough for me to really see her.

She was a middle-aged white woman with two thin gray plaits hanging on either shoulder and some kind of bandana tied around the lower half of her face.

"I told you it was him," she mumbled in a rough old lady cackle.

"You can't tell from this far," she answered herself. "You can't see nothing no more unless it's right up in front of your face—"

"Hush. We both know you're the blind one. Can't see nothing smaller than the side of a barn. *I* can see him just fine."

Amaranth took a half step toward her. "Mrs. Watson, I'm—"

"Stay where you are!" the old woman shouted, swinging the barrel of her gun in Amaranth's direction. "Ain't nobody talking to you!"

"And it's Dr. Watson, anyway," I muttered. I don't know why; a bad habit of correcting people, I guess.

The old lady's beady eyes locked on me. She laughed a witchy chuckle that ended when she turned her head and spat on the ground.

"Sounds just like him, I'll give you that."

"Told you. It's him."

She took two more steps and stopped about fifteen feet away from us.

"You," she said, gesturing with the shotgun. "Come here."

She'd done so much talking to herself that I hesitated.

157

"Me?" I asked.

Another wet cackle, another stream of spit steaming on the snow.

"Yeah, sounds like him all right," she muttered to herself. "Yeah, you. Come closer. So I can see you better."

"I'll come closer, Doc," I said loudly taking a small step in her direction. "I'll come as close as you want... if you stop waving that gun in my face."

The old lady went still. She didn't move for such a long time I was scared she'd died standing with her shotgun raised and her eyes open. I didn't dare move either, but I rotated just my eyes first at Amaranth and then Katie, trying to decide if I should inch closer to her, or if we should just grab our guns and run.

Then Doc Watson lowered her arms abruptly like they'd gotten too tired to hold up any longer.

"You're a bossy one, aren't you?" she said.

"I'm telling you, it's him—" she added to herself.

"Who is she talking about?" Amaranth whispered.

"Told you she was crazy," Katie replied.

"Crazy but not deaf," the old woman cried. "I told y'all to 'hush up' and I meant what I said. In fact," she lifted her gun again. "You can git. Git off my land—"

I stopped my slow movement in her direction. "They're with me, Doc. If they go, I gotta go, too—"

"No," she interrupted quickly. Desperation and sadness made her tone almost like a plea. "Fine. Bring them then. Just come here."

I'd been half-stepping before then, but the plaintiveness in her voice made me feel strong. Like I had some hope—some power—in the situation, even though I didn't have any idea yet what it was.

"Gun down," I insisted. "On the ground, doc. You know I can't come any closer while you're pointing that thing at me. How about we all just leave our guns, right here, okay? Then we can really talk."

"Oh!" It sounded almost like she was crying. "Oh, yes! Yes!" And to my surprise she tossed the weapon away like the steel barrel had burned her.

When we stood only about three feet away from each other, I stopped. The respirator still dangled from my fingers, but I'd lost the hood of the protective suit when I pulled it off. My face—broken glasses and all—was exposed and naked. The old woman devoured my features, and then stepped even closer to me. I saw filmy blue eyes floating in weather-beaten skin before she grabbed me by the neck and cupped my cheek with a furry mitten.

"Oh!" she exclaimed, happily. Her eyes filled with tears and she blew hot, bad breath into my face. "Oh, Robert! It *is* you! You've come home!"

And she threw her arms around me and pulled me into her chest, nearly crushing me in her embrace, saying "Robert, Robert!" over and over again.

Robert? Who the hell...?

Finally, she stopped squeezing the life out of me and settled for crushing my hand. "Come on, come on. Into the house. You can bring your friends, too. I don't mind, I don't mind. Any friends of my Robert, are friends of mine—"She stopped short and glared at a person I couldn't see. "I told you I didn't kill him all those years ago. That's someone else out there, buried under that tree!" she shouted belligerently. "I told you I didn't kill Robert—and now here's the proof!"

Amaranth gasped. Her pale face seemed to lose the little color left in it.

"What's the matter?" the old vet demanded.

"Nothing, Doc. Nothing." I draped my arm around the old woman's shoulders and shot Amaranth a warning glance. "She's tired. Long journey. Lots of snow, lots of crazy people out there, you know?"

The old woman grimaced.

"Go pick up that stuff my Robert brought me, girl,"

she ordered, her eyes dancing with suppressed excitement. "My Robert knows I like presents—but leave them guns out there, just like he said."

She led me slowly toward the house, pinioning my arm under hers, her grip surprisingly strong. As she opened the old creaky old door and pushed me into a room as dark and close as an ogre's cave, I thought I heard Nate laughing.

16

PRESENTS FOR DOC WATSON

I caught only a quick glimpse of the place before she slammed the door and shut out the gray sky's light.

It was filled with stuff.

Boxes and piles of objects that scraped the ceiling on all sides surrounded us; most were taller than me. We stood in a narrow tunnel between the mounds of stuff through which Doc Watson moved as easily as if she were alone on the wide concourse of a shopping mall. But when the door closed and I couldn't see anything anymore, the smell of the place came at me from every side: stale air, rot, decay and dog crap. It was suffocating and vile. My eyes teared and I would have slapped my respirator back on my face if I could—I just didn't want to piss the old lady off. More barking sounds rushed us and I felt canine paws on my shins.

"Hello, babies. Hello! We got company, yes! Company!" she exclaimed. A wet nose nuzzled me, and then I was licked by a rough tongue. "Go! Go on!" the old lady said, shooing them off toward a pinpoint of light ahead of us. "Go on!"

The animals retreated on her command and we pressed forward, walking on something that wasn't the floor—I could tell by the way it crunched and crackled beneath our boots. The old woman grabbed my arm again and dragged me through the debris with sure steps. And she talked to herself and answered herself the entire time.

Someone fell against my back.

"Nester!" Amaranth hissed from behind me. "Help. I can't..."

I reached for her hand and caught a tower of stuff instead, sending it sliding. Amaranth squealed as we were showered in miscellaneous garbage for what felt like forever.

"What? What's the matter with her?" Doc Watson asked, oblivious to the avalanche.

"Nothing, doc," I said. "Just need some light."

"You used to know your way around this place with your eyes closed."

Suspicion had crept into her tone. She was invisible to me in the darkness, but I could smell her: a heady mix of body odor and dog scent

"But that was a while ago," I said lightly. "You said so yourself. That I've been gone a while. And you've gotten some new presents since then."

There was a long pause while she thought about what I'd said—and I thought about what we'd do if she didn't buy it—but at last she giggled again. "Of course, you're right, Robert. Of course."

I exhaled my relief so loudly that the old lady must have heard it. But she simply squeezed my forearm again and then released me. I heard the sound of a match, a dim flame lit the outline of her shape and then a candle illuminated the room...

Sort of.

It was still dark, but now I could see that we stood in the center of what was probably once the main room of the farmhouse. A dirty fireplace stood right in front of me, filled with ash and partially-burned wood. Even though it was zero degrees outside, it didn't look like it had been used in

162

a long time. The room was warm— almost hot. I guess all those piles of things made a weird kind of insulation that kept the cold out. A big bowl of kibble rested on the hearth, and half a dozen golden retriever puppies circled it playfully. Their mother lay in front of an old recliner like a living footrest. She lifted her head, but didn't seem that interested us.

The recliner had once been a burgundy color but was now ripped and stained, with an old quilt draped over one arm and a plate of something half-eaten resting on the other. There was a little table near the chair, covered with papers. A photograph rose out of the remains of meals past like the wedding cake topper of a disaster: a young white woman in a long white dress and young black man in a tux. Even in the dim light I could tell the dude in the picture looked a lot like me: bald brown head, nerdy black glasses, very tall and very slim.

Beyond that, every other available space was covered floor-to-ceiling by the hoard. I'd seen stuff like it on television, but I never imagined myself standing in the middle of one. There were boxes and papers and all kinds of dusty, old and decaying objects towering in unsteady piles everywhere. I looked up: they reached the ceiling. I looked down. We'd been walking on them: crushing wrappers, empty food cans, papers and all kinds of little parts and pieces beneath our feet. I saw roaches scuttling in and out of what looked like an empty sardine can on the floor near the fireplace, and I wouldn't have been shocked to see a rat or two either.

I turned slowly, taking in the scope of the mess. There was barely enough space for me to do it. Random stuff, everywhere: a rusty iron, a pair of dusty lamp shades, the head of a dirty mop, an oven mitt with a price tag still on it, a one-story tower of partially empty food containers and soda cans. It was like being inside an ADHD kid's brain: too much, unfocused and overpopulated.

Amaranth and Katie couldn't even make it into the clearing where the old lady's chair sat. They stood at the edge of the tunnel of junk we'd come through with their mouths open and their eyes wide, clinging to each other like sisters. But at least they had their respirators on. The smell was nose-burningly amazing. Imagine visiting the town dump on a day in August after all of the trucks for the entire city of Washington, D.C. have dropped their loads. Then imagine letting all that garbage bake in the hot sun for seven days. That was the smell. Enough to make you throw up in your mouth.

I wanted to slip my mask back on so badly but the old lady was staring avidly at my face. Up close, I realized she wasn't nearly as old as I had thought. Maybe in her fifties?

"Let me have my presents!" she said gleefully as she slowly lowered herself into her chair.

I stretched out my hand, but just the simple act of transferring the backpacks from the girls to me made one of the piles tremble. A pair of shoes—brand new and child sized—tumbled off the top and brained Katie. Doc Watson didn't even seem to notice. Her face lit up like a little girl's as I kicked aside some crap and set the backpacks on the tiny strip of floor in front of her.

"Wait!" I said before she could unzip the first one. "You have to do something for me first, remember?"

She glowered at me: a straight-up pout that Elise would have envied.

"What?"

"I need some medicine. An antibiotic. For my—" I hesitated, wondering how much I should say about Liam and the whole situation. "Horse."

"You know I don't do that anymore!"

"Oh come on," I cajoled. "For me?"

Behind me, I heard just the tiniest burst of laughter. I'd have blamed it on Nate, but when I turned Amaranth

164

had a smirk on her face. I shot her a *What?* even though I knew why she was laughing. She'd never heard my "flirt" voice. Neither had I, for that matter.

Didn't work anyway.

"No," the old lady harrumphed. "I haven't used the office in years. Not since. Well, you know..." she stopped talking and stared at the dead fire like she could will it back to life.

"Well, that's too bad," I said sadly, picking up the backpacks by their straps. "I think you would have liked what I picked. Don't you think she'd like it, Amaranth?"

"I know she would have," Amaranth said quickly, following my lead. "Good stuff."

"Yup," Katie seconded weakly, but she looked far less sure.

"Yeah? Thought I heard bottles. It ain't just alcohol, is it? 'Cause I never touch that stuff anymore."

I glared at Katie—yet another bit of misinformation—but there wasn't anything for it now.

"Of course there's more than just that." I said quickly. "You'll see. But I need those drugs, Doc."

The woman's mouth twitched with temptation, but she didn't look at us. I waited, but she stared steadfastly into the ashes like she'd forgotten I was there. Her eyes volleyed back and forth and I knew there was a conversation going on in her head, but this time, she didn't share it.

"Come on, ladies," I said to the girls. "We're done here."

I turned and so did they. Katie stretched out her hands to feel her way down the dark tunnel and immediately set off another avalanche.

"What's the matter with you?" Doc Watson jumped to her feet and lunged at the girls. "You're messing everything up!" Before any of us could comment on the irony of that statement, she spun back to me. "I get

165

everything in the bags?"

I glanced at Amaranth and Katie. That wasn't the plan; the ammunition and water and food we'd brought had been our backup stash. But if it got us out of there with the drugs quickly, maybe that was worth the sacrifice.

Amaranth nodded. Katie frowned, her calculations flitting across her face.

"I'm keepin' mine," she said.

"Everything in these two," I said.

Doc Watson's eyes flitted over Katie—well, her backpack really. Then they fixed on me again, measuring me carefully. "Gimme that watch," she said pointing to Liam's timepiece, still ticking accurately on my wrist. "As a deposit," she stood up. "And I'll take you to the office. You see if I got what you want, and then we'll talk about what it's worth to you."

It was even more treacherous getting out of the house than it had been to get into it. The stuff we'd disturbed caused obstructions in the narrow tunnels and now we had to climb over the piles. The puppies trailed us, barking and nipping at our heels and generally making nuisances of themselves. They were cute—maybe about three months old—frisky, curious and the color of honey. But in the general mess of the woman's house, they just added a layer of hazard we didn't need. When Amaranth picked one up to keep from stepping on it, Doc Watson snapped, "Hands off the babies!" so stridently, Amaranth dropped the little thing like it was hot.

"Have you been to town? What's the news?" Doc Watson asked, like we weren't engaged in the slog of our lives just trying to make our way to the door. "My groceries haven't been delivered this month."

"Groceries aren't coming." I shook my head. "Town's gone."

She laughed at me. "What do you mean it's 'gone'?

166

Town's don't go anywhere—"

"They do when the bombs go off, Doc."

The woman frowned and the eyes she fixed on me were suddenly clear, lucid and curious. "Who'd bomb a one-horse town like Kinder?"

Katie's fingers curled around my arm. I could barely make her out in the darkness, but I got the message: the old lady didn't have a clue about anything happening in the outside world and we wouldn't help ourselves any by enlightening her.

"Jokin', doc. You know how I love to joke."

Somehow we made it to the front door without stepping on a puppy or getting suffocated by old paper, lacerated by empty bottles or knocked unconscious by anything worse. As soon as we stepped outside again, I settled my respirator back on my face. If the house was this bad, I could only guess what the abandoned veterinary office might be like. The grown dogs surrounded us, barking and jumping menacingly.

"Be still!" Doc Watson snapped her fingers once and they silenced, trotting along behind her, their tongues lolling out of their mouths. They were mutts that had the look of strays who'd found their way to her farm and been taken in. Kind of like us at the Mountain Place.

Our strange party circumnavigated the cottage, and then crossed a short covered walkway to a smaller building. I saw the cottage's side door, its frame barely visible behind another heap of junk. I guessed there was a way to walk more easily between the house and office, but that doorway was buried in walls of junk both inside the house and outside of it. The portico was littered with all kinds of things— all of them rusted, faded and damaged by rain and snow and sun. But Katie was right: it was a tinkerer's paradise. I saw a skateboard and a lawn chair, a few old tires and an old sink. My Robotics Club could have built one heck of a project with just those scraps and a decent power source. Scholarships would have flooded into our email boxes and Jindal Patel and I would have been neighbors in Cambridge: me at Harvard, him at M.I.T.

There were two signs on the office door. One said "*Dorothea Watson, DVM*"; the other read "Out, Back at" with the hands of a clock hung at 3:10. Both looked weathered, lopsided and sad.

Doc Watson stopped short. Her face changed, her expression shifting from wariness to fear. Like someone confronting the memory of a traumatic experience.

"Been a long time," she said aloud and I almost answered her before I understood she wasn't talking to me.

"But it's okay now. That other must have been—a bad dream. He's here now. He's standing right—right—" She reached out and grabbed my arm, feeling along my forearm for reassurance. "Just a nightmare," she answered herself and shuddered.

"I don't want to go in—" she told herself. It was the voice of a scared kid, trembling and on the verge of tears.

"No, and we don't have to. Let *them* go in. See if they can find what they want. We can stay right here and make sure—"

She glared at me suddenly, unaware that the conversation she'd had with herself had been aloud.

That's your future, Nester. Gollum mumbling about his Precious.

It was Nate's voice, but I didn't see him. I focused on the old vet instead.

"You go," she said firmly, looking into my eyes. "If I got anything for your horse, it'll be in the cabinet." She reached deep into her clothing and pulled out a worn leather strap with two keys on it. "In the supply room in the back."

"What's the name of it? The antibiotic?"

"Name?" She frowned in confusion.

"Yeah. Are the names the same as for humans?

168

Azithromycin or Amoxicillin or—"

"Trimethoprim sulfa!" She spat out the name triumphantly, like she was pleased with herself. "I thought I had forgotten but," she pointed to her forehead, "it still works! Now," she continued, shoving me toward the door. "Go on in. Get what you want. So I can get what /want."

"Yeah," Amaranth agreed in a low voice. "Let's hurry up and get out of here."

The key turned the lock, but the door was stuck— it had been so long since it was opened I guess— and I had to use my shoulder to muscle it. It gave suddenly and I stumbled into a small dusty space that must have been the waiting area. There were a couple of chairs and a little coffee table in front of a chest-high counter with one of those flip-up doors that led to a work space with a desk, an old-fashioned desktop computer and a landline phone. Behind that was a door—to the supply room, I guessed— but there was also a door directly in front of us that probably led to the exam room. For patients larger than dogs, I suspected, Doc Watson must have made house—or barn—calls.

The biggest surprise was that the entire place was clean. A little dusty and stale-smelling, yes. But nothing like the cluttered insanity of the house.

Weird.

Out of habit, I reached for the panel of lights on the wall: to my surprise, a sputtering roar split the air. A moment later, florescent lights flickered on over our heads.

"Power!" Amaranth gasped. "How—"

"There must be a generator outside somewhere." I pulled off the respirator and wiped my sweaty face again. "A lot of hospitals have them for backup power. Never thought about animal hospitals having them, but I guess it makes sense." We stared at the glowing ceiling like we were witnessing a miracle. "Lights," I shook my head. "It's

169

been so long, it's almost—"

"Unnatural," Amaranth finished. "I'm starting to get a bad feeling about this whole idea—"

"Me, too," Katie said. Amaranth raised her eyebrows in surprise at their agreement, but Katie ignored her. Instead, she wiped a long streak of dust off the counter and muttered, "Think she has anything that would help?"

"Even if she does, it might not even be any good." Amaranth sighed. "I shouldn't have listened to you guys. I should have started for Benson, even if I had to go alone. Maybe we're looking for the wrong thing here. If she's got a running generator, she's got some kind of fuel. Maybe we can use it to get the tractor running and then—"

"Most drugs last beyond their expiration dates," I interrupted. The tractor was a bad memory; I didn't want to talk about why it was out of gas and rusting in the snow. "My mom told me that once, I just don't know how much longer. It's still the best shot we have, right? If there's something here—anything at all—that might work, we can get it back to the Mountain Place in an hour and—"

"Liam will get well," Amaranth offered at the same time that Katie said, "Liam will be all right."

The two girls studied each other for a moment, warily, like competitors entering the ring.

I lifted the flap on the counter, letting myself into the work space, mucking the clean white tile with my wet boots. The liquor in my backpack was ridiculously heavy, weighing me down as I struggled with the keys. I shrugged it off my shoulders and set it on the floor beside the supply door and bent to the second lock. The key fit easily and the door swung inward, admitting us to a long, narrow room lined with waist-high storage drawers topped by white countertops. The surfaces were all smooth and blank. I slid open a drawer and found it full of supplies, syringes and needles in sterile packages, gauze and other small instruments. In another drawer were surgical instruments of all sizes.

"What the hell is that?" Amaranth asked, pointing to a rack of tools hanging in a glass case. "It looks like a saw."

"It is. It's a bone saw. Most of the time docs use an electric or battery-operated one. But I guess sometimes they still use the old fashioned kind—"

"Stop, Nester.   Just...stop." Amaranth pushed me aside. "We're—we're not going to need a bone saw. Let's—let's get what we came for, give the old bag her presents and get out of here." She stopped in front of a tall white cabinet with a padlock looped between its two handles. "I bet this is it. Give me the keys."

"You're looking for Trimethoprim sulfa—" I prompted when she threw the doors wide.

"I know!"

"It's probably in boxes—"

"I don't see—"

"Let me."

The shelves were carefully organized and neatly arranged. Supplies like paper towels and hand sanitizer rested on the floor. On the upper shelves the bottles and boxes of various drugs were arranged in alphabetical order like they are in a pharmacy.

"Here," I said, seizing a big can.

"You said a box."

"I was wrong. It's in a powder. Probably so it can be mixed with feed."

"Will it work?"

I ignored her and squinted my glasses up my nose to read the label.

"It says here it expired... August 2009. But maybe if we use enough of it, it'll still work. This jar is half empty, so it's probably useless. But there's three more of them," I said reaching back to pull out the others. "Unopened."

"You think she'll let us take—"

"We'll barter for it. For Katie's backpack. You can tell

171

she wants it, greedy old witch—"

"Then we'll have nothing. If anything happens on the way back—"

"I don't like it either, but we need these drugs. Besides, nothing's going to happen—"

"Wait!" Katie had been silent, letting us banter back and forth. But now her voice was loud and clear. "Y'all hear that? It sounds like—"

The supply room's door slammed closed.

"Hey!" I sprinted toward it, grabbing the knob, but of course, the door was locked. I could hear her laughing on the other side.

"You always did underestimate me! Well, you're not going to leave me again, Robert Watson!" she cried gleefully. "I killed you once, and I'll do it again, if I have to!"

Killed?

"Hold up, hold up, okay? Uh, look, lady! I'm not Robert Watson!" I shouted through the door. "I only said that because— because—" Telling her I was a liar didn't seem like the best strategy so I abandoned that approach for a more useful truth. "Look, our friend is sick. Really sick. If he doesn't get this medicine he'll probably die. And I— we all—we'd do anything to save him—"

"You're a liar, Robert. You always were. The stories you've told me! You're a much better actor than you are farmer, I'll say that!"

"No, really, ma'am, I'm not Robert Watson! My name is Nester Bartlett and we're friends of your neighbor, David Harper. The guy who lives at the Mountain Place, next door—"

"David Harper? The soldier?" The old lady sounded confused.

"Yes!" Amaranth answered her at the same moment I did. "He's telling you the truth, ma'am. He only pretended to be your Robert to help Liam, Mr. Harper's son—"

"It's the truth," Katie added.

172

"Yeah, you can believe Katie. Her family rents that little... uh...house. At the edge of your property—"

Katie's dusky skin turned flamingo pink. "Well—we don't exactly rent it—"

"Ha!" the old lady cackled. "Got Robert and those damn squatters, too, right, pets?" We heard the dogs bark and whine in answer. "Well, this calls for a celebration. Treats for everyone!" she cried. I heard the familiar clink of glass against glass and that's when I realized that I'd left our trade outside the supply room. "But... there's nothing in here but liquor and... some kind of bullets. I hate liquor! It's been the cause of nothing—but— trouble—" I heard the sounds of smashing glass. "Oh, you are a liar Robert Watson! You always were and always will be!" Her voice broke like she was crying. "You never did give me anything but misery...and I hate you for it! I hate you! You'll pay for all the times I cried. You'll pay!"

Then the lights went dark and the office door slammed shut behind her.

17

THE WHOLE TRUTH

"Thanks a lot, Nester! Thanks a frigging *lot*!" Amaranth hissed. "You had to try to be a Romeo—"

"Hey, for a while it was working—"

"Working? Is that what you think? Honestly, Nester. Stick to what you *know*."

In another circumstance, I might have asked her exactly what *that* was, but I shrugged it off and inspected the room. There were no windows and no other doors. A tiny bit of light bled in from under the crack in the door, but other than that, we were in complete darkness again.

"Katie, you got a flashlight, right?"

"No. Had to leave it. Couldn't find no more batteries for it. We've used them all for the radio. You think there's anything behind these cabinets?" Katie asked, rattling one.

"Yeah, more wall," I answered. I wasn't trying to be sarcastic, but Katie got real quiet like she was ticked off. Instead of answering, though, she stared up at the ceiling like she expected an escape hatch to magically materialize.

"That crafty old witch played you like a basketball!" Amaranth ranted. "And now here we are, locked in a room, without weapons or a way to communicate with anyone—"

"Maybe there's like an air vent we can crawl through. Them panels like in the movies—"

"And maybe not," I muttered. The ceiling of the room was low—and I'm tall—so stretched my hand up and felt along it. "Not." I concluded. "This is pretty much a normal one story house converted into a workspace. Most normal houses don't have ceiling air vents. You see that in movies because it's a convenient plot device, but in real life—"

"Wish you wouldn't talk that way," Katie murmured. "Makes me feel stupid and I'm just tryin' to help—"

"And I wish you would come clean for once!" I shot back. "You and your brother always seem to tell half the story. About yourselves, about your past, about what's going on, about what to expect at this house—"

"But I tol' ya she was crazy—"

"You told me she *talked* to her dead husband! You didn't tell me she probably *killed* him and *ate* him for all we know! And you didn't tell me that you never actually had the right to live on her land, or about the dogs or—" Panic rose inside me and I had to close my eyes and breathe a second before I lost myself to it. "It was me she wanted to keep here. Or Robert. Or whatever—" I continued, getting confused by the confusion. "She might have let you go if I'd known what *not* to say—"

"You would have said the wrong thing anyway, Nester. You usually do," Amaranth sighed and dropped to the floor like she weighed 600 pounds. "But it doesn't matter anyway. It was a trap from the beginning—"

"Cut it out, Amaranth," I warned.

"Why? It's true. The problem with you, Nester, is you still think things are going to be easier for you because you're smart. You still think it's like it used to be and that you can outwit, outplay, outlast—"

"And you think you can screw your way out of every situation," I shot back before I could stop myself.

The ugly words hung in the darkness.

"Yeah," Amaranth sounded completely defeated.

175

"Yeah, you're right."

I wished I hadn't said it. For a long while, no one said anything.

"Look, we've got what we need," I said at last, patting the lid of the antibiotic powder. "We just need to figure a way out of here. There has to be something in your bag that would help, Katie."

"Don't know what. All's I got is some food and water, a tarp in case we had to make shelter. Rope and knife. That's it." She paused. "What do you think she's going to do to us?"

"Nester's probably going to meet the same fate as old Robert, whatever that was," Amaranth quipped. "You and me...who knows? Puppy chow?" Surrender dripped out of her like melting snow.

"What happened to the chick who went strolling out in the front of a pack of junkyard dogs?" I demanded. "Where'd she go?"

"Couldn't find anyone to screw, I guess."

"Amaranth—"

"Look, I don't know what you two are talking about and I don't wanna know. I just want to find a way out of here and get back to the cabin," Katie muttered. "If you don't got any ideas about how to get out of here, I wish you'd both just shut up—"

"*You* shut up. We probably wouldn't be *in* here if you could tell the truth! Why didn't you tell Nester that this old lady was some kind of homicidal maniac?"

"Well, if there's some stuff we ain't told you, we had our reasons for it—"

"Or maybe it's in your blood."

"What's *that* supposed to mean?"

"Yeah, yeah, I know. Your father went to jail for 1st degree murder and bank robbery. Marty showed Nester the stuff he found in the convict's bag, the pictures of the two of you when you were babies and the letter—"

"Amaranth!"

She stopped. I felt her turn to challenge me in the darkness...then her brain kicked in.

"Oh shit," she said.

I couldn't see Katie, but I could feel her, her stormy eyes wide and locked on me, piercing the blackness, demanding answers.

"Nester? Is this true?"

I sighed, wishing Amaranth Jones had an "off" switch. Right then, I'd have flicked it, put her up on a high shelf and left her there until she was a quaint antique.

"Yeah," I sighed. "Marty found some pictures. In the guy's pillowcase. Of the two of you. After we'd left him. After he escaped. Marty said the stuff might not have even belonged to him. That he might not have been your father. He said the guy could have taken them from someone else or—"

I heard a soft sniffle... then nothing.

"Remember he said he needed to get to Kinder. I guess he was going to town. To look for you."

Silence.

"Marty didn't want you to know." The darkness and her silence made me want to ease them both with words. "He wanted to protect you. Said it would hurt you and that you'd been hurt enough. That there was so much he couldn't do for you. This was supposed to be something he could."

It was awful. Standing there in the darkness, listening to her absorb the sort of information that re-orders your universe, feeling like the biggest jerk to ever walk upright for spilling my guts to Amaranth. I wished I had a cyanide capsule in a tooth filling like in the spy movies because I was pretty sure that if we ever got out of Doc Watson's supply room, Marty was going to kill me.

"I got one question," Katie said at last in a low quiet voice that betrayed no emotion at all. "Did he–that man—

did he know who we were, when we—when we—"

"I don't think so. I don't *know*. But I don't think so—"

"What did Marty say?"

I hesitated just a second too long.

"What did Marty say?" she demanded, her voice rising to a shout.

"He said it didn't matter to him. Didn't matter who he was. Didn't matter if he was looking for you or not. Didn't matter if he came back or not. He said as far as he was concerned the dude was just another threat. And—" I hesitated, but softening the truth now didn't seem particularly useful. "That he'd kill him if he did."

I heard a rush of movement. "We need to get out of here," Katie said urgently. "I got to talk to Marty. We need to get out of here—" she attacked the door, throwing herself against it like she could bust it down like a TV cop.

"That's not going to work. It opens *in*, not out. Feel right here. Where the lock is—" The idea hit me as soon as I said the words. "Wait. This is a pretty simple lock. Hey, if we could pop the mechanism, jimmy it with a credit card—"

"Katie, gimme your knife. Let me see it," Amaranth said, bumping into me as she moved toward the door.

Metallic scraping sounds tickled the silence. Thirty seconds later, there was a click and Amaranth turned the knob.

"Sometimes, I wonder how you normal kids survive," she said, swinging the door open.

"What do you mean?"

"I mean the stuff you don't know."

"Picking locks wasn't considered a valuable life skill in my household—"

"My point exactly," she said. "You're sheltered. Too sheltered for your own good. And yes, I know—" she continued quickly, so I wouldn't have to say it. "I'm the opposite."

178

The outer office was dark, too, but at least the windows let in some light. Katie hurried to rattle the knob of the front door. "It's locked too. From the outside. But I guess we could break the glass—"

"Are the dogs out there?"

"I don't see any yet."

"But they're out there. Patrolling the hoard. They'll come. And when they come, she'll be right back out here with that shotgun or that stupid assault rifle Amy made me bring," I added with a sigh, studying the mess of broken liquor bottles. "Too bad we can't get the dogs drunk."

"Why not?" Amaranth said after a pause. "Why can't we get the dogs drunk?"

I shook my head at her. "And just how do you propose we do that?"

"That's a cabinet full of animal drugs, right? Surely we can find something that would knock them out? Mix them in some food or water or something?"

I looked around me. "You see any?"

"Maybe in the exam room?"

"We can check, but I doubt it. This place obviously hasn't been used in years. And even if we could find something, how are we going to lure them to it without making noise? And then it might take a while for them to eat it. And even longer for the drugs to work, assuming they're still effective. Which is a gamble."

Amaranth rolled her eyes. "All right. You're the brainiac. Give us a solution, please, Mr. Peabody."

An idea—crazy and desperate, but possible— tickled the back of my brain.

"Where's the knife?" I asked, grabbing it from Amaranth and hurrying back into the supply room.

"What are you doing?" Amaranth asked.

"Taking the door off the hinges. We're going to use it to make a dog run— to keep the dogs from running anywhere but straight into the exam room."

"You're going to let them in here? With us?" Katie's eyes stretched wide.

"Yeah. We're going to barricade them into that room," I said, jerking my head toward the exam room.

"But how are we going to do that?"

"There's only one way I can think of. One of us will have to be the bait."

"And then what? We drive them into the room, but how do we get out?"

An image popped into my mind: my mother in the emergency room at the pediatric center. Details flooded through me, igniting the smallest of hopes. I hopped over the counter and opened the door to the exam room.

It was a large space with something like a gurney you might use for a person in the center of the room, a sink and more cabinets. But there was another door beyond it. I pushed it open, feeling my heart leap with real possibility for the first time.

It was an animal surgical set up: operating table, lights, rolling carts and an IV stand... and in holsters bolted into the wall, two cylinders that looked like fire extinguishers. One said oxygen in bright green letters and the other—

"Yes!" I cried when I lifted it and read the label.

"Change of plan," I yelled to the girls. "I hope everyone's respirator is working. We're going to drive them into the exam room and then we're going to send them to nighty-night and get the hell out of here."

18

WHO LET THE DOGS OUT?

"Run!" I screamed,

Katie launched herself out of the office and ran like hell.

"Come and get me!" she screamed, dancing crazily across the portico. Five of those ugly junkyard beasts appeared from out of the hoard and she took off, dodging the stacks of debris like a skier on a slalom course, weaving her way through the crap and back to the open door of the veterinary office.

The dogs raced after her, snapping at her heels, growling and barking and drooling like wolves. One of them nipped her ankle and she stumbled. But in the next second, she recovered and sprinted the last few steps across the threshold.

"Now, Amaranth!"

Amaranth slammed the door closed. Katie kept running, through the waiting room and into the exam room where I waited. Then Amaranth slammed that door, too, shutting Katie and me in with the wild barking beasts. I hoisted Katie up onto the rolling gurney that served as an exam table beside me as the dogs leapt and snapped at our toes. We were surrounded.

"Ahhh!" Katie shrieked as a dark mutt with a bit of German shepherd in his ears jumped, digging his fangs into her calf just above the ankle. "Get—him—off—" she cried, tears of pain forming in her eyes. She shook her leg, trying desperately to get the dog to let go but it dug in, tearing at the muscle, salivating at the taste of her meat.

"Let go!" I screamed, lifting the container of gas and bashing the dog as hard as I could. It fell back with a whimper but the others leapt and snarled and rattled the steel.

"I'm gonna fall off!" Katie screamed, struggling to keep her balance as the table shook, rolling forwards and back. "Hurry up, Nester!"

I turned the valve on the gas, releasing the pressurized contents in a long steady stream that quickly filled the room. It made no difference: the dogs crowded us, barking and leaping. The table wasn't high enough to be much protection: their paws scraped the top and their jaws weren't far behind. Katie stood on one foot, shrinking against me while I sprayed the anesthetic like pesticide.

"It's not working!" she screamed. "It's not working!"

The shepherd mutt snapped its jaws at Katie again and she screamed, jerking away from the animal so violently the table rolled a full foot. I lost my balance and fell off the cart, hitting the floor on my back with the raging animals all around me, the gas spraying in a wild and violent hiss.

"Nester!" Katie screamed as I coiled myself into a tight ball, protecting my face and internal organs as they animals converged on me, biting and tearing at the thin fabric of the protective suit. I lost her voice, lost everything but the menacing sounds of canine fury and the sensation of snatching teeth. I barely noticed when the barking got quieter and quieter and the teeth retreated.

I opened one eye and peered around my hands.

"I think it worked!" Katie yelled. Her voice sounded

muted and distorted under her mask. "I think—"

The door burst open. Doc Watson's massive shape loomed over me. Her cheeks were red and her eyes were hard with anger, but beyond that, all I could really see was her shotgun—and she was pointing it right at me.

"What do you think you're doing?" she shouted. "You've destroyed my—"

She never saw Amaranth emerge from the office behind her and she never knew what hit her when Amaranth smashed the liquor bottle against her head, baptizing her in gin. Doc Watson dropped like the *Titanic*, hitting the floor in a clatter of arms and legs.

"Fast thinking."

"Let's get out of here," Amaranth replied.

"Wait..." Katie slid slowly off the table, wincing. "I think... I think I need some help."

"How bad is it?" I asked.

I carried her until we had cleared the house and the junkyard, leaving the old lady and her dogs out cold and locked in her veterinary office. We found our guns exactly where we'd dropped them in the snow.

"It's bleeding and it hurts like fire. But I can walk. Slow but I can walk," she said without looking into my eyes. "I just want to get back. Fast as we can."

I knew it wasn't just for Liam's sake anymore.

"Katie, I'm—" Amaranth began, but Katie shook her head.

"Don't want to talk to either one of you right now," she muttered.

She was right. We'd both have plenty of explaining to do when we got back to the Mountain Place so there wasn't really any point in making big speeches now. Instead, I bound her ankle with some of the bandages Amaranth had swiped from the supply room and grabbed

183

the canteen.

"Looks like you're the guinea pig."

Her expression was one big question mark.

"The antibiotics. I'm giving you a dose right now, just in case. I don't think the Doc would keep a rabid dog, so you're good there. But all this trash and filth..." I shook my head. "Bad germs everywhere. Do you know how much you weigh?"

She shook her head.

"I'm going to guess between 80 and 90 pounds," I said quickly reading the dosage instructions and peeling back the canister's inner foil lid. Thankfully, it had a scooper inside. I dumped two scoops into the water and shook it hard. "Down the hatch."

Katie looked more scared of that water bottle than of anything we'd faced.

"You think it's okay?"

"I think so. I mean," I couldn't stop myself from clarifying. "They might not work, but I don't think they'll kill you."

Katie's green tea coloring went more green than tea.

"Drink it," I commanded, and she obeyed, grimacing at the taste. "I don't think I can carry you much further. Are you sure you can walk?"

She nodded and I pulled her up beside me. "I have no idea how long they'll be asleep. We need to be far away when they wake up—"

Katie dropped my hand like I had cooties. "Let's go."

I nodded at her. If she'd given me any kind of opening, I might have tried once more to explain. But there was no invitation in her tight lips and steely eyes. Until she talked to Marty, I wasn't going to get a thing from her, and after she talked to Marty... well, I was probably going to be the one tied up in the shed.

"Do you think she'll come looking for us?" Amaranth asked. "You told her we were from the Mountain Place. Do you think she'll come? For payback?"

I remembered how I stared down at the unconscious old woman just before we left her there, thinking about what Amy had said. She was right: the world had changed. There weren't any rules anymore and it seemed like everyone was trying to cheat us, use us and hurt us. It was a world full of desperate and traumatized people—just like us— unhinged by the end of the world they once knew and doing things they'd never have believed themselves capable of back when the toilets flushed and there was food and sunshine. I'd changed, too— and not for the better. It wasn't just Nate appearing and disappearing; it was the growing bleakness inside me, consuming my hope and smashing down everyone else's too.

And yet, here we were, still fighting to survive. Fighting so hard that I'd aimed her own shotgun at the brains of an old lady—a woman who in another lifetime would have been my grandmother or my great aunt and medicated by some nice strong anti-psychotic drugs— thinking about whether I should pull the trigger.

But instead of shooting, I had loosened Liam's watch from the woman's wrist. We'd been gone for five hours, I noted as I slid it back on my arm. Five hours—twice as long as I had hoped. I didn't look at the girls as I turned away from the old vet, grabbed a couple of thick black trash bags and swept all of the items Amaranth had brought from the supply room into them. We left her lying there.

I had been expecting protest; I had expected one of them to chastise me for my naivety and foolishness. I knew what Amy would say when she found out: she would let me know in no uncertain terms that I was a "wimp" or a "wuss" or worse—and she'd send me out to double check our perimeters against the old lady's attack. But neither Amaranth nor Katie had said a word.

We walked. The snow and cold slapped me in the

185

face. The sky was a darker shade of overcast, foretelling the coming of night. My protective suit was nothing but Tyvek shreds, so I stripped it off. But the effort of our escape had made me sweat. When the blustering wind hit the wet, I felt like I had a layer of ice cubes between my skin and my clothes. I shivered but kept moving, tracing our own tracks back through the snow where I could find them, tamping it down to make it easier for Katie to make her way.

"Is it me or is it colder?" Amaranth looked up at the darkening gray sky.

"It's you," I answered, even though I was pretty sure it wasn't. All kinds of thoughts went through my mind—snippets I'd read about nuclear winter and a whole special I'd seen on TV once about how, when our planet was young, there was some massive volcanic eruption that filled the skies with ash, blocking the sun. For *three years.* Almost every living thing on the planet died. The plants from lack of sunlight and the animals from starvation as the Earth was plunged into an ice age.

I could see it my head: the flat screen TV on—the big one in the basement where Nate and I used to game—flickering with computer-generated images of what life would have been like when the Permian era came to an end. It was so bad, the scientists nicknamed it the "Great Dying." They talked about other occasions in history when ash or dust or debris in the atmosphere had impacted the weather, sometimes lowering temperatures miles and miles and miles from the center of the disaster. But right when they started to discuss the theories about what would happen to the Earth's temperatures in the wake of a nuclear disaster, Nate had wanted to turn the channel.

"No. I'm watching this."
"But it's boring."
"It's not boring. It's science. It's like, the history of

186

the planet and stuff."

"But Adventure Time is on the Cartoon Network."

"You've seen all of those."

"They're funny."

"Then go upstairs and watch it on the TV in the family room."

Nate was silent long enough for me to hear the announcer say something about a nuclear cloud covering all or part of the Earth for months—or even years—when Nate lunged for the remote near my fingertips and pressed it. A moment later Cartoon Network programming erased the thoughtful images of planetary destruction.

"Hey!" I cried. "Turn it back."

"You've been watching that for an hour!" Nate stuffed the remote on the long-suffering bit of couch where he often rested his ever-widening buttocks and glared at me like he was daring me to shove his fat butt aside to fish it out.

Dude didn't know me very well.

I stood up. "Turn it back," I hissed. "Turn it back, right now—"

"No. It's my turn. If you want to watch that, you can go upstairs—"

I grabbed him by his T-shirt and yanked, but he was too heavy, so I had no choice but to lock my arms around his neck wrestler-style and drag him by inches off the sofa.

"Help! Help! Mom! Dad!" he shrieked when he realized he was losing. He flailed his arms around, catching me in the side of the face with a fingernail and breaking open a white furrow of ragged skin. "Help! Help!"

With one last mighty heave, his butt left the sofa. He hung suspended for a few seconds with his T-shirt bunched high over his belly, my arms hooked beneath his armpits and his feet still on the sofa—and then I let him go.

He dropped like a stone. It was only two feet or so, but he landed hard on his side, his head striking the edge

187

of the coffee table. I knew by the way the wood rattled that he'd probably hurt himself, but right then, I didn't care. I snatched the remote and changed the channel, throwing myself back on the sofa and crossing my arms over my chest as my little brother started to wail.

"I'm telling! I'm telling!" He pulled himself off the floor unsteadily, holding his hand to the side of his face. "See what you did?"

When he moved his hand, I saw the blood and the raised welt on his temple.

Crap, I thought, no longer paying attention as images of a gray, radioactive sky accompanied the narration about what would happen to whatever was left alive after Armageddon. I wasn't worried about that anymore. I wasn't even listening. My mind was occupied with one thought, repeating in my mind like an iPod on continuous replay. Mom's gonna kill me.

"Mom's gonna kill me," I heard my own voice saying. "Mom's gonna..."

"Nester?" Amaranth's voice had the leading edge of a query in it. I know that sound. I wished I could escape, but there was nowhere to go.

"Yeah?"

"I'm sorry."

There wasn't really any response for that, so I didn't offer one. I glanced back at Katie. She was at least six steps behind, struggling but determined.

"I don't know why..." she said after a long pause. "It wasn't even really the gin. It was more like...I knew I could. It was something I knew I could do. " She shrugged. "That was your weakness. It is for most guys," she added, trying out a self-deprecating smile that didn't quite fly. "I haven't done a single thing right since we got here—you know it's true. I guess... I guess I just wanted to feel like I used to feel for a second." Her voice got soft. "Kind of... powerful."

188

"Whatever," I grumbled. As far as apologies went, it didn't exactly win any awards; she'd called me *weak* and easy to manipulate and since I'd fallen right in, there wasn't much point in arguing the facts. I didn't want to talk about it anymore. I wanted to forget it, to pretend the whole thing never happened.

"She's right about me, you know," she said after another long pause. "Katie. And you're right, too. The only one who's blind is Liam—" she tried to laugh. "I sometimes think it might have been better if I hadn't found his dad's backpack when the riptide caught me. Back at the river. If I'd just gone under the water. Stayed under—"

"Stop talking crazy," I muttered. "In fact, stop talking. It happened. It was a mistake. It won't happen again. Forget it, okay? Because that's what I'm going to do. Forget it." I paused. "We should let Katie catch up."

Amaranth stared back at Katie. "Amy's right about at least one thing, Nester."

"What?" I kept my eyes on Katie, making her way slowly after us, each step becoming more and more labored. The bite was deep and I hoped like heck the antibiotics worked. Her brother was already going to be pretty p.o.-ed with me for telling Amaranth his secret. If anything happened to Katie, he'd have my head on a plate.

"We've got to become killers or we're going to die."

That got my attention. My eyes swung to her face, but she wasn't looking at me. Her gingery eyebrows were contracted like she was thinking very hard about something or someone I couldn't see.

"What—"

A rapid volley of gunshots echoed through the dark woods, interrupting me.

I lifted my weapon, whirling around in the snow, trying to determine where the sounds were coming from. They seemed to ricochet off of every tree.

"Where's the Mountain Place?" Amaranth asked,

189

scanning the horizon.

"This way!" I took off running and they followed, pounding after me. As we ran, the shots seemed to be getting louder and closer.

My foot caught on something—an obstacle buried by snow— and I fell, landing on something hard and yet strangely soft at the same time.

"What the—" I began making the snow slip and slide around me as I tried to right myself. I looked down: I was staring into the wide open eyes of a dead man.

It took me a second to stop screaming and scramble up off him, and another second to look him in his scarred and tattooed face.

He'd been dead awhile—several days at least. He was stiff and blue and had died with a hard look on his face, as though he'd been determined to kick Death's ass until the bitter end.

"Is that...?" Amaranth whispered.

"Yes."

"Should we...?" she glanced back over our shoulder to where Katie was limping after us, running as fast her bitten leg would allow.

"What do you want to say?" I asked. "What is there to say about any of this—?"

More shots, deliberate and individual, sounded in the thickets ahead of us.

"That's definitely coming from the Mountain Place," Amaranth said, taking off at track-star speed. I shot off after her, pounding up one snowy incline after another. The shots sliced the winter's silence, even louder and closer than before.

Remember what Liam said. Nate ran beside me, holding his imaginary gun at the ready. *That he always found the Mountain Place—*

"By scanning the trees for the top of the Lookout!" I said the words aloud but if Amaranth or Katie thought I was crazy, they didn't say. Instead, I turned slowly in a circle scanning the nearby peaks.

"There!" Amaranth cried, pointing.

The shooting stopped. In the sudden stillness, I peered at the rising slope of the next hill and saw the rounded dome of the cupola just barely cresting the tops of the nearby trees. Thick black smoke billowed around it, clouding the dark sky.

The Mountain Place was on fire.

19

WHERE THERE'S SMOKE...

"No!" Amaranth shrieked. She took off, sliding down the snow-covered slope like she had skis instead of feet.

"Marty!" Katie caught up to me and then passed me. There were tears on her face.

But I stood for a moment longer, listening.

The shooting had stopped. I couldn't hear anything else—no screams or voices—just the acrid smell of burning things. My first thought—stupid, I know—was that we needed to call the fire department or the cabin would burn to the ground. There was a flash of a second, when I reached for my pocket, like I could pull out a cell phone and dial 9-1-1. And then I remembered that I was the fire department, and I started running too, slipping and sliding in my haste to get down the hill and up the next one in time to save the closest thing to a home we'd had since the end of the world.

We emerged from the woods to find the cabin's cupola smoking like a backyard barbeque. I ran, passing Katie and Amaranth, until I neared the barn, then slowed, abandoning Doc Watson's shotgun for the assault rifle Amy had given me. I flattened myself against the rough wooden frame and peered around the structure toward where the cabin should have been. Instead of its familiar rear door, though, I saw only columns of smoke, pouring out of the doors and windows and ballooning out of the Lookout. My throat was tight from running and from anxiety, but there was just enough air left from me to scream Amy's name.

"I'm here!" her voice was faint, but I could see her ahead of me, a dark figure crouched in the nearest clump of woods bordering our compound. I edged my way around the barn and dashed toward her.

She held the handle of the laundry tub in her hands. "I'm going to try to get to the well!" she cried. "We have to try to put it out but—" she peered out at the cabin. "I'm not sure where they are. The shots seemed to be coming from the front of the house, from the road, but I haven't heard any in a while."

"What happened?" I asked, just as Katie and Amaranth tumbled around the barn and joined us in the trees.

"All I saw was one. Started walking toward the house. I yelled a warning, but..." Amy's expression hardened. "He didn't stop. Just kept walking toward the house with his hands up— and a shotgun swinging from his shoulder. Some story about needing help. I'm sure it was the same man." She glared at me. "The one you let go. Only this time he was back with his friends—"

"It wasn't the same man," I told her, glancing at Katie.

"Of course it was—"

"No. We found his body. Less than a quarter mile from here. In the woods. He's been dead for days."

Doubt and confusion flicked across Amy's face. "Same. Different. It doesn't matter," she said. She swallowed hard, reigned in ambiguity and proceeded. "The guy came up with some story about needing shelter and I told him I

193

would shoot. He kept talking. Some b.s. about not wanting anything but to get his friends out of the cold. Started pleading and stuff... all the while just walking toward us. When he got too close..." She raised her chin and gave me a look that dared me to challenge her actions. "I fired and he fell. And then I heard screaming and out of nowhere bullets came whizzing at me. We're not exactly an army here, but I fired back. Marty came up to the Lookout and we gave them everything we had. Then, everything stopped. We were just thinking that maybe they'd moved on when they started throwing stuff."

"Maybe Molotov cocktails. They're pretty easy to make if you have a little kerosene," I whispered, trying to make out the house through the smoke. I could see the well and considered Amy's idea of running for it— but it was a waste of energy. One or two buckets wouldn't make any difference and besides, it was so cold there was sure to be a layer of ice on the water's surface by now.

"They got lucky and got one right through the little window in the front room," Amy continued. "Then a second one landed in the Lookout. I had to jump—"

"You jumped from the Lookout?" Katie sounded genuinely impressed.

"No. Down to the roof of the porch. Thank god for snow and gymnastics. One of the first things you learn is how to fall," Amy added, like it was no big deal but I was reminded of just how good an athlete she was. "I wasn't as worried about breaking a leg as I was about getting shot—"

"Where are the others?" Amaranth stared at the smoke nervously.

"The root cellar. When I hit the ground and I wasn't dead, I ran for the wheelbarrow in the barn. That's how we got Liam out since Rod and Marty..." she frowned and I knew without her saying it that she was thinking of how frail Rod was, but all she said was: "That was hard. We got him settled but," her eyes met mine. "Tell me you got what

194

you went for, because he's worse."

"We got it,' I said, skipping the story about crazy Doc Watson and the possibility that the drugs wouldn't be strong enough. "And Elise?"

"Marty went back in for her. I guess they're all in the cellar by now. I came back out to scout." She stared in the direction of the road like she could somehow see through the smoke into the woods. "They're still out there. They just decided to fall back and let the fire do its thing."

I followed her gaze, but only for a moment. It was the house that drew my attention and held it, not the intruders lurking in the trees.

"I don't see fire. Did you *see* fire?" I asked her.

"Look at it," Amy said, rolling her eyes at me like she considered the question beyond stupid.

"I am. I see smoke but not fire. Did you actually see fire? Flames? Think, Amy. It's important."

She frowned, her dark eyes searching my face like she wasn't sure if I was just being obnoxious or not.

"I..."

"Remember BTB, back in middle school on the last day of seventh grade?" I continued urgently. "Someone set off a—"

"A smoke bomb!" Amaranth and Amy said together. The ghost of a smile lit their faces as the memory erased our present danger. For a second, we weren't fighting for our survival; we were a bunch of stupid kids, screaming with joy because some doofus had risked expulsion to start summer half an hour earlier.

"Exactly. Didn't you say the man said they wanted shelter?"

"He said they wanted to get out of the cold."

"Then it doesn't make sense they'd burn it down—" Amaranth began.

"They just want us out of it," Amy finished and when she looked at me the stink-eye she'd been giving me for

195

days was finally gone. "Okay. So what do we do?"

Yeah, genius. What do we do?

"Uh..."

A rustle in the leaves behind us distracted me from admitting I had no answer. Amy raised her assault rifle like she was ready to shred the black trees. "Who?" she demanded.

"Me," a familiar voice drawled, and Marty appeared, his face dark with soot. He choked a cough behind his palm, taking in Katie's dog-bitten boot and our makeshift bag of supplies wordlessly. A complete stranger wouldn't have seen much change in his features, but it seemed to me I saw relief relax his stony face just a little. He nodded at his sister, and then frowned.

"She ain't here?"

"Who?" Amy demanded.

"The little girl who don't talk. Looked high and low and didn't find her," he said, pausing to cough and rub his dirty hands over his throat. "Thought she must have come out on her own—"

Amaranth, Amy and I exchanged a single frozen glance, then Amaranth dove forward, screaming, "Elise!" at the top of her lungs.

"Shh!" Amy hissed. "We can't give up our position! You'll lead them right to us and they'll pick us off one by one—"

"You heard him! Elise is still in there!" Amaranth cried. "We have to get her out of there."

"I know," Amy took her hands. "I *know*. But you can't get everyone else killed in the process—"

"The smoke in there's pretty bad. Respirator was damn near useless. Can't see nothing," Marty deadpanned and the girls all shot him the same murderous look for his honesty that I'd been seeing so much of lately.

"I don't care. I made Elise a promise a long time ago. To take care of her like a sister. I know I haven't been doing

196

that great of a job at it, but I'm sure as hell not going to just leave her in *there!*" Amaranth jerked free of Amy's restraining hands and stood up, making herself a target.

"Get down, Amaranth," I barked.

"But Nester, we—I promised her—"

"I know. But she won't come to you, Amaranth. And she probably hid from Marty." I peeled off my gun and handed Amaranth the medical supplies. "Marty, take Katie down to the cellar. Give Liam a dose of the antibiotic right away. Amy and Amaranth can cover me while I get Elise. Then we'll figure out what to do," and I dashed toward the house before the smart part of my brain could remind me how dangerous my mission was.

I was almost blind as soon as I got within three yards of the house and had to feel my way up the few steps to the back door and into the mudroom. I touched the kitchen door carefully, but I didn't feel any heat, so I swung it open, peering around the kitchen like I expected to see Elise standing there.

But of course I didn't. I couldn't see anything. It was pitch-black. Smoke curled all around me, thick and acrid. I hit the floor like they taught us a long time ago in elementary school, wondering what the heck they'd used to make such an effective bomb, and I wished for Google like I wished for a gas mask. I had neither, so I just crawled forward on my belly. A flashlight—or even better, a headlamp—would have been nice, too, but I had to settle for my own eyes.

I didn't waste my breath calling her name; I knew Elise wouldn't answer me. She'd been scared into silence for so long that flames and smoke would send her further from us, deeper into whatever was going on in her own mind. But I also knew she was still in that house somewhere: she was too scared of everything outside of it to leave it on her own.

Since the lower level cabin was really just one big open space with very few places to hide, I didn't waste time there. I tightened my respirator and crawled through the kitchen toward the stairs.

The smoke was thicker on the second level as the noxious hot air rose toward the roof. I coughed but the respirator couldn't filter the gray bile fast enough. The first cough made me draw a deeper breath to recover—and that made me cough harder. I flattened myself down even more, wiggling like a snake on my belly as fast as I could through the two small bedrooms, reaching all the way to the darkness under the beds, throwing things out of the little storage chests at the edge of each of them. When I was done, the rooms probably looked like they'd been hit by a cyclone—or maybe like Doc Watson's place looked when her disease had first begun.

I didn't find Elise... but I didn't find any flames either.

I crawled back up the hallway toward the hatch that led to the Lookout. If it had been a Molotov cocktail– a little fireball in a bottle—the Lookout would have been engulfed in flames by now. I touched the door that led to the cupola tentatively, expecting it to feel like the sand on the Fourth of July—too hot for skin—but there wasn't any heat, just more thick smoke, blinding me and shutting off the oxygen to my brain. There was only one last place to look.

The gun cabinet.

Something Amy had said resurfaced in my mind.

That's one of the biggest ones I've ever seen. Fireproof, bullet proof—

If she were in there, there couldn't be much oxygen left. I tugged on the cabinet's handle but of course, it was locked.

I pulled off my gloves. My fingers were shaking and I could barely see the steel dial of the digital lock. Marty had reluctantly told us all the combination when he realized we were there to stay, but the smoke was so intense I could barely see the digits. More by memory of the placement of the numerals on the black key pad than by sight, I pressed #3006—it translated to "Doom" alpha-numerically—and turned the handle.

She was curled up in the corner of the massive case with her fingers clasped tightly around an assault rifle. Nate sat beside her.

What took you so long? He asked, rolling his eyes at me.

"Elise?"

I lifted her out of the case as gently as I could and tumbled down the steps, choking and disoriented, my lungs screaming for fresh air. I forced my feet forward toward the nearest door—the front one—and opened it onto plumes of smoke taller than I was, but no flames and no heat.

Fire or not, there was no hope of getting out that way. I slung Elise over my shoulder and backed up, stretching my hand out, hoping to feel my way toward the rear of the cabin. I stumbled into the table and chairs and fell down, thumping my head against something hard enough to pop the respirator off my face. Elise rolled limply away from me and for a moment I lay there, stunned, gasping for breath. My head ached and I couldn't see. My lungs felt like I'd swallowed down a live flame that was burning me from the inside out. I reached for Elise with the last of my strength.

"Nester! Nester!"

Amaranth's voice was high-pitched and annoying, but it gave me direction.

Somehow, I dragged us both across the floor. It felt like I was pulling a Sumo wrestler on my back, but Amaranth's voice kept getting louder and louder, until at last when I thought I might pass out if I had to move another inch, we tumbled out onto the snow.

The "fresh" air was awful—still silty and thick, but

compared to the smoke in the cabin, I inhaled it gratefully, sputtering and coughing as the smoke cleared my lungs.

"CPR—" I choked at Amaranth, pointing to Elise. "CPR—"

"I don't know it!"

"Breathe—breathe—" I pointed to the little girl's slack mouth and Amaranth understood. She straddled Elise and covered her mouth with her own.

"Breastbone, two fingers down—"I coughed. "Cup your hands—"

She did what I told her, pumping the smoke out of Elise and then forcing her own breath into the girl's little body until finally with a massive hacking cough that sounded almost like vomit, Elise inhaled on her own.

"¡Suéltame! ¡Déjame en paz!" She screamed, clawing at Amaranth like a tiger.

"Elise! It's okay! It's me! It's me—"

"Elise!"

She stopped and turned to me with wide eyes.

"It's okay, Elise. Amaranth was trying to help you. Get the smoke out. Do you understand?"

Elise nodded. Her eyes filled with tears and her mouth worked like she wanted to say something else— but Amaranth didn't give her time.

"I'll take you to the cellar with the others." Amaranth stretched a hand for Elise, but once again, she shrunk away from her, sidling close to me. Hurt crunched Amaranth's face again, but she continued calmly, "You've got no coat, sweetie. We've got to get you inside."

I unbuttoned my coat and wrapped it around the little girl's shoulders.

"Where's Amy?"

"She went to check on Rod and Liam. She'll be back—"

"No, that's good. It's going to take all of us who are able to do this fast enough."

Amaranth's eyebrows shot up in surprise. "You've got an idea?"

I nodded. "It's time to fight smoke with fire."

20

LIGHT IT UP

"There aren't enough of us who are strong enough to beat the bushes for them— and even if there were more of us, that wouldn't be a good idea—"

"Ambush," Amy interrupted. "We don't know where they are. We don't even know how *many* there are—"

"Five or six, I'd say," Marty interjected and for once neither Amy nor Amaranth rolled their eyes. Instead, Amy nodded.

"That would be my guess, too—"

"Then it's a waiting game," I continued. "They're waiting for the smoke to clear. For us to try to make our way back into the house—"

"And then they're going to try to pick us off one by one," Marty concluded.

While they thought about that, I looked around me. The root cellar's doors were just a few feet beyond the garden, in a small clearing in the nearby woods. I didn't want to think about how they'd gotten Liam down the ladder, but now he lay on one of the cots, swaddled in blankets and oblivious to everything.

I didn't have to touch him or look at his foot to know how much worse he was. He looked sick— not I-got-shot-sick, but seriously-ill I-need-a-hospital sick. His skin was the color of old paste—a weird bluish gray, with a nasty clammy sheen of sweat slicking his forehead and cheeks. His eyes were closed, and he seemed to be shivering and sweating simultaneously.

"Got to go..." he mumbled. "Got...to... go... find them—"

"Yeah, buddy," Rod said. "Katie's getting your go-bag. Then you can go find them—"

Rod looked like he'd aged thirty years in the hours since I'd seen him last. As if reading my mind, he looked away, staring steadfastly at Liam like he was the only one we had any reason to be concerned about.

"What's the play?" he asked.

"The play is simple. We're going to make our own bomb and send them running."

Cries went up around me.

"How do you—" Katie began.

"With what?" Rod asked.

"We're gonna get ourselves killed," Marty finished, but he didn't seem upset about it. In fact, he was looking at me with the same ease he had since we'd marched the convict out to the shed and decided against killing him. I cut my eyes at Katie, but she was dabbing some analgesic cream on her calf and pretending not to see me. She hadn't told him that she knew. Had she told him that the man was dead? I wondered, but only for a second. There wasn't time for that *ish*, as Nate would have said.

"I don't think we're going to get killed," I said. "I think I know how to do this. See, I—"

"It was you, wasn't it?" Amy interrupted. "The kid who set off that smoke bomb the last day of middle school. That was you."

I hoped my skin wasn't as red as it was warm. "Yeah."

"No way!" Rod grinned and stretched out a shaky set of knuckles for dap. "My man! One day, you're going to have to tell me how you got away with it."

I grinned, but Amy frowned skeptically.

"I see containers we can use, and kerosene, so I know we can make something that will work," she said matter-of-factly. "I only have two questions."

"Only two?" Rod asked drily.

"They're biggies," Amy crossed her arms over the loops of ammunition crisscrossing her chest and gazed up at me. "First, how are we going to launch them without getting shot to pieces?"

"From the house. The front windows. Upstairs." I replied. "Even the Lookout if it's not too far to throw—"

"We're going back in there? But you barely made it out last time—" Amaranth said. She stood close to the stairs leading out of the shelter, as far from Liam as she could get, her head turned away. But every now and then, I saw her steal a glance at him, and then blink quickly, biting her lips to hold her feelings down.

"The smoke is clearing. When it does, we're going in—"

"But they'll see us," Marty interrupted. "They'll see us and shoot at us—"

"No they won't. Because we're going to make our own smoke screen. Just outside the cabin, not inside."

Rod's sparse eyebrows lifted. "Okay, so I know you can make a smoke bomb, but this other one, the bomb that's going to 'send them running', you know how to make one of those, too?"

I nodded. "Between middle school and high school, I took this chemistry summer camp. We made—"

He held up his hand, stopping my explanation with a curt, "Got it," before turning to Amy. "What was the second question, babe?"

Amy hesitated while she gave him a long, sad look that made everyone in the room get quiet. Something personal and intimate was communicated between them, completely without a word being said. Finally, Rod's cracked lips lifted in a smile. "Out with it, Amy. As Marty might say, 'time's a-wasting.'"

Marty opened his mouth to refute that, but I dropped a hand on his shoulder, and he let it go.

Amy took a deep breath. "The second question. Those trees are dead or dying. They're going to light up like a matchbook. How are you going to keep from burning down the whole cabin?"

"Wind's blowing from the northwest," Marty replied as if the significance of this fact should be obvious to all.

"So?"

"So it's blowing away from the cabin, not toward it," the boy finished, nodding at me. "And the snow will help. Hard to keep a fire going in snow. Will spread in the tree tops, but not on the ground."

"So it'll spread through the orchard," Amaranth stole another glance at Liam. "Near Lilly's grave."

"Lilly won't know the difference. Like Nate never felt the gravel," I said. They all looked at me, shocked at the blunt words. "I don't see any better options," I added quickly.

Liam shivered, his mouth twitching like he was contributing to the conversation, but we all knew it was the fever, tossing him in his own nightmares. The infection was eating at him and he was dying. That was as clear as to me as the other fact: that effects of the radiation that were slowly eating Rod away from the inside out.

Katie stood up and hobbled over to me. "It'll be better without the orchard. We'll be able to see folks coming better. " No one pointed out the obvious: that we'd be more visible from the road without the trees, too. She lifted a trusting face to mine. "Tell us what we gotta to do."

Making the fire bombs was easy enough—it was the

205

smoke bomb that was tough. BTB, we'd have crushed up some golf balls, but in the apocalypse golf balls were hard to come by. It took me a second to remember the other way—a mix of sugar and potassium nitrate. And fortunately, fertilizer is full of KNO_3... and that wasn't something we had a shortage of.

"We used pure stuff in camp," I muttered, mixing the two into an empty paper towel tube taped to a large piece of cardboard. "Hope this still works."

"Well it'll be a stink bomb at least," Rod quipped. He sounded like his old self: a one-liner for every situation. It was weird and welcome at the same time.

When we were done, we stood our efforts in a line: three large smoke bombs and half a dozen fire bombs made of kerosene-soaked scraps of fabric stuffed into empty Mason jars.

"Okay," I said. "I'll set the smoke bombs. I'm useless with the fire bombs. I throw like a girl."

"Really?" Amy groaned and the other girls rolled their eyes at my stereotype. With good reason: they all had better arms than I did.

"Sorry," I muttered. "Just an expression. What I meant was what we really need is a flame thrower. To be sure to reach the trees. Who's got the best aim?"

Rod unfolded himself slowly. "I do," he said, rotating his arm and reminding us all briefly of the jock he'd been once.

"Can you do it?" Amy's question was fair, but Rod glared at her like she'd insulted him.

"Katie's got a good arm, too," Marty piped up. "And I'm good with this." He pulled an old-fashioned slingshot out of his pocket. "I've killed squirrels with a rock at 20 yards," he said, a slight edge of pride in his voice.

"It's further than it looks. If they land in the snow, they're useless. All we need is one—"

"We can do it," Rod said. He stood a little straighter,

like he was determined to win our confidence.

"Okay, then it's you, Marty and Katie. When the smoke is thick enough, make a run for the cabin. Straight to the front windows. Light 'em up and throw as far as you can."

"And Nester, Amaranth and I will cover you from the woods, in case they run toward the house—"

"No," Amaranth's voice was shaky but determined. "I'll go with you, Amy. Nester needs to stay here." Her eyes settled on Liam. "You have to do something. He's running out of time."

"We gave him the antibiotic, but he ain't no better," Katie said quietly.

"Well, it hasn't had time to work yet," I replied, grazing my fingers against his scorching forehead. His eyes moved under his eyelids so rapidly that it looked like he was having convulsions. In spite of the blankets, he shook at my touch like we'd left him out in the snow for hours. Liam's heel was a large patch of colors: green and red and yellow, but all edged with black.

"You were right," Amy said quietly. "It's gangrene and now, maybe blood poisoning. Even if the antibiotics work, you're probably going to have to cut it off."

The idea made my stomach turn even more than the ugly rotting skin I was looking at. A part of me shut out the cellar and the faces of the other kids. Instead, I was home listening to my stepdad deliver rant number 22 while we watched a PBS documentary about slavery and the Civil War.

"You kids need to understand where you came from. What your ancestors endured in slavery."

I could see Irv sitting in his recliner with his feet up, one hand curled around a soda, the other holding the file of one of his cases. His glasses were perched on the edge of his nose and his bald head shone under the track lights.

"There's a direct line between that—" he nodded toward the tintype images of slaves laboring under the Georgia sun—"And these—" he nodded to the files of death row appeals in front of him. "Believe it."

I didn't argue with him. I knew he wasn't wrong, and besides, the documentary was interesting. Unforgettable, really because it made events that happened 150 years ago seem as real as the present moment. The treatment of slaves, the economics of plantations, the ideological and political differences above and below the Mason-Dixon Line—I'd have watched it even if Irv hadn't made me.

But right now, the only image that came to mind was a photograph of a dude carting a wheelbarrow full of severed arms and legs out of a military hospital like it was just another day.

That photograph was seared into the "real-life horrors" category of my brain—right there with the images of lynchings Irv had added to my mental Instagram feed and the stuff we learned about the Holocaust in 5th grade.

"I can't do that," I told Rod, shaking my head so hard my brain started to ache. "I can't—"

"You have to. If you don't he's gonna die," Rod said.

"If I *do*, he's gonna die!" I spat back. "Look at him! You think he's strong enough to survive something like me sawing his leg off? Even if I knew how to do something like that—which I don't—he probably wouldn't make it—"

"But he might. It's turning black, Nester, infecting his whole body! If you don't do something now, he *will* die. You have to at least *try*—"

"Are you listening? I. Don't. Know. How."

"There's an ax in the shed," Katie said softly.

"Not an ax," I said before I'd even thought about it. "You need a saw—"

"The meat saw?" Marty suggested.

208

"Maybe. Some kind of bone saw, really—"

I stopped talking. Amaranth and Katie exchanged a glance, and then looked at me and I knew what— or rather *who*—they were thinking of.

"We have to go back," Katie said. "We have to beg her to come and—"

"She won't. She'll kill us before we get to her front door this time. If she's even alive. Amaranth hit her pretty hard..." I shook my head at them.

Five somber faces stared back at me, each begging me in its own way. I looked down at Liam, shaking and shuddering as the infection consumed him and heard his own plea: *I'd rather die. Just let me die...* They all wanted me to figure out a way to save someone who didn't want to be saved.

I swallowed hard. I felt like I'd known all along Liam's fate would come down to this moment, this decision... and me. I looked into their faces, trying to find my way to an answer. Then I thought of Nate and how many times I'd wished for one more day, one more hour of his stupid, annoying, juvenile b.s...and I knew that, even if the sun never came again and we all slowly died here under the gray sky, I had to try.

"I'll try," I muttered, grabbing the smoke bombs. "But first, I'll set these and let you guys get started defending the cabin. Then I'll try. I promise. I'll try to—"

Elise yanked on my hand and then pried the smoke bombs out of them without saying a word. She shrugged out of my coat, handed it to me, and then headed for the cellar's doors.

"Elise..." I sighed. "No..."

But she shook her head at me and pointed to Liam.

"This is crazy," I muttered. "The saw has to be sterilized and—"

"He's right," Rod said. "We'll need to build a fire—"

"And there's more of that peroxide—"

209

"Yeah, that'll work. We'll get it as clean as we can—"

"And can't you use fire to like... stop the bleeding after it's done?"

Rod nodded. "Cauterize. Yeah, like in those westerns where they dump the gunpowder in a wound and light it up."

"We've got gunpowder, if that's best." Amy turned to me like I was part of this macabre conversation. "Will that work?"

I sighed. Instead of making me feel better, their blind faith in me scared me to death. "I need that book. The survival medical book with the pictures—"

"You'll have it in a few minutes," Amy said. "Anything else?"

I hesitated, knowing I was breaking yet another confidence. "He asked me not to. He said... it would change the way the way we looked at him. All of us—" I said but my eyes strayed toward Amaranth before I got control of them and directed them at all of their faces.

"But we wouldn't—" Katie began.

"We would," I said firmly. "He said he could already tell from the way we were treating him because he was wounded." I paused. "He said he'd change, too. Like his father did."

There was an awkward silence.

"I don't care," Amaranth said at last, her voice trembling. "And you—you can tell him that—"

"I don't think I could convince him."

Amaranth stared at me a long moment like she was taking apart every syllable I'd spoken.

"Well," she said at last in that tough girl, I-don't-give-a-damn voice we'd all heard a million times before. "This is one time when we're not doing what Liam Harper says."

"Maybe he's right—" Rod began. "No, I know he's right. Things will change here." He glanced at Amy quickly,

210

and then looked away. "That's inevitable. But if our positions were reversed— if it was one of us lying there, I don't believe he'd let us die. Even if we thought that was what we wanted. Because no one... no one really wants to die. No one."

There were tears rolling down Amy's face. The anger that had coated her like a tortoise's shell shattered all at once. She turned away from us, her shoulders shaking.

"I'm... all right," she said into her hands, shrugging away the hand I stretched toward her. "I'm... all right." She took a deep breath, wiped her face quickly and turned back to us, her face wet and red. Rod gave her a quick smile, but she wouldn't even look at him.

"And if anybody can save Liam, it's you, Nester," she said in a fragile voice. "And...we...aren't losing another one. We're *not.*" That was when she finally looked at Rod. This time he was the one who looked away.

"Let's get these intruders out of here as quickly as we can, so Nester can do what he's got to do," Rod said. "Nester, let Elise set the smoke bombs," he continued. "She's a smaller target. Amy has one job: get in, find the book and all the supplies she can and get back to you as soon as it's safe. You and Amaranth cover us while we run for the house. Okay?"

It was the speech of the quarterback in the huddle or a general to his troops. The speech of a leader, even though he was weak and nearly out of breath. I was immediately sorry. For how sick he was. For dismissing him as weak. For ever disliking him even in our prior life BTB. A united sense of purpose rippled through the group and I wished I could share it...but it seemed to me I'd drawn the shortest stick.

Liam trembled, offering us a few words of muttered delirium as his contribution to the conversation. His lips looked dry and parched so I lifted his head, dribbling a bit more water mixed with animal antibiotic between his lips.

211

They were all looking at me, waiting for my sanction of a plan that had one huge flaw: even with the book, even with the best tools in the world, I knew I could never do it. But another plan, equally crazy and probably equally fatal was forming in my brain, its details clicking together like the parts of a Transformer after it's been blown apart by a Decepticon.

"I'll cover you," I said. That much was the truth.

Rod nodded. "Good deal. Okay, everybody. Let's go."

21

FIRE FIGHT

So, let's just get this straight—even though I know it's like *Duh, Nester*—I gotta say it.

TV and movies lie.

They make it look so slick to be in a gunfight. People pop up from their cover taking all kinds of crazy shots and then dive back down, in a hail of incoming bullets totally unharmed. You know why? Because it's a movie and they know *for sure* they're not going to get shot.

I wasn't sure of that, not at all. For a while, there seemed to be bullets flying everywhere— and I knew that I'd completely misjudged our opponents. They weren't out of ammunition; they were just saving it to annihilate us completely, up close and personal.

This stupid plan is going to get everyone killed.

The thought kept running through my mind. The stupid plan was my stupid idea and now I'm going to get everyone killed, just like I got Nate—

Stop thinking 'bout me, man, Nate hissed in my ear. *Now ain't the time for your guilty conscience. Man up, dude—*

I started firing the assault rifle as soon as Elise jumped out of the woods into the clearing and dove to the ground to light the first smoke bomb. I sprayed the wooded area in the direction of the road like in *Scarface*: just as wild and even more desperate. And they answered back, firing at me in a volley that made me hit the dirt with my hands over my head until I remembered that the others were counting on me and I made myself reload and fire again and again.

Unlike *Scarface*, though, I was scared—so scared my hands shook and I flinched with the sound of every shot. My body vibrated with the weapon's backfire and I just wanted it to be over, over one way or the other so I could erase the sound of gunfire from my mind and think clearly again.

The smoke was working: I couldn't see the cabin anymore or anything between me and it. I couldn't tell if the others had made it inside— or if they were bleeding out in the snow, casualties of this desperate plan.

"I'm out," Amaranth said, dropping to her belly in the little space beside me and pulling another box of rounds from her coat pocket. "Looks like they've got a decent tactician, too—"

"And a decent arsenal."

"Who are they?"

"How the hell do I know?" I shouted, firing and firing. I didn't even know what I was firing at anymore, I didn't see anyone coming toward the cabin, but someone was out there, still shooting at us. The Alamo popped into my head: the tragic saga of a bunch of dudes who barricaded themselves into a church and got themselves killed when they realized that they were totally outgunned. I was starting to think the Mountain Place would be our Alamo— only I wasn't sure there was going to be anyone left to remember us or use our last stand as a rallying cry.

"Wait!" Amaranth said when I paused from my wild shooting. "Look!"

A bright orange flare lit the treetops.

"They did it!"

The shooting stopped. We watched as the flare grew, multiplying through the dense woods as the flames consumed the dead trees.

I stood up, peering toward the narrow lane that led to the road and saw a wall of yellow orange fingers sending more dark smoke into the sky.

"Where are you going?" Amaranth asked, grabbing my arm.

"I need to take the road. Before the fire makes it impassible. I can't go the way we went. The terrain's too uneven—"

"You're going *back* there? I thought you said—"

"I have to. I can't do what needs to be done. I know you guys think I can, but I'm telling you, I don't have the skill. *She* does—"

"But after what we did..." Amaranth shook her head. "She won't help you."

"Then I'll have to *make* her."

Amaranth blinked at me. "Nester, are you sure—"

"Yes."

"She'll probably kill you both."

I didn't reply to that, since she was probably right.

"Nester...when Liam said he was worried about... about us looking at him differently...he wasn't talking about all of us, was he?"

I didn't want to answer that question, but she pressed on.

"Did he say my name? Please, Nester. Please. I need to know." Her eyes searched mine, clearer than I'd seen them in days. "Did he mention my name? Is he worried it would make a difference... to *me*?"

"I think he's worried about being seen differently by all of us. As being a burden or liability. But," I nodded, "he said your name."

"Thank you." she said quietly, locking eyes with me.

"You got this?"

215

"I have to. Our family is in there."

Then, before the fire got any worse or I lost my nerve, I turned away from her and hurried toward the cellar for the tools I needed to make the next step in my secret plan work.

All those hours I'd spent surfing YouTube weren't a total time suck. I remembered a dumb video I'd watched on a snowy day about a girl who'd made a sled out of a pizza box and trash bag. I didn't have a pizza box but I had cardboard and I had garbage bags. I whipped the squares of cardboard together with some duct tape, taking care to make sure I made my sled as wide as Liam and almost twice as long. The garbage bags were just enough to cover the cardboard and keep it dry, but I knew they'd rip if things got rough. I used some of the rope in Katie's backpack to form a harness to keep Liam on it, a little more to fit myself as the beast of burden. It wasn't comfortable, but that didn't matter.

I bundled Liam into every bit of fabric I could find: the blankets he was already wrapped in, plus some spares I found stored under the cots in the cellar. Even as thin as he was, he wasn't exactly a lightweight and I struggled a bit when I lifted him. But I was a lot stronger than I had been BTB and I managed to get him up the stairs and onto my makeshift sled without dropping him or passing out from the effort. Before I closed the doors of the cellar, I hurried back down to the metal cabinet to inspect the weapons. Once—not so very long ago—I wouldn't have known what to choose. But the plan tickling at the back of my brain required particular kinds of firepower—if I was going to have a better chance than a snowball's in hell of getting me and Liam out of Doc Watson's alive. I grabbed a shotgun and more rounds for the assault rifle. The cabinet had seemed full the first time I'd looked in it, back when hiding liquor had been my main concern. Now, it looked

216

ransacked and nearly empty.

I raced back up the stairs. I no longer had a protective suit or a respirator—but considering where I was going and what was likely to happen when I got there, a slow death from radiation poisoning wasn't at the top of my list of concerns.

I slipped the rope harness over my neck and started for the path that led to the road, dragging my burden behind me.

I found the first two bodies near the tree line. Even from a distance, I could tell they were small—but it didn't take much to be smaller than the convict. Even dying, the man was taller than most. But it wasn't until I was right up on them that I understood they were children—probably not much older than Elise. A boy and a girl both dressed in the mismatched fashions of our life in the new age: whatever will cover you and keep you from freezing to death. They'd both been shot, apparently as they tried to dash through the woods from the front of the house to the wooded areas bordering the open fields. The boy landed on his back. His eyes were open and he looked dirty and hungry and completely terrified. The little girl was face down and I didn't turn her. It bad enough to see two pigtails stained with her brains.

My stomach twisted and my head started to pound. For a second I thought I might be sick, but I reminded myself that I had a job to do and pushed myself forward.

I hadn't gone far when I nearly fell over two more bodies: boys, I thought, though one of them was shot up so badly I couldn't be sure. A backpack lay on the ground beside one of them, split open by the force of the shell that ripped through the body. An empty plastic water bottle spilled out of it, along with a flashlight and a popular graphic novel series from a reality that felt so long ago and so far away that it might as well have existed in someone else's imagination.

A kid around my own age sat propped against a tree. He was dead, too. I recognized him: the bespectacled kid we'd seen in the forest on the way to Doc Watson's. And then it all made sense in a sudden horrible, sickening moment of understanding.

They were the same kids: the ones Amaranth had wanted to talk to. Wanted to help. Now...

They were dead. We'd killed them.

Amy's words rushed back to me:

"He said he didn't want anything but to get his friends out of the cold. Started pleading and stuff... all the while just walking toward us. When he got too close..."

Our intruders weren't desperate convicts still wearing prison uniforms or marauding abusers like Richter and his men. They were a bunch of scared hungry kids who had watched Amy shoot their friend. They'd probably used the last of their resources in a desperate gamble for revenge and shelter... and we had killed most of them, then set the forest on fire to keep the others away. Would they still be alive if I'd let Amaranth talk to them? Had her impulse been the right one? Or would they have killed us first, given the chance?

Behind me the trees smoldered and burned. From time to time I was distracted by the distant pop of crackling branches or the sound of a large limb falling to the ground. But the fire was already dying down, consumed by the wet cold of the snow. It was just smoke again, rising off the snow, the smoke of dying embers consumed by the icy land.

This has to work.

I repeated those four words over and over in my brain and shut off everything else—the bodies of the kids we'd killed, the damage and exposure we'd created by the fire, Nate and everything about my life before the bomb. I understood more completely than ever Amaranth's infatuation with the whiskey: I wished for a blackout to overtake me and turn me temporarily into someone else— but there wasn't any alternate version of me or any ghost that could help me do what I had decided to do.

I slogged slowly and steadily over the snow-covered road, meeting no one. When I turned, I couldn't see the Mountain Place at all, as the last of our fire smoldered and went out. The wind carried the faint odor of burning wood.

Just like the Mountain Place, there was no road leading into the Watson farm, just a break in the trees you had to be familiar with to find.

"It's only about a mile once you get to the road," Marty had explained as we planned our last trip there. "Used to be a sign that said 'Watson's Veterinary', but the trees covered it over. Can't really see it no more. But there was a big rock there—tall as me— it's gonna be snow-covered by now, too."

Those reasons had led to our decision to take the other route before—the one that by-passed the little shack that Katie and Marty had called home—but that path was too wooded for me and my sled.

I glanced at my watch as we lurched out of the trees and onto a wide expanse of white that must have been the road. I could walk a mile on a level surface comfortably in about fifteen minutes—or at least that's what I'd done on a treadmill BTB— but in the snow, dragging Liam behind me, I calculated twice that average and started walking.

He was heavy, and my makeshift sled didn't glide as well as I hoped. The snow grabbed at the bottom of the edge of the cardboard and the friction made it feel like I was dragging a Mini Cooper on my back instead a sick kid. Liam frowned and winced and mumbled like he was talking

219

to me as we crept along the road.

"We're almost there, Lilly..." he yelled in a sudden loud rush of breath, his eyes flying open.

"You're right, man," I agreed. "We're close now. But keep it down, okay?"

"Mom... the Mountain Place... I promised..."

"You kept that promise, Liam," I replied over my shoulder. "Lilly's at peace, remember? She's at peace. Now, close your eyes."

He obeyed but I could tell from the way his body twitched and jerked that the fever was escalating.

I needed to move faster—I needed to get him out of the elements—but I had no options. No cars, no snowmobiles, not even a pair of skis materialized to assist me. So I walked, straining with the effort of his weight. And I talked.

"This might get messy, Liam," I told him in a voice that was only a little above a whisper, but it seemed to carry for miles in the stillness of the empty air. "Real messy. See, the doc thinks I'm her husband... which isn't entirely a good thing." I chuckled. "Funny. Me as anyone's husband. Let alone some white lady who looks like she's old enough to be my grandma. But these are strange times, man, you know? Like who would have expected this: me dragging you around on a garbage bag. If you'd have told me I'd been doing this..."

You want to make God laugh?

Nate trudged beside me in his parka and girl's hat, the pom-poms bobbing with each step. My eyes stung with a sudden heat, and if I hadn't been sure that my arms would close around nothingness, I would have stopped and hugged him so hard it would have lifted his feet off the ground.

"How?" I said out loud.

Tell him your plans, Nester. Tell him your plans.

If anyone had seen me, out there on a deserted

road, dragging an unconscious kid on a jackleg sled and laughing my ass off, they would have probably either crossed the road to avoid me or shot me to put me out of my misery.

"You're right: joke's on me."

Always was, bro.

"Yeah, you're probably right."

I knew I had the right opening when I walked right into the rock. I'd moved out of the center of the road when I realized the snow was less deep on the shoulder, and ended up bumping a shin against it as I struggled forward. I glanced at my watch: I'd been walking forty-five minutes and I had at least another fifteen before I was within sight of the farmhouse.

I checked Liam: he was alive, but that was all I could say about his condition with absolute certainty. I checked myself, assessing my willingness to carry out the course of action I'd imagined in my mind.

You good, man?

I nodded.

You can do it?

"I have to," I said and turned off the road.

The dogs were barking before I was even in sight of them and I knew she would be alert. The second she saw me, she'd shoot— and once she realized it was me she wouldn't *stop* shooting until I was a smear on the snow.

"Gotta leave you for a minute, Liam," I whispered, bending close to his ear.

"Are we there?" he asked. "Home?"

Home.

This place couldn't be further from anyone's idea of home. I almost said that, until he shivered so violently that his teeth rattled in his jaw. Suddenly telling the truth didn't matter as much to me.

221

"Yeah," I answered, pulling the blankets up around his ears. "Almost. Hang tight, man. Hold on just a little longer, okay?"

I check the assault rifle one more time, then lifted it high and stepped into the Forum.

"I am Spartacus!" I yelled, like I couldn't—wouldn't be beaten and the dogs raced toward me.

I shut off my brain and pulled the trigger, struggling to hold the weapon steadily as it sprayed bullets in rapid succession. One after the other, dogs squealed or yelped then dropped. I blocked it all out—the awful sounds of the rounds finding their targets and the roar of the debris sliding into the snow, the tremors of the rifle as it bounced and leapt in my hands and the dogs dying as they fell— I let it all of it slip past me like it was happening to someone else and I was just watching, like—like—

In a movie? Or on TV? A video game?

Nate—or Nate's ghost—had suggested that very thing to me once and I'd called him an idiot. Now, it turned out he was right. Killing living things was easier if you could convince yourself it wasn't real.

It was done in seconds and I'd already retreated back into the woods for Liam when I heard the report of her shotgun.

One, I counted.

"No! No!" she screamed. "No!" The shotgun exploded again. *Two*, I counted.

"I'll get you!" she yelled. "I'll get—you—"

But then there was silence—or at least, she didn't fire again. I heard her moaning and keening over the dead animals, a heart-breaking human sound—but I closed my eyes and pretended. She was a story. An actor in a story I was watching. A good one, but an actor and that was all. An actor with two more rounds left in her shotgun. Two more shells that needed to be fired before the hero could dive in and take control, quickly, before she could reload.

I needed those shots. I needed her empty... and I needed it now.

I slung the assault rifle back over my shoulder and grabbed the shotgun. My aim was a bigger joke than my plans, but I hoped it wouldn't matter.

I crept closer, moving along the perimeter of trash, taking aim at a large pile of junk with a chair leg sticking out of the top of it like a flag pole. I aimed right for the center of it— a target about as wide as a drive-through window from the world BTB and fired.

Kaboom!

I missed it by a mile, hitting instead another pile further away that broke apart and scattered into a hundred little pieces like I'd dropped a bomb on it. She fired in my direction immediately, missing me only because I'd never fired the shotgun before and the recoil had knocked me flat. I landed on my back in the snow, my shoulder aching from the recoil. As soon as I recovered myself, I grabbed the shotgun again and fired it randomly into the junkyard without even taking aim—anything to make her take that fourth shot—and kept running as the old lady's fourth shell sliced through the trees.

"Come on, man, you're up," I muttered as I scooped Liam's limp weight and slung him over my shoulder. I was hurting him, but there wasn't any other way now. Hopefully, I'd catch a break and it wouldn't be much longer.

She was already stuffing fresh shells into the shotgun's barrel when I started moving as fast as I could under Liam's weight through the crap toward the front door of her house.

"Robert!" she screamed as I slipped inside.

I couldn't see. I tried to use my hands, but Liam slid off my shoulders as I felt my way along. I had to drag him through the tunnel of her possessions. The hoard fought back, raining down its fury at being disturbed.

"What...?" Liam opened his eyes as I eased him into

223

her chair by the dark fireplace, and staring at his surroundings in a dazed delirium.

"Hold this," I told him, pressing the shotgun into his hands. His head slumped forward, but his fingers curled tightly around the weapon. Years of training, I figured...but the sickly color of his skin told me that our time was up.

She came after me at the speed of vengeance with the shotgun ready. But I was ready, too.

I gathered two of the golden retriever puppies in one hand and pulled my pistol with the other.

22

ROBERT WATSON'S GHOST

"One more step and I'm killing them all!" I shouted.

I heard her rack the shotgun.

"And I'm killing you," she hissed at me.

I closed my eyes...and tried to believe that I could do it. That I was the person who could shoot a puppy in the head. *To save my friend's life. To save my friend's life. To save...*

Liam jerked to attention behind me, rising out of his blankets like Death himself.

"Put the gun down!" he shouted to the characters in his dreams. His wild eyes focused on the cluttered room. He lifted the shotgun but he was too weak to keep it steady. "I should have killed you the first time, Richter! I told you to leave my friends alone!" He screamed and fired.

I hit the dirt with a yell as the sound blasted through the room. A shower of glass and paper and I don't know what else exploded like a tornado around me and for a while I was deaf from the sound and blinded by whirling debris. Liam collapsed back onto the armchair as the avalanche of the piles of the hoard trembled and fell, sliding from their peaks and covering me. I struggled to keep my head above it as the stuff rained down on us. Something scratched me; something else—heavy—crashed down on my foot. I yelped, taking in a mouthful of dirt and dust while I flailed my arms, trying to keep from being suffocated in the woman's garbage.

Finally, it stopped. Being tall helped: I was buried up to my armpits, but I could breathe, see and move. I swam through the junk toward the armchair and used both hands to sweep the crap off Liam.

"Liam?" I patted his face, trying to bring him around, but he'd been knocked senseless by the combination of the weapon's recoil, the oxygen-sucking debris and his own weakness. I couldn't see Doc Watson at all.

"Doc!" I yelled into the room, suddenly scared that Liam's wild shot had actually hit her. "Doc!"

A muffled sound from the spot where I'd last seen her— like a yell from underwater—answered me. I pushed off toward it, but the stuff was harder to move through than the wet snow had been. When I got close enough, I started digging frantically, throwing the papers and objects aside carelessly: food containers, unopened boxes, clothing—all of it got tossed aside as I searched for something that looked human.

At last my hand closed around her arm. I dug anew, in the direction of her face, clearing an airway under the suffocating pressure of the stuff.

"Doc! Doc!" I cried, when I saw the blood on her face. "Doc! Are you all right?"

She opened her eyes slowly and blinked at me. "What happened?"

"The stuff fell," I answered quickly. "Are you okay? Are you hurt? Are you shot?"

She stared at me blankly like "hurt" and "shot" had no meaning.

226

"Here!" I stretched my arm toward her. "Let me help you..."

I had to clear more stuff off her legs before I got her to her feet. There was a deep gash on her forehead, and she swayed a bit, holding my hands tightly.

"All right?" I asked again.

She peered at me. "You—you're not Robert," she said at last.

"No, ma'am," I replied. "My name is Nester Bartlett."

"I—I—thought..." she touched her forehead, studying me silently. "You're just a boy," she murmured at last. "What are you doing here?"

Something unexpected shone in her eyes, as though the clouds of her crazy had parted. I was looking into the eyes of something I hadn't seen in what felt like forever: a lucid, concerned adult.

"I need your help, Doctor Watson," I nodded toward Liam. "My friend hurt his foot—well, he got shot too, but fortunately the bullet just grazed him—but he had this bad blister on his foot and I guess I didn't take it seriously enough because it got infected. We've done everything we could, but it's still turning black and now he's running a really high fever."

I knew I was talking too fast, but the words tumbled out of me as well as all the emotions I hadn't had time to feel. There were tears running down my cheeks and I let them fall, continuing in a long sentence without pause or punctuation.

"I'm scared the infection is getting worse and spreading into his blood and you're the closest person with any kind of medical equipment so— "

"Okay, son. Okay," Her eyes darted to Liam. "How long has he been running the fever?" she asked, swimming through the debris toward him and grabbing his wrist. I could tell by the way she squinted that she was taking his pulse.

"Less than a day."

"Were you able to take a reading?" she asked clinically.

"The last time I took it was 104 degrees. That was hours ago." My chest was heaving. I felt foolish—like an overgrown baby, bawling and out of control—but I couldn't stop. The tears kept coming, rolling thick and hot down my cheeks. "Please...help him. Please..."

She pulled the blankets from around him and lifted his pants leg, peeling away the bandages around his heel.

"Okay," she breathed. "I gotta be honest with you, Nester. Your friend's not in very good shape. I'm going to do the best I can, but—" she shook her head. "I just don't know," she quirked an eyebrow at me. "You understand what I'm trying to tell you?"

I wiped my face and nodded.

"Are you okay?"

I nodded again. I suddenly wanted to confess: to tell her that I was sorry about shooting her dogs; that I planned to threaten, intimidate, pistol-whip, and even shoot the puppies if I had to. Anything to make her do what she was volunteering to do for Liam right now. But instead, I sniffled and wiped my face again. "Thank you."

"We've got to get him to the surgery out in the office." She looked around the room. "Do you think you can clear us a path?"

It felt like it took forever to dig our way out of the room. I scooped out handfuls of stuff but the only place to put them was on top of the remaining piles and those were still unstable. Time and time again, my efforts slid back into the morass. Finally, I developed a new strategy: I packed the stuff down, densely enough that I could stand on it. The ceiling rose to meet me as I walked like a hunchback on top of it.

"Pull me up and then get your friend," Doc said. "The

228

surgery is around the house—"

"I know."

Confusion raced across her face like a couple of the rats from the junkyard—quick blurs that were gone before I could decipher their meaning. "You know...?" she began, frowning, but I kept moving, picking my way carefully atop the piles until I could jump down in front of Liam. She must have decided to save her questions until later, because when I turned around, she was gone.

My legs were shaking from the effort of climbing over the piles of junk with Liam's weight, but when I reached the veterinary office, it looked like we'd left it. The supply room door was still off its hinges and the canisters of anesthesia lay empty on the floor. Doc Watson had stripped off the heavy overcoat and now wore a white lab jacket with *Watson* embroidered on it in blue script. She was scrubbing her hands intently, a deep frown etched in her face like she was trying to remember something.

"Lay him down."

I lay Liam on the surgical table that I'd stood on when we barricaded the dogs into the surgery and pushed it toward the stainless steel light fixture hanging in the center of the room. I watched as she grabbed the IV stand, pulled a clear bag of what I guessed was saline from a small insulated cabinet, and carefully eased a needle into the bend of Liam's scrawny arm.

"Is that still good?" I asked.

"What? The saline? Of course. It's just salt water, really. Store it room temperature, and if it doesn't get punctured it'll last forever." She smoothed Liam's hair off his forehead. "This boy's too thin... and his coat—I mean skin—is off."

Liam shuddered, his eyes racing under his eyelids.

"Easy, fella. Easy," she murmured as she placed surgical instruments on a tray like she'd used them as recently as yesterday. I recognized the scalpel and the

229

battery operated bone saw and my stomach did a long slow flip to my shoes.

"You're going to have to hold him," she said pulling on some latex gloves. "The anesthetic canisters are empty. Might not have been any good anyway, but..." she frowned. "Something... happened here...I can't remember..."

"I'll help you clean it up," I said.

She smiled, her face softening and I realized she had once been young, once been pretty. "You're a good boy, Nester," and before I could feel guilty, she added, "Hold him. This going to hurt."

"Then you're going to—"

"I'm taking the foot," she said.

His fevered screams filled the room as she sliced into the skin along the arch and up to a spot just above his ankle, but I knew how much worse it would get.

"It's okay, Liam, it's okay!" I repeated the words over and over again, but I don't think he heard me. I don't think he knew anything but the agony of the saw as its motor churned and sputtered, severing muscle and bone. I wished for an escape—or even for Nate to appear and watch in sick fascination. But there was nothing, nothing but the whir of the saw and the awful sound of Liam's shrieks. I pressed him down, keeping my arms locked on his shoulders as he twisted and struggled and fought the excruciating pain.

And then, in less than a minute, it was over. I looked down and she was using the scalpel to trim the flaps of skin, and then folding them over the bone, making a stump. Liam's blackened, swollen foot sat on the metal tray with the bloody instruments looking strange and unreal, like the prop from a horror movie.

Liam was vibrating, shaking so hard it seemed like he was having convulsions.

"What do I do?"

230

"There was some Benamine—it's for pain. I'll go look," and she left us alone.

"What... didn't...? You didn't..." Liam's eyes made a wild, wide circle of the room, coming to rest on the tray where the remains of his foot stood upright, mocking me. "No! No..." he cried. Then he vomited and blacked out.

As I cleaned him, exhaustion swept over me, erasing all the other feelings that had tumbled inside me only moments before. I shrugged out of my weapons and took off my coat, wadding it into a pillow to raise Liam's head high enough to prevent him from choking if he threw up again. Then I moved out of the surgery through the exam room and on to the office.

"Doc?"

I hopped the makeshift barricade Amaranth, Katie and I had made only hours before and peered into the supply room.

"Doc?"

I was alone.

I opened the door and stepped onto the portico.

"Doc?"

She was on me before I could react. Something hard and dull thudded against my temple, knocking my glasses off my face and making the world dim. My knees buckled. Everything reeled but I reached up to strike back, landing a punch that only slowed the onslaught, but didn't stop it. Another blow dropped me and I hit the ground, stunned and dazed.

"You killed them! You killed my dogs!" she shrieked, striking me again and again. "I almost believed you! I almost believed you were just some poor, lost kid. You almost had me fooled. But I know it's you, Robert Watson! You killed my dogs, again!" Her screams mixed with sobs. "You... killed...them... again... and I will kill you again... and again... until you stay... *dead*!"

I tasted my own blood as she pinned me with her

weight, straddling me, striking me again and again while she screamed her rage over me. Every blow pounded through me, echoing from my head down to my toes and making it hard for me to find the strength to fight her. I lifted my arms, but she struck at them battering them down. Darkness surrounded me. I barely felt the pain anymore, just heard the thudding sounds of the assault.

And then, miraculously, from somewhere far above me, a gunshot.

"Get off him!" someone yelled, but the woman was too caught up in her rage to heed. "Get off him or I'll shoot!"

I knew the voice but I couldn't believe it. I had to be dreaming...

The thing crashed into the side of my face again with full force. "Killed—my—dogs—" she hissed like no one had spoken and raised the object again. I finally saw what it was: an old skateboard. And then I heard another shot.

It was just one, clean and merciful in its way. Doc Watson paused with the skateboard held high. Her face rearranged itself again, and once more I saw the calm professional woman who'd performed the operation. The woman who'd recognized me for the scared kid I was. And then she slid sideways off me and lay still.

I could breathe, but I couldn't see. I felt around for my glasses and stumbled to my feet, wiping my face. My hand came away wet with blood. I staggered, stumbled, righted myself, stumbled again.

A gaunt man stood in the doorway in a snow-dusted coat. He wore some kind of broad-brimmed hat and scraps of fabric wound around his face. A revolver was stretched out in front of him, trembling in his hands.

The ghost of Robert Watson—the real one—that was my first wild thought. And when he called me by name, I wasn't even surprised. Nate had been talking to me for weeks. Why wouldn't this ghost?

232

"Nester!" the man repeated. "Are you okay?"

"Rod?" I stretched out my hand like I was going to pull the mask of fabric off his face but my sense of distance and depth were off. My hands caught the air and I fell, landing hard on my hands and knees.

The figure pulled aside the swatch of cloth and showed me a lopsided slash of mouth set into a crisscross pattern of burned skin and red lesions. The face was ugly and disfigured and the most welcome one I'd ever seen in my life.

"What—what are you doing here?"

"Saving your butt, apparently," he muttered, and then I blacked out.

23

PUPPY LOVE

It was just a few seconds. I came to myself again quickly, but my head ached and I was pretty sure Doc Watson had done me some damage beyond the bruises on my arms. One of my fingers was bent at a weird angle, and the pain was like nothing I'd ever felt. Broken, probably.

Rod tried to help me, but his arms were shaking with the effort of holding the pistol steady, and I counted it a miracle both that he'd made it here and that he hadn't shot me by mistake. He wore just his coat, hat and gloves—no protective suit and no respirator—and I finally recognized the colorful bit of fabric around his face as a bit of Amy's JFK cheerleading sweater. His cheeks were bright red with exertion and cold and a fresh lesion, blooming on the burn-scarred path of skin below his left eye.

"You okay?" he asked breathlessly.

There were two Rods standing there. It took a second for me to understand that the tape had given and my glasses were in two pieces again. I stepped over the crazy old vet with a weird cocktail of emotions—anger, sadness, gratitude and regret—and nearly tripped over the skateboard. It was wet with blood. My blood, I realized. I stretched out my hands, lurching for the door of the office. Once inside, I gripped the counter for support, making my way back into the surgery with Rod moving slowly behind me.

"What are you doing here?" I asked. I reached for the faucet and stuck my head under the running water, watching my blood join the clear liquid swirling down the drain. My head ached like fire, and my hand hurt like it had been dipped in acid. I stumbled back toward the supply room as Rod answered.

"Amaranth. She told us where you'd gone. Said you'd need some help. She didn't think Doc Watson would do it and thought you'd welcome some back up. She's also sure the old lady has gas stockpiled. If we can find it we might be able to get the tractor going again. Maybe make for the hospital in Benson instead. When we got here and saw the dead dogs and the front door wide open and no sign of you, we split up. I came here and she went into the house to see if she could find you," he glanced out the window. "She was just here, though—you were out of it. She went around the back to see if the gas tank is there."

I staggered away from him, heading for the supply room where I found the painkiller Doc Watson had gone to look for and returned with it, hoping like heck it was still good. Liam and I both were going to need it.

"So," Rod nodded at the severed foot. "You did it."

"She did it."

Rod considered that information. "Will he be okay?"

"I don't know. It's too early to tell. She—she was different for a while. Went to get these..." I showed him the drugs. "I guess she saw the dead dogs and the crazy came back."

"We would have been here sooner, but...'" he paused. "I guess you saw the bodies? Of our intruders?" he asked softly.

235

I grabbed some medical tape and wound a strip around the nose bridge of my glasses. They didn't go together as well as they had before and I foresaw a day when I'd be in serious trouble. Unless of course, somewhere in all Doc Watson's piles of stuff there was a pair of glasses with my exact prescription.

"Yeah."

"Amy really thought it was a different threat."

"Is she okay?"

Rod hesitated. "She will be. She's tough..." he slipped to the floor like his knees had turned to Jell-O, but when I approached he waved me away. "I'm okay," he said weakly, offering me the remains of his sarcastic smile. "When I saw that old broad beating the shit out of you man, I had to *run*," he chuckled. "That's what messed me up. Before that, I was just fine..."

He had probably done the right thing, killing her. But it just felt like one more thing that wasn't—shouldn't have been—real. I focused my attention on Rod again.

"Why you?" I asked.

"This is the thanks I get for saving your life?" Rod grimaced. "I guess I'll be going now—"

He tried to pull himself up.

"Hey, I'm not trying to be ungrateful, man," I began offering him my hand. "It's just—"

"Amy and Marty are alternating with defense. Katie's ankle is still a bit tender from the dog bite, but it doesn't seem to be infected," he answered before I could ask. "She says she thinks the antibiotic is helping. That gives us some hope for him, right?" He nodded toward Liam, whose breath rose and fell like he knew we were talking about him. "And Elise..." he shrugged. "She's helping Katie put the cabin back together. Not saying much, but...all things in their time." He quirked the last leftover hairs of his eyebrow at me, then looked over at Liam. "I'm here because we're short on manpower, Nest."

236

"Yeah," I agreed.

We stood there in silence for a moment.

"Since we're sort of on the subject of me... there's something I've wanted to ask you. About me." When I just stared at him, he looked away. "So... the lesions are getting worse...as you can see."

I busied myself with bending my crooked finger into place and splinting it quickly to the one beside it with some tape.

"Yeah," I said, hissing with the effort.

"But I can still do some stuff. Sometimes I don't feel too bad. Yet. Just nauseous. Sometimes." He let out another short bark that was supposed to pass for laughter. "No... all the time. I guess that's good in a way. More food for everyone else, right?"

I nodded, feeling his question loom between us, heavy and dense as a black hole.

"From the time we left the Hole, to the day we got here was what—ten days? It was hard to keep track with the sky always gray and no real night or day, but it wasn't more than that. Right?"

"I don't know," I lied. I didn't want to help him; I didn't want to have this conversation. "Maybe I should check on Amaranth? That house is a hazard—"

"When did we see Lilly's first sore? It was either the second or third day, wasn't it?"

"It was a couple of days." I squinted out the window and saw Amaranth on the portico. She was dressed like Rod, without a mask or a protective suit: just a coat, hat and scarf, but the proportions were wrong. It took me a second to realize she had a couple of puppies stuffed into her jacket. I don't think she saw me through the blinds, but I could tell that she was crying. Still, she walked deliberately towards us with her shoulders squared with determination. "There she is," I said. "Amaranth."

"So from first exposure to the day she—the day she

237

died, Lilly lived a little more than a week," Rod finished after a pause. "I saw the first one the day we got here—after two weeks of exposure. So I probably have..."

He calculated in silence. I did the same, almost automatically, factoring the ratio, multiplying it out, wishing that for once I could shut off my brain and stop the algebraic equation that presented itself like a word problem in my mind. If lesion 1 appears on day 2 and death occurs on day 10, then lesion 1 on day 10 equals death on—

"There are too many variables, Wasserman," I said. "Lilly's disability made her more vulnerable. You're an athlete—"

"Was." He gestured to his burns. "Before this. Now..." he shrugged. "Three weeks? Two if things get rough, and four, if I'm really, really lucky?"

I wanted to rebut but I respected him too much to lie. How do you tell a fifteen-year-old kid that he's living on borrowed time?

"Yeah," he muttered and turned away from me. His fist opened and closed, the fingers curling and releasing, curling and releasing, but nothing else moved until he turned around suddenly and said, "You got to promise me something, Nester," like he'd never stopped talking. "Two things, really. First: that you'll look out for Amy. Her family is dead. She doesn't have anyone left but me... and when I'm gone she'll be alone. She's tough—tougher than I ever knew—but she's fragile, too. She's gonna need somebody." His single eye found mine. "You're alone, too. You'll look out for her, right?"

"Man—"

"Say it, Bartlett. Say you'll look out for her. When I'm gone."

"Yeah," I sighed. I imagined myself trying to take care of Amy Yamamoto—a girl who probably said only two words to me in our life Before—and who had turned into a

238

kind of sexy scary commando ninja in our life After. A part of me thought it would have been easier to promise to look after Rod's pet dragon or something. But another part of me knew that I would—and would have even if Rod hadn't asked.

"Yeah, okay," I said. "She doesn't even like me, man. But if anything happens to you, I'll give it my best shot."

"It doesn't matter that she doesn't like you. Just that you'll do it."

I touched my forehead and came back with another light smudge of blood. "I gotta get a bandage or something," I muttered. "What's the second thing?"

Rod paused for so long I thought he was having some kind of episode. "Forget the second thing," he said as Amaranth came into the room. "Either way, it'll take care of itself."

I watched her face as she took in the room: Liam out cold on the exam table, the blackened severed foot and my own ragged appearance. I expected her to ask me about him, about what happened, but to my surprise, she made a beeline for Liam and kissed him gently and sweetly on the forehead, on the cheek, on the mouth. Like Rod and I weren't there. She whispered something in his ear, and then planted another soft kiss on his lips. When she turned to us, her eyes were bright emeralds coated with tears.

"I brought you some things," she exclaimed like she was the Welcome Wagon. She pulled a puppy out of her jacket. "I guess you two are going to be here a while, so you might as well make friends. And let's face it, Doc Watson kept them for a reason: they're an excellent early warning system. "

She put the little bundle into my hands. I couldn't tell if it was the same little pup I'd threatened to kill a short while ago, but when it licked me and yipped and wagged its tail, I was glad I hadn't.

"We're going to take one, too," she said, dropping a

239

wriggling bundle into Rod's arms.

"No," Rod said quietly. "How will we feed it?"

"We'll find a way. I have a feeling about it." She turned back to me. "We found these in the root cellar. And batteries. In a Faraday cage under the cots." She pulled a fresh walkie-talkie out of a pocket of her loaded backpack. I heard a crackle of static. "The Mountain Place is going to stay tuned to frequency 32." She turned to Rod. "I just talked to Katie. Told her we made it okay." She stretched the device toward Rod. "Amy wants to talk to you—"

"I can't." Rod shook his head and turned away. "Not right now."

Amaranth studied him sympathetically before turning back to me.

"There's one last thing." She pulled a folded piece of paper out of her pocket. Liam's name was written on the front in a girly script. She held it for a second like she was debating with herself and then finally handed to me. "Read it to him when he wakes up. Please," she said.

It felt really junior high school, but under the circumstances, what could I do? I took the note and stuffed it into the back pocket of my jeans. Amaranth hesitated, and then she kissed me on the cheek. "Thanks, Nester," she said quickly and turned to Rod. "I'm ready."

Rod stretched out his right hand. It took me a second to realize that he was offering me not his knuckles or his palm but a handshake—it just wasn't the kind of gesture we normally shared. I should have known then that something was wrong, but my head felt so heavy and sore that nothing seemed to be making the sense it should have.

They left. I watched them cross the portico: Rod as slow as an old man, his hand heavy on Amaranth's shoulder. He said something to her and she nodded, hitching her backpack higher on her shoulder with a determination I recognized. She lifted two opaque containers with difficulty and realized they'd found some gas. They moved forward, picking their way through Doc Watson's "lawn" until they disappeared.

Exhaustion tumbled around me. My brain hurt, my body was sore and spent from pulling Liam through the snow. The horror of my friend's agony echoed in my ears, along with the sounds of gunfire. All I wanted was to put my head down and sleep. I remember locking the door and shutting off the lights to save the generator's power. I covered Liam with blankets and took a few for myself. Then I guess I finally did pass out, because for a long time there wasn't anything else.

24

GOODBYES

"Nester, man, wake up."

As soon as my eyes popped open, I reached for the guns the way I once would have reached for my cell phone. My face hurt—Doc Watson had cut me up pretty bad—and my brain sloshed around in my skull.

"Come on, Nest. Snap out of it! It's me."

He was dressed like he was on that last normal day: the green shirt in a husky boy XXL, jeans, lime green sneaks.

"Look at you. Lettin' a little old lady beat you up! Check him, Mom."

She wasn't there... and then she was, holding Nate's hand, looking exactly as she had the last time I saw her: her black hair in a bun, the brown pants that stopped at the knee and flat boots. She wore her white lab coat like a jacket. She didn't smile. I thought she was mad at me—for finally really getting Nate killed—until she said,

"Don't tease him, Nate. Remember why we're here."

Nate sobered. I expected him to say something—for one of them to say something—but they simply stood there, holding hands and staring at me.

"So?" I asked, my voice a croak from sleep and effort.

"What? What do you want to say?"

"Oh, Nester," Mom shook her head. "You've always been just a little too direct. I used to think you'd outgrow it, but now I guess it's just the way you are."

A part of me wanted to run to her and wrap my arms around her and apologize for every obnoxious, insensitive thing I'd ever said. But another part of me knew she wasn't really there. Knew she was a dream or a ghost. I shrugged and stayed rooted to the spot, trying to memorize every single detail of her. Because the truth was, I already knew why she was there. Why they were both there.

"All I wanted to say—all Nate and I want to say— is..." she hesitated, blinking a little. "That we're okay. You don't have to worry about us. You don't have to feel bad. We're okay. It wasn't your fault. It's time to let that go."

"But I was supposed to look out for him."

"And you did. You did a good job, Nester. I'm proud of you. It wasn't your fault."

"And I was just messing with you, man. I don't blame you. For none of it." He stretched his knuckles toward me like he was giving me dap. "So go on. Do what you gotta do."

"Which is what exactly? What am I supposed to do?"

"What you're doing. Take care of the others as best you can," Mom replied. "And yourself, since—" They looked at each other, and then Nate erupted into a wild, immature giggle. When he spoke it was in that tattletale voice that had always made me want to snap off his head and hand it to him like he was a Lego toy.

"Nester thinks Amy is hot. And Katie, too. And even Amaranth—"

"Hush," Mom whispered, but now she was smiling like she had a secret. "Nester will make the right choice when the time comes. But it won't be here. You have to move on and soon. Southwest to Alabama—"

"Alabama?" I spat out the word like it was poison. I'd

243

never been there, but Irv started talking in my head about the legacies of racism and pernicious stereotypes of white supremacy and for a second I got too wrapped up in that monologue to listen to what my mother was saying. "You want me to go to Alabama?"

"Mobile, Alabama." My mom's lips weren't moving and her voice had changed, getting deeper and more masculine like she was ventriloquist operating a dummy. Only I didn't see a dummy—well, Nate, duh—but you know what I mean. "Repeat. Mobile, Alabama. Longitude: -88.243561 Latitude: 30.68723. All survivors..."

"Wait. What's happening? What are you talking about? Why Mobile—"

"Goodbye, Nester," Mom said her voice already fading away.

"Good luck, dude," Nate seconded before they both vanished.

"Wait!"

I heard my own voice loud in the room. I sat up, staring around me. But of course they weren't there. It was some kind of weird dream or vision or something.

"...survivors. Emergency shelters and assistance available at the Coast Guard Aviation Training Center in Mobile, Alabama, Coordinates Longitude: -88.243561 Latitude: 30.68723..." The voice was male, military-sounding and almost robotic, crackling out of the walkie-talkie like it was coming not just from far away but out of another century. "Repeat. To all catastrophe survivors. Emergency shelters and assistance available at the Coast Guard Aviation Training—"

"Coast Guard?" I repeated.

The room spun a little when I stood up, but after a few seconds it slowed back to steady. I glanced at Liam's watch: I'd been out for many, many hours. Almost a full day. My body felt like it belonged to someone else: numb and unfamiliar. I held on to the wall just in case it gave out on me and crept back into the surgery.

Liam's open blank eyes stared glassily at me. They were empty and flat. Dead-looking.

"Liam!" I screamed, grabbing his wrist. In my anxiety I felt no pulse—nothing, nothing at all. "Oh God, oh my God, oh my God." I muttered searching the room for—I don't know, a doggy defibrillator or something to jump start his heart. All the while, Liam gazed flatly up at me, and the radio message repeated in staticky endless loop.

And then he blinked.

I stopped yelling and looked at him—really looked at him. His face was still pale, but not sweaty. He wasn't shivering or muttering, and as I watched, his chest rose and fell in one, long even breath.

His eyes weren't flat, I realized. They were just fixed on me in a level stare...until he blinked again.

"Liam?"

His mouth twitched a little like he was trying to speak, then his tongue flicked out to wet his dry lips.

"Ur," he whispered and I could tell by the way the muscles in his neck tightened that he was mustering every ounce of his strength, trying to sit up or talk or both. "Uf—"

"Save it, man," I laughed, gone giggly with relief. "You've been down for a while. It's gonna take a minute to build back up to bossing everyone around, you know?"

His eyes closed for a long minute. I used the time to stop searching for electrodes and start looking for my canteen. I dribbled a bit between his cracked lips and he drank quickly and greedily.

"Repeat. To all catastrophe survivors. Emergency shelters and assistance available at the Coast Guard Aviation Training—"

I listened to the whole thing again, committing the coordinates to memory. Mobile, Alabama. Even without consulting the atlas in Liam's father's bookshelf, I knew that had to be at least 1000 miles away. How on earth we'd get there, through the snow and cold, I didn't have a clue. Or at least not yet. We'd figure it out. We'd get there. As soon as Liam was strong enough. Just thinking about that journey replaced fear with a grim kind of excitement. It would be intensely difficult—I knew that. But Mobile, Alabama offered the first hope of a world where things were normal that we'd had since the bombs fell.

"Where...." Liam managed in a voice like a rusted hinge.

"Your neighbor. Old Man Watson's place."

"Antibiotic...working..." he said.

"Looks like it, yeah," I said and hoped he'd leave it there and not press to know everything that had happened. I turned away from him, searching through the supply drawer until I found a thermometer. When he opened his mouth for the next question, I popped it under his tongue.

99 degrees.

"That's good," I said, exhaling for what felt like the first time in days. "But here," I scooped up some more of the doggy antibiotics and poured them into his mouth. He grimaced and swallowed them down with a big mouthful of water.

"Foot. Hurts like fire..."

"Yeah. I—I'll give you something for the pain in a sec—"

"Others?"

"Back at the Mountain Place," I answered.

"Weirdest dream..." he said, his voice a steady whisper. He closed his eyes, frowning as though he were trying to make the images come together in a way that made sense. "Richter again. Gunfire. And junk... everywhere—"

It made my head throb, but I laughed anyway. "For a dude who was pretty delirious, you've got a lot of that right, man," I said before giving him the thirty second recap.

"Amaranth?" he asked after a pause. "Here, too?"

"Yeah," I said, remembering the folded piece of paper still tucked in my pocket. "She wrote you a note." I quirked an eyebrow at him. "Isn't that how she introduced herself? She gave you a note?"

He was too weak to smile, so I did it for him.

"You want me to...?"

He blinked a yes.

I opened it, scanning it quickly. Then I crumpled it up. My heart started a desperate thump in my chest and it was all I could do to stay at Liam's side. I wanted to run out into the junkyard, screaming her name at the top of my lungs—and she wasn't even my girlfriend.

"Maybe later, man—"

Alarm and agitation creased Liam's face. I saw him tensing his body, struggling for the energy to force himself up and off the gurney.

"Read!" he demanded in a clear strong voice.

I sighed and smoothed the paper out.

Dear Liam,

If you're reading this, you're better—and that's the most important thing. Nester and Amy have done a good job holding us all together and Katie and Marty are like you. They have skills. Elise is a little girl. I'm sorry that she has to grow up in this awful world. I'm sorry that she has to learn to kill to survive, but I know she will learn. I see it in her face.

That leaves me. And Rod. He's dying, Liam. We all know it even though no one says it. His last wish is to go back. To see if he can find his mom. I know she is probably dead, but if I don't go with him, he will go alone. I can't bear the thought of him dying out there in that wasteland by himself. And I can't bear the thought of staying here, knowing I have so little to offer you all. I knew how to survive in the old world. I'm broken in this one. I can't let my brokenness sink the rest of you. I won't.

I told you once that I never wanted to be a killer. Richter made me question that. I saw a side of myself I never knew was there. Its ugliness scares me. So much that I wanted to erase it. To drown it.

But I know now, I can't. I have to face the truth: I'm my own worst nightmare. I'm as bad or worse than the people who dropped the bombs or my father or Richter. There's no difference.

The only way I can live with that is to leave here. Deciding to go with Rod is the first thing I've done since we got to the Mountain Place that feels right. That feels like I can live with myself. That I can look in the mirror and be at peace.

Since the day I first saw you, looking bewildered on the steps in front of JFK High, I knew you were different. I didn't know what it was, just that I liked it. Now I know what it is: you're a survivor, like your Dad. Legs or not, foot or not, you and he are brave enough to face what has to be faced and find a way to live with it. Me, I'm a coward, living on victim status. I understand that now. I'm no good for you and I know that.

I'll never forget you, Liam. I'm glad I got to find out just how really special you are and I hope, when you remember those days, you'll smile.
-A

"What— she—my foot?" Liam's brow crimped in confusion. "You said... antibiotics worked... What? Why—"

His eyes strayed away from me, circling the room for an explanation. Then his face froze, his eyes widening in horror.

The remains of his diseased foot still sat on the

counter looking like the mummified relic from a pharaoh's tomb.

"Liam," I began. "Man, we had to! Don't—"

But it was too late. He struggled up to his elbows and looked down. When he saw the stump where his foot had been he screamed.

"You *promised*!" he hissed. "You—"

"I know but it was the only way to save your life—"

"I told you—I told you—"

I shook my head. "I know. You said you'd rather die. But you don't mean that—"

"I do!" he shrieked. "Can't—can't—survive! Can't run—"

"What about your Dad, Liam? He—"

"Dead!" he cried and then collapsed back on the gurney, out of breath. "No way— No way—" he sobbed.

"You don't know that—"

"Found... dog tags...." He managed. "On that body at the edge of the river—"

I frowned. We'd been close to the Mountain Place, floating on that overburdened canoe. We'd seen the body at the edge of the bank, dressed in military fatigues like Mr. Harper had often worn. I could hear Lilly in my memory, insisting that Liam inspect the body closely. It had decayed so much that the face was unrecognizable, but Liam had checked and the man had legs. Real ones.

"But you said that wasn't him—"

"Wasn't!" Liam cried. "But—he had the tags! My father never took them off—"

"Well, maybe they got ripped off. In some kind of struggle or something—"

"Backpack floating in the river?" Liam yelled. "How could he survive without his gear? And—and he couldn't run, Nester. He couldn't—run—" he gulped a deep, ragged, pain-racked breath. "And I can't run, either..." The sound of his sobs filled the small room, heartbreaking and bereft.

"You should have—let—me—die!" he wailed. "Amaranth... Dad... Lilly..."

"You heard the radio, Liam," I tried to make him look at me, but he had closed his eyes. "We have to get to Alabama! Think of your Mom, Liam! She's probably there right now, man! Waiting for you! If we can—"

His head wagged a negative. "Can't get to Alabama. Can't *walk*—"

"I'll—I'll make you a prosthetic, Liam. It won't be titanium but it'll be good, you'll see. It'll be my project. Like for the Robotics Club. Yeah, there's a yard full of possibilities out there. I'll start right now," I was talking too quickly but the defeat in his voice had me spooked. "You'll see. By the time we see the others, you'll stride up the Mountain Place like—"

"No! No! No!" he moaned. "Can't go back. Can't let—let them—see. Should have let me die—"

I couldn't listen to any more. It opened up a black hole of grief and loss, tore away the one thing I'd been certain of: that we needed to save his life at any cost. That we couldn't lose another one. And for all of that, we'd lost two more. They were hours and hours ahead of me now, and pursuit was probably impossible, even as slowly as Rod moved. And then I remembered the gas and the tractor, and I knew for certain that they had started it and taken off for home on the snowy roads.

"Should have let me die," Liam sobbed again and again.

I backed out of the surgery, then turned and ran, leaving him, while the walkie-talkie message repeated on continuous loop. The little puppy yipped and tried to follow, but I left him, too, and dove out into the junkyard, shaking with doubt and regret.

The yard was cold and desolate. The generator chugged uncertainly and I knew that eventually the gas would run out and it would stop. We'd have to abandon

250

the veterinary office for the cluttered house. I moved toward the farmhouse with a sense of purpose, if not peace.

Liam was right: walking was out of the question. And so was returning to the Mountain Place—not until he'd come to terms with his loss and learned to accept the hard reality of his survival. He needed to grieve and he needed to rage and there had to be space—a house with a fireplace so we could fight the winter's chill. And we had one, I just needed to clear it out and clean it out, if not completely, at least enough to be livable.

I imagined Amaranth and Rod making their way back down the winding roads. Tears rose to blur my vision. I'd never been much for prayer, but my lips moved of their own accord.

"Please God, let them find peace," I murmured. "Amen."

Then I wiped my face, shut off conscious thought and set to work.

There was a lot of trash—but a lot of useful stuff in the hoard, too: candles, clothing, and even some canned goods that looked salvageable. I worked until my back ached and my stomach growled, but I only managed to clear the foyer of the small farmhouse before I knew I had to return to the office to face Liam's pain.

By then, though, I knew that the hoard was the answer. In it, I would find the parts and pieces I needed to make a prosthetic foot—one strong and flexible enough to walk a thousand miles.

End of Book Two
Curious about Book 3? Keep reading!

Book Three

AMARANTH'S RETURN

The Doomsday Kids series follows Amaranth on her journey back to the wasteland to help Rod find his mother before he dies. Beginning on the tractor, the two do their best to avoid the places where they met their greatest terrors on their journey to the Mountain Place—only to find new horrors await them. Among the new survivors they meet, there are friends and enemies, including the handsome Jax, who appears to be a little of both. The Doomsday Kids will also be reunited with two characters from their past, one of whom will offer Amaranth the chance to reconnect with Liam and the others—but at a terrible price.

AMARANTH'S RETURN
Available now

LETTER TO YOU, THE READER

Dear Reader,

Thank you for reading *Nester's Mistake*! If you enjoyed the story, help me spread the word by reviewing/rating it on your favorite book website! You may have noticed: EVERYONE is writing a book these days and it's hard for readers to know which books are worth their time and which should be avoided like the plague! Whether you found Nester's Mistake to be "5-star," "1-star" or somewhere in between, please take the time to share your opinion.

Reviews are immensely helpful to me as I continue working on this series, too. What did I get right? Wrong? What resonated with you? What should happen next? Thanks for participating in the writer/reader exchange by sharing your thoughts on this story.

The Doomsday Kids books are a labor of love for me. It is my hope that the books make heroes of kids and teens from all different backgrounds, with all kinds of problems and issues. In my experience, bravery, self-sacrifice and heroism can be found in people of all colors and creeds.

Stay tuned to future books. Each story is told by a different "doomsday kid" and in each book, the kids struggle not only for their own individual survival, but for the survival of the other Doomsday Kids. Will they ever find safety again? Find out!

Sincerely,

Karyn Folan

P.S. Want more Doomsday Kids between books? Join our newsletter by visiting the website: www.thedoomsdaykids.com. You'll find excerpts, deleted scenes and get the chance to win all kinds of free stuff, including the special Doomsday Kids backpack!

OTHER FICTION BY KARYN LANGHORNE FOLAN

Forever Young (with Scott G. Kyle)

Paparazzi Princesses (with Reginae Carter and Bria Williams)

Diary of an Ugly Duckling

Unfinished Business

Street Level

A Personal Matter

Breaking Point (with Paul Langan)

Pretty Ugly

CPSIA information can be obtained
at www.ICGtesting.com
Printed in the USA
LVOW10s1802120517
534313LV00009B/572/P